Caribbean Adventure Series
Book 1

BLUE WATERS

A Rick Waters Novel

ERIC CHANCE STONE

2020 by Eric Chance Stone

Published by Lost and Found Publishing

All rights reserved. No part of this publication may be reproduced, distributed, or transmitted in any form or by any means, including photocopying, recording, or other electronic or mechanical methods, without the prior written permission of the publisher, except in the case of brief quotations embodied in critical reviews and certain other noncommercial uses permitted by copyright law.

Printed in the United States of America

ISBN: 978-1-7341626-1-5

First Edition
10 9 8 7 6 5 4 3 2 1

ACKNOWLEDGEMENTS

I thank my late mother, Sylvia Stone, who got me into reading in the first place and let me borrow her guitar when I was in the fourth grade, she never got it back. Sorry mom. She taught me my first three chords, how to dream and share my stories in songs and later in books.

I thank my dad, who's never-ending support allowed me to follow whatever path I wanted to in life, and gave me the freedom to express myself in my own terms.

I thank my mentor Wayne Stinnett, who got me started on this journey of discovery. Wayne shared all his knowledge with me and never asked for anything in return. It was because of him that I am a novelist. Wayne reminds me often that I am a storyteller just like he is and that writers are people with literary doctorates. Thanks for keeping it all in perspective for me. Your insight and kindness will fill your life with great karma. - https://waynestinnett.com/

I thank Cap Daniels, who's positive attitude and encouragement never ceases to amaze me. When I felt like it was a pipe dream, he would remind me in no uncertain terms that if I keep writing, it will become a reality. He's always there to answer a question or give me his opinion on any subject. - https://capdaniels.com

I thank Chip Bell who not only hired me to write a song for his books but also inspired me to write as much as I could every day. - http://www.chipbellauthor.com/

I thank Steve Kittner, who's friendship has always been there. He's a great writer and very supportive. Thanks for all the kind words along the way. - https://amzn.to/35DAQhR

I thank my beta reader, supporters, friends and fans. Their honesty and willingness to help astonished me. You all are so important and I thank you again from the bottom of my heart. In no particular order: Frank Rush, Lucy Rush, Gary Haas, Pat Biondi-Pennington Wood, Hancy Deacon, Bob Bitchin, Bavette Battern, Dennis Battern, Judy Seidler, Bruce Seidler, Kathleen Semenuk, Phil Semenuk, David Dangler, Gary Howman, Alicia Taylor, Doug Hendrix, Mike Keevil, Dan Mason, Allison Bankston, Charlotte Lanier, Janice Hagar, Eric Babin, Karen Saylor, Sandy Block, Diane Rutledge, Mike Tenbroek, Steve Coder, Pam Knight, Doug Clark, Katy McKnight, Heidi Benson Stagg, Kathy Zeller, Dotty Riddle, Todd Alexander, Julie Jones, Thomas Michael Jackson, Dianne Jackson, Linda Reed, Chuck Reed.

I thank my editor Marsha Zinberg, who brought this book to life. Her ability to convey what needed changing made this book the way it should be. - https://writetouch.ca/

I thank my formatter Colleen Sheehan who went beyond the call of duty as a formatter and answered any question I had without hesitation. - https://ampersandbookinteriors.com

I thank my narrator Nick Sullivan who's sense of humor is always uplifting. His ability to narrate as well as write is astounding. He's also a wealth of knowledge and selflessness to share is greatly appreciated. - https://www.nicksullivan.net/

FIND THE OFFICIAL SYNOPSIS MUSIC AT:

GUM.CO/BLUEWATERSMUSICFREE

BLUE WATERS

CHAPTER ONE

"911. What is your emergency?"

"My name is Rick Waters. I'd like to report a dead body."

"What is your location?"

"I'm several miles downstream near Rodair Gully on the Hillebrandt Bayou," replied Rick. "If you can send someone with a boat to the Steinhager boat ramp off of FM 365, I can lead them to the location."

"Ok, please hold, Mr. Waters," said the dispatcher.

She came on the line again a moment later. "Mr. Waters, we're sending an ambulance and a couple of Jefferson County deputies with a boat to the Steinhager boat ramp. Please keep your phone free in case they need to speak with you."

"I understand. I'll head back to the ramp and wait for the deputies."

As Rick trekked back to his jon boat and began to motor down the bayou, he mentally reviewed the odd chain of events that had led to his gruesome discovery that morning.

His day had started like many others recently.

A few hours earlier he had slowly been awakened by the morning sun that had shone through the cloudy camper windows of the old Ford, catching dust particles in its beam. As the warmth from the dim light fell on his face, he remembered an aggressive mosquito had buzzed in his ear and his mouth had felt as dry as the West Texas desert. His cockatoo, Chief, was rustling in his cage as well.

Before bedding down, Rick had parked the truck by the boat launch, just below the overpass on FM 365. He'd been playing pool at the Boudain Hut into the wee hours and had won a couple of hundred bucks from some rednecks. Rick was a great pool player. Not a shark, but a well-rounded competitor.

Up until a few months ago, he'd made his living as a baggage handler for Delta Air Lines and had gotten bumped from station to station because of his lack of seniority. Most recently, he'd worked near Destin, Florida, at the Okaloosa Regional Airport. But that didn't last long, because he was bumped, yet again, by a senior ramp rat from Detroit who wanted to semi-retire to the blue waters of Destin.

Rick had never been good at keeping a job long-term. So, he'd taken the last of his money and hopped in his red 1962 Ford F-100 with his jon boat and old two-stroke outboard in tow, and driven back to Fannett, Texas, where he was born and raised.

There was no place like home, they said, but the muddy brown waters of the Hillebrandt Bayou sure made him long for a boat ride on the emerald blue waters over Crab Island back in Destin. Crab Island had been only a few feet above water, with a smattering of palm trees and salt grass until

Hurricane Eloise swallowed it up in 1974 and moved it knee-deep below the surface. It had become a favorite destination for locals and tourists alike, where they'd anchor boats of every size, stand waist-deep in the water, and drink beer all day.

After reluctantly rising from his slumber, Rick had put Chief in his travel cage, placed him in the jon boat and launched it. He'd slowly motored down the slow-moving waters of the bayou near La Belle, Texas, taking in the scenery with Chief. Several lazy gators basked in the warmth of the morning sun on the banks of the bayou. It had been a glorious start to the day.

He kept his cockatoo in the cage. It was far too dangerous to let him ride in the open, since he'd make a nice, tasty treat for a gator if he ever fell overboard.

Rick was a jack-of-all-trades: a commercial diver, treasure hunter, fisherman, boat captain, and part-time detective. Logging water time on the barges and tugs in the Houston ship channel had qualified him for his captain's license, and he also did boat deliveries when the opportunities arose.

He'd also obtained his PI license online and possessed a concealed carry permit in Florida that had reciprocity in thirty-six other states. A few cases here and there intrigued him, and he'd made a little money. With his license, permit, some tiny, hidden surveillance cameras and a field recorder, he was in business.

He refused to take sleazy assignments, such as spying on spouses to see if they were cheating. That wasn't his style. Instead, he chose more ethical jobs, like helping to find missing persons or tracking down stolen vehicles. Rick liked to help people; he believed in Karma and the old adage, "Do unto others as you would have them do unto you."

Rick had continued motoring his skiff deeper into the bayou. His little jon boat was dependable but not very luxurious—a working man's boat. His dream was to one day own a huge charter boat. He had once been on board a few huge sport-fishing boats at a boat show in Destin and was blown away at the comfort and opulent interiors of some of them. One that really caught his eye was a used, fifty-five-foot Viking sport fisher. He was so taken by it that he'd printed a small photo of it and kept it taped to the dashboard of his old Ford with the words "One Day!" written in the corner with a red Sharpie.

Now, as he drew closer to the boat ramp where his morning had started, he could make out two deputy cruisers, an ambulance, and a pickup with a large inflatable on a trailer. He waved at the deputies and one helped him tie his jon boat off to the dock.

"I'm Rick Waters. I called 911."

The officer stuck out his hand and shook Rick's.

"Deputy James LeBlanc. I'll be heading up the investigation. Where's the body you found?"

"It's easier to show you than tell you. You'd never find it unless y'all follow me, as I explained to the dispatch," said Rick.

"Ok. How did you come across the body?" asked LeBlanc, as he scribbled on a small notepad.

"Well, after I caught a mess of catfish, I thought I'd do a little exploring with my metal detector. Treasure hunting is a hobby of mine. You never know what you'll find down on the bayou. It's way down the bayou where the Hillebrandt meets the Taylor in a place called Rodair Gully. I pulled my jon boat to the bank and started metal detecting a small open area in between some mossy live oaks and tall cypress trees, and my detector went off after several passes over an old campfire, but I assumed it was burnt beer cans. Then, after I changed the settings on my detector, it pinpointed a large object of some sort. That's when I started digging."

"So why did you choose this particular spot to pull up the jon boat?" asked LeBlanc.

"No real reason. I just saw an opening between the cypress trees on the bank that would be an easy place to drag the boat up."

"And after your metal detector went off, you dug up...?"

"A barrel. A fifty-five-gallon drum, to be exact, sealed and only about a foot below the surface. I rolled it to drier ground and loosened the latch ring around the lid of the drum. I heard a small, whooshing sound when the pressure escaped.

"The body was in the barrel?" asked LeBlanc.

"Yeah, and the smell of burnt flesh was almost too much to handle. I nearly lost my breakfast," said Rick. "Oh, and here, take this," he continued, as he handed the deputy a gallon-sized resealable bag. It held a leather pouch filled with contents from the crime scene.

"What's this?" asked the deputy.

"I found it inside the barrel, sitting on top of a burlap sack. It looks like a gris-gris bag, like the ones I've seen at voodoo shops in New Orleans."

"You disturbed the crime scene?" asked the deputy in a sharp tone.

5

"I had no idea it was a crime scene. I always wear mechanics' gloves while detecting and had them on when I opened the barrel," said Rick.

"What else can you tell me?"

"Once I opened the barrel and saw the body, I knew something purely evil had happened here, though not recently. The soil above the barrel wasn't freshly disturbed, and clovers and salt grass were thick where I first dug."

"Were there any footprints other than your own you could see?" asked LeBlanc.

"I wasn't paying that much attention to that, but the grass and weeds were tall, and it didn't look like anyone had been in the area for some time. After I removed the leather pouch, I resealed the barrel and covered it all up with saw palmettos."

"Did you disturb the body?"

"Not at all. I just closed up the barrel and called 911."

"Thanks, Mr. Waters. I'll round up the boys and we can follow you to the body."

Rick nodded and waited for the deputies to get their inflatable launched.

As he waited, he tidied up the mess he had created while fishing, and put his metal detector and digging bag back in his truck.

It was a comedy of errors watching the deputies get their boat ready. Testosterone mixed with narcissism made a mighty strong cocktail. Rick sat in his boat, patiently waiting while they finally got in the water and cranked up the huge outboards. Every bird within a mile jumped, including Chief. Those outboards were loud—even for four-stroke engines.

It took twenty-five minutes to get to the low part of the bank where Rick had pulled his jon boat up earlier.

The deputy driving the inflatable followed, then throttled the outboards slowly and nudged up to the bank, keeping just enough pressure on the throttle to keep the boat steady against the bank, and one by one, each man stepped onto dry land. They tied their flat boat to a large chinaberry tree, and the second-to-last man handed over a soft stretcher, a body bag, and a few leather cases of what was probably forensic gear. The driver stayed on board.

Rick opened his phone to the saved GPS location, and they all began the trek through the tall salt grass. There was idle chatter about gators and snakes, and Chief, seeming to understand, clung tightly to the inside of Rick's jacket, peeking his head out every now and again.

When they reached the site, Rick removed the palmetto branches he had used to cover the barrel before he had contacted the deputies.

The forensics team set up camp next to the rusty old barrel. Then a deputy wearing latex gloves reopened the seal.

A sweet, sickening smell combined with a burnt char odor filled the air. The deputy slowly pulled back the burlap sack and then stumbled backward. The dead body, skull and bones, were curled up in a fetal position. Rick turned away and held onto a nearby tree for stability from his lightheadedness. When he regained his composure, he moved closer. The smell was unmistakable: the smell of death.

The bones were black with soot, but he could see the skull; it had three bullet holes in it from a small-caliber gun. The lower jaw was missing. The forensics guy snapped many close-up photos as another deputy rooted around the edge of the barrel with a stainless-steel grabbing tool, until he came across something shiny. He tugged at the object, and a badly burned, sequin-studded belt appeared. He gently grabbed the belt with the tool and slowly pulled it out. On the end was a belt buckle, charred but clearly crafted out of silver and tarnished brass.

The deputy in charge of forensics took several more photos of the evidence, tagged each piece, and then stuffed them inside a plastic baggy.

Deputy LeBlanc gasped when he got a better view of the belt.

"It says 'CJ' on the belt buckle," the deputy murmured, seeming to pull himself together after a moment. Then he shook his head in disgust. "I think I know who this girl is." He pulled out his smartphone and began to key in something.

LeBlanc must have pulled up a missing persons website, scrolled for a while, then stopped. The look on his face told the story, and he showed Rick and the other deputies what he'd discovered.

Name: Cara Johnson
Sex: Female
Race: Caucasian
Age: 23
Eyes: Green
Hair: Blonde
Height: 5'6"
Weight: 109 lbs
Description: Wearing Wrangler jeans with a sequin belt buckle with the initials CJ and a black Cowgirl

Legend embroidered snap western shirt.
Last Seen: March 25th at Casa Olé, 5898 Eastex Frwy, Beaumont, TX, around 7:40 pm.

If you have any information about the whereabouts of Cara Johnson, please contact your local Jefferson County Police Department.

Cara Johnson was the daughter of Benjamin Johnson, a wealthy real estate developer from Port Arthur. The story of Cara's disappearance had been covered by every news agency for months and was the talk of the town.

Cara had been a popular young woman, and a rising star on the horse barrel racing scene. Her adoring father had lavished her with all the gear and outfits she needed to outshine the competition. According to the reports, Cara and her friends had gone out one night after celebrating her win at the local rodeo in Beaumont. They headed to Casa Olé, a favorite Tex-Mex place, for late-night drinking and appetizers. Cara had forgotten her phone in her truck and went out to get it after she ordered a Cadillac margarita. She was never seen again.

"I knew her personally," LeBlanc told the others, looking up from his phone. "I met her at Cutter's Bar. I danced with her once and I remember that belt buckle vividly. I had even commented on how pretty it was, trying to impress her. She just smiled as we continued to two-step. I saw her a few times after that at Cutter's, but she was with another guy every time. I assumed they were dating, so I didn't bother her," said LeBlanc.

The look on the deputy's face matched that of the other members of his team as they moved the remains into a body bag. It was tragic to find a dead body, but the discovery hit home even harder when the person was one, they had all heard about, and one of them had even known personally. A huge sense of anguish mixed with disgust filled the air as they zipped the body bag closed.

Rick knew Cara's father, Benjamin, and knew *of* Cara but had never met her. He'd actually met her father at AJ's Oyster Bar in Destin, Florida, while Benjamin was on vacation there. Rick knew Benjamin's reputation more than the man himself because of his frequent TV appearances and stories about him in the newspapers—usually defending his plans to clear-cut land for development or fill in some wetland for the next strip mall or parking lot.

Rick didn't like his development methods but couldn't fault a guy for trying to make a buck either. They had exchanged business cards at AJ's back in December after Rick noticed Benjamin wearing an East Chambers baseball cap. E.C. was a 3A high school football team Rick was more than familiar with. He had gone to Hamshire-Fannett and the team from East Chambers were bitter rivals, but it was a Texas connection, so Rick had introduced himself.

That would've been only three or four months before Cara went missing. What a horrific ending to such a young girl's life!

Contemplating the ways in which she could've been murdered revolted him. *Was she raped? Did she know she was gonna die? Was she tortured?*

Deputy LeBlanc thanked Rick again for his help and shook his hand.

"We'll need a full statement from you," said the deputy. "Can you head down to the sheriff's office? The address is on the business card." He pulled a card out of his shirt pocket and handed it over.

"Sure, no problem, I'll motor back and let y'all do your thing. Who should I ask for down at the station?"

"Ask for Captain Garner. I'll call ahead and let him know you're coming in. Thanks again for all your help."

"No worries. Sorry it was someone you knew. That really sucks!" said Rick.

"Yeah, it sure does." LeBlanc said, sighing. Then he recovered himself and turned back to his men.

Rick returned to the boat ramp, maneuvered his old skiff onto the trailer, secured the hand crank and outboard, and climbed up in his truck with Chief still nestled under his jacket. Then he beelined it for the sheriff's department in Port Arthur.

A bell chimed as Rick pushed open the front door of the sheriff's office. He spotted a uniformed woman deeply engaged with a computer, sitting behind a long partition at the center of the room.

"Excuse me," he began as he approached her. "I'd like to speak to Captain Garner. He's expecting me."

The woman was typing something and intently focused on the screen. She glanced up at Rick, held up one finger and continued to type. A minute went by.

"How can I help you?" she finally said.

"I need to speak to Captain Garner," he repeated.

"Ok. Put your name here." She pushed a clipboard with a pen attached to a chain toward him.

He wrote down his name, the time and the date, and gave it back to her.

"Go ahead and have a seat. He'll be right out."

Rick sat down and thumbed through the classifieds in an issue of the Thrifty Nickel paper while he waited. The wall in front of him was covered with missing persons photos, mostly of kids, and a list of Texas's most wanted. He winced, recalling his gruesome discovery and pondering how Cara's life was taken in such a sickening way. He quickly looked away and went back to scanning the paper.

After a few minutes, a burly, gray-haired man peeked around the corner of a door he held open down the hall. "Rick Waters?"

"Yeah, that's me."

He shook the man's hand and followed him to a small office. The desk was piled six inches high with a sea of papers and file folders.

"I'm Captain Bryan Garner. I understand you're here to give a statement?"

"Yes, I'm the one who found the body down on the bayou this morning."

Rick respected the authorities but knew, based on crime books he had read, that he would be considered a suspect just for reporting the crime. He tried to brush aside his uneasiness at that possibility. His PI instincts reminded him that the authorities would likely rule him out quite quickly as a person of interest, due to the lack of his own DNA on the scene and the time of death, once it was determined. Because of that, along with his general distrust of police and the justice system, he erred on the side of caution.

Rick assumed the body had likely been there for several months based on decomposition and the long growth of weeds where the barrel had been buried. At the presumed time of Cara's death, he had been working at the Okaloosa Airport in Florida, so his alibi was solid.

"So, tell me how you came across the body, and please be thorough. You never know what little detail may help us in this case," Garner began.

"I started my morning early, just after sunup. I had spent the night in the back of my pickup camper. I keep a small mattress back there for sleeping. I wanted to get an early start, so I could catch some catfish to sell to Pine Tree Lodge."

"I love that place," said Garner.

"Yeah, well, they use only wild-caught catfish, and it makes a difference."

Damn! The catfish! I need to get those to Pine Tree while they're still swimming.

"Ok, please continue. So, you started off at the Steinhager boat ramp?" asked the captain.

"Yeah, I launched my jon boat and started setting limb lines. After a couple hours I had pretty much filled my live well and decided to do some exploring. I have a metal detector and I love hunting for artifacts on the banks of the bayou. I decided to motor down deeper in the bayou than I ever had before, so I could find a new place to explore.

"As I travelled downstream, I came to a place where the Hillebrandt and Taylor bayous meet. On my map, it's called Rodair Gully," continued Rick. "I found a low part of the bank to tie off my boat and took my bird, metal detector and digging bag to the shore and started walking through the salt grass until I came upon a clearing."

"Bird?" asked Garner.

"Oh, yeah, I have an umbrella cockatoo that thinks he's a dog and goes everywhere with me. His name is Chief. He even barks," Rick explained.

"That's funny," said Garner with chuckle. "Ok, so you're hiking though the salt grass. Then what?"

"Well, this clearing was surrounded by live oaks covered in Spanish moss and a few old cypress trees. In the center was an old campfire, so at first I steered clear of that with my metal detector," said Rick.

"Why did you steer clear of it?"

"Well, in the past, when I've run a detector over an old campfire, I always find burned up beer cans. Everyone loves to throw their aluminum cans into a fire to watch them melt."

"That's true. I've done it myself."

"I did a round-square sweep of the entire area and got zero hits on my detector.

"What's a round-square sweep?"

"I think y'all call it an expanding-square pattern. It's a search pattern where you start by taking one step forward and sweeping the area, then take two steps ninety degrees clockwise and sweep, then three steps ninety degrees clockwise, et cetera, until you have covered the entire area. I learned it in a scuba diving search and recovery class."

"Yeah, ok, I'm familiar with the expanding-square pattern."

"I was beginning to think my detector had a glitch, so I decided to focus on the campfire area, and then the thing started going off big time. I adjusted the settings but it continued to peg out, so I knew it was something other than beer cans. When I pulled out my shovel and dug, I hit something hard, so I used a couple of branches to make a fulcrum to get it out. It was a sealed, fifty-five-gallon drum. I cracked open the seal and the smell that came out almost made me puke."

"What sort of smell?" asked the captain.

"You know. The smell of death. That rank sort of sweet odor when you stumble upon a dead animal in the woods or something. At first, I thought maybe someone buried a boar carcass or something. But after I got the lid all the way off, I found the gris-gris bag," said Rick.

"What's a gris-gris bag? I'm not familiar with the term," said Garner.

"I learned about them in New Orleans at Marie Laveau's House of Voodoo on Bourbon Street. They're small leather pouches for good or bad luck, depending on the herbs or other items in them, and the words spoken over them while they were made. Here, I took some photos and notes I can show you. Read this."

Rick handed him his phone with a photo of a list he had written detailing the contents of the bag.

The captain read it aloud.

> *Tail fur from a goat or lamb*
> *White cloth Voodoo doll with X's on eyes*
> *Rubber-banded herbs of some sort*
> *Dried chicken foot*
> *Several bones from a small animal*
> *3 black feathers*

Vial of dark liquid
Carved wooden hand with glass eye in palm

"Ok, I get it now," Garner said, after glancing at the photos. "Can you forward those to my email?"

"Sure. Where should I send them?"

After Garner gave him the address, Rick highlighted all the photos and messaged them to the captain, then he continued his story.

"So first I went through the leather pouch, with mechanics' gloves on, mind you, and then I pulled back the burlap sack. That's when I found the body. I was so shocked; all I could think to do was call 911. Then I guess I sort of came to my senses, resealed the barrel and covered it in branches, then headed back to the boat ramp to wait for the deputies. I gave the bag to Deputy LeBlanc and he and his men followed me to the crime scene. After that, he told me to come here and speak to you, so here I am. That's about all I have for you," Rick finished, letting out a sigh of relief, as if he was exhausted from telling the tale.

"Wow, that's quite a story. I'm sure you're rather disturbed by it all, as am I. If you think of anything else, please call me."

Garner handed him a business card.

"Oh yeah, not that it matters, but I'm a part-time PI, so if I can help in any way, please let me know. I want to find out how and why this happened as much as anyone," Rick added.

The captain rolled his eyes in dismissal of Rick's offer to help, then said, "We'll keep you posted if anything arises or we have more questions for you."

CHAPTER TWO

Rick left the sheriff's office, hopped into his truck and set his GPS for Pine Tree Lodge. He knew how to get there by heart but set his GPS out of habit.

Randy, the manager, was out back and offered him a beer, but Rick declined. "I have some errands I have to run," he told him, "but check this out," he said, indicating his catch.

Randy carefully counted the catfish and weighed them out. "You have fifty-eight channel cats, Rick, weighing a total of 134 pounds." He pulled a calculator from his pocket and mumbled aloud while doing the math. "Ok. At $3.50 a pound, that comes to $469. How about we round it down to four big bills and I clear your bar tab?"

Rick couldn't remember what his bar total was but figured it was close or probably higher than that. He didn't want to haggle, so agreed to the price. They shook hands, and as Rick put the money in his shirt pocket, he overheard a young girl crying while speaking to someone on her cell phone. He recognized her as a waitress from the fish camp.

"I'll try and get the money," she said. "I'll try." She wiped her eyes as she put the phone in her pocket.

"Are you ok?" Rick asked her.

She sniffled and looked at him sheepishly. "Yes... I mean, no. I don't know."

"What's wrong?"

"I'm behind on my rent, and my landlord says if I don't come up with it today, he's gonna put my stuff out on the lawn. I'm still two hundred dollars short, and we're almost out of diapers and baby food."

Rick reached into his pocket and pulled out some money. He handed her three hundred-dollar bills.

Her eyes grew wide.

"I can't take that. I don't even know you."

"Sure, you do. You served me beers here a couple of times. You were always friendly to me and even bought me an appetizer once when I was short on cash, before Randy started letting me keep a running tab here. Consider us even."

She grabbed Rick and wrapped her arms around him. "You saved my life."

"Nah. Just call it a good day. Pay it forward someday, hon."

Rick got into his truck and headed toward the Boudain Hut. But on the way, he dropped off his jon boat at the storage yard, where he also stored his old Firebird from high school. After backing the boat down, he unhitched it beside the Pontiac. It was almost happy hour and he was itching to play some pool.

At least I have a little scratch in my pocket. I can always make more tomorrow.

Rick scrolled through his music app for something to listen to and chose some George Strait. That always got him in the mood for a honky-tonk.

His Ford was rusty and beat up, but his sound system was beyond badass. His phone was synced to the new stereo receiver he'd bought while working in Destin, and he had two eight-hundred-watt subwoofer enclosures behind the seat as well as another power amp running the six-inch door speakers. But his sound system wasn't the only thing that rocked. So did the engine.

When he was living in Destin, he'd woken up late for a shift at the airport, bolted to his Ford, fired it up, and put the hammer down. Apparently, it hadn't warmed up long enough, and as he drove over the Destin Bridge and onto Okaloosa Island, he heard a loud bang under the hood and saw a rod fly right through it. The old Ford seized up and was dead in the water, so he had called Dave Meeks, the only mechanic he knew.

Dave worked out of a shop in Panama City and ran sound for bands when he wasn't turning wrenches. They'd originally met at a David Allan Coe concert in Panama City where Dave was running the monitor mix at Pier Park. They had talked about the crappy new music coming out of Nashville and hit it off immediately. Dave was a good ol' boy and a hard worker, and Rick appreciated that. When Rick told him about throwing the rod and being stuck on Highway 98, Dave immediately sent a tow truck.

Later that day, Dave had given him the bad news first.

"Dude, this straight-six is a goner. I have another engine you might like though, and with a few motor-mount mods, I can fit her in. Also has a brand-new tranny."

"How much?"

"Well, I was rebuilding her for a guy's '68 Mustang and I personally have twenty-five hundred in the build. It's a sweet engine. He gave me five bills as a deposit, then he got busted for selling meth, and he's in the big house again. Three strikes, so I'm stuck with it."

"Holy shit! Will that fit in my truck?" asked Rick.

"Hell yeah, dude. No worries. It also comes with a rebuilt B&M racing tranny and a Hurst shift kit. I just need to swap out the motor mounts to make her work for your Ford. If you can give me thirty-eight hundred, it's all yours." Rick figured his rebuilt truck would be the fastest '62 Ford F-100 in Bay County. Hell, maybe Okaloosa County, too.

Two weeks later, the Ford came back, sporting new twenty-inch American Racing rims and Z-rated tires. Except for a few rust holes and faded red paint job, she was one of the most jaw-dropping trucks on the road.

That entire rebuild and truck transformation was a great benefit of his time in Florida, and Rick smiled fondly at the memory as he arrived at the Boudain Hut —a typical Texas honky-tonk gun-and-knife club. He liked the place; it was pet-friendly and often had good local bands that played real country music. The bar was known for its boudin; a combination of cooked rice, pork, onions, green peppers and Cajun seasonings in a sausage casing.

It seemed like a good night to make a buck playing some pool, but it was still early. Rick sat down and had a couple of Lone Stars before the good players arrived. The hundred-dollar bill left over from his catfish sale was still in his pocket, and he hoped to parlay it.

"Rick Waters?" said a voice behind him. "It's me, Gary Haas."

Rick spun around and his face broke into a warm smile when he recognized his old high school friend.

"Oh my God, how long has it been?" asked Rick.

"Too long, buddy. How have you been?"

"I've been good. Pull up a chair—let's catch up."

Gary grabbed a barstool and sat down. He waved over the bartender and pointed at Rick's beer.

"Two more of these on me, please," Gary told him.

"Would you like to see a menu?" asked the bartender.

"Nah, I'm on a liquid diet for the time being," said Gary with a grin. "So, who's your friend?" he asked, looking up at Chief.

"This is Chief—he's an umbrella cockatoo. I got him off of Craigslist from a guy in Orlando. The guy had taken a job out of the country and couldn't take Chief with him, so I bought him. Got a good deal too. Only eight hundred bucks. A bird like this from a breeder or pet store would cost at least twenty-five hundred. I think the guy saw that Chief and I had an instant connection and really wanted to sell him to someone who would take care of him. I've kept in touch with the guy and texted him pics and video clips of Chief from time to time."

"That's so cool, man. So, what else is new in your world?"

Rick told Gary about working in Destin, his recent move back home to Texas, and how he'd fixed up his old Ford. As they sipped their Lone Stars, Gary filled Rick in on his two failed marriages and his new job at the refinery.

But Rick couldn't resist sharing his most recent news. "You won't believe this," he whispered, leaning in to Gary.

"This morning while I was out on the bayou, I found a dead body."

"What? You didn't start with that?"

"Well, it's kind of a downer. They think she was a local girl from Port Arthur named Cara Johnson. Have you heard of her?" Rick asked.

"Damn dude! Yes, I knew her, and I read about her disappearance. I used to spend some time down at the rodeo helping a friend of mine who rides bulls and I saw her barrel race many times. Pretty girl. That's so tragic. I figured after being missing so long, something bad happened to her."

"Yeah, it'll probably be on the news tonight," said Rick.

After a few more beers and a lot more conversation, the sound of pool balls smashing together caught Rick's ear.

"You wanna play some pool?" he asked his friend.

"It's been a while, but why not?"

Rick got some quarters from the bartender and told him to keep the tab open. They both grabbed the straightest sticks they could find and Gary racked on the only open table in the bar.

Rick broke and ran the table but scratched on the eight ball. Then he racked the next game and Gary broke. Gary made two solids and a stripe and chose solids. He made the next couple of shots but missed on the third. Rick again ran the table and sank the eight ball.

"Wanna make it interesting?" said someone to Rick from the next table over. The guy had apparently seen Rick run the table twice but thought he could beat him.

"Sure," said Rick. "You don't mind, do you, Gary?"

"Nah, go ahead. I gotta head out soon anyway. I'm gonna get some food to go and grab a cab," replied Gary.

"Just hang out for a bit if you can and I'll give you a ride home. You still over in La Belle?"

"Yep, no worries. I can hang for a bit."

The large, barrel-chested guy who'd challenged Rick stepped up to the table. He was cocky and Rick could tell he was a bit buzzed.

"How about twenty bucks a game?" asked the man.

"Ok, twenty it is," said Rick. "You can break."

The guy chalked up his pool stick as Rick racked the balls as tight as he could.

The man broke and sank two solids. He made his next shot but missed the following one.

Now that money was on the line, Rick concentrated more than when he was playing Gary. He sank all his stripes and deposited the eight ball in the corner pocket with ease. Rick's giant opponent huffed loudly in anger when Rick reached down to grab the twenty. Then the guy stopped him.

"How about double or nothing?"

"I need to get going; besides, I want to give my buddy a ride home," said Rick.

"So, you won't give a guy a chance to win his money back? Pretty cheesy," the stranger said.

"Ok, fair enough then. My friend just ordered his food anyway. It'll be a while."

The man racked the table and Rick chalked up his stick. He broke the balls and won the game without ever missing a shot. The big guy was furious and a little embarrassed, as his friends were snickering and patting him on the back.

Rick picked up the forty dollars and was ready to leave when the guy said, "So, you think you're a hotshot pool shark, don't you?"

"Nah, just a fairly decent player, I'd say. You made the bet rules, not me," responded Rick.

The last thing Rick wanted to do was to get into a brawl with this thick-necked monster. The guy was clearly agitated and his ego was hurt.

"One more game—five hundred dollars, winner takes all!"

"Dude, I don't have that kind of cash on me," said Rick.

"Well, there's an ATM right over there." The man pointed toward the corner.

Rick knew he only had about two hundred in his checking account but he did have a credit card with a zero balance. It was a risk, but one he was willing to take. He had a little under two hundred in his pocket, so he withdrew three hundred and fifty to be safe. The ATM charged him six bucks for the withdrawal. A rip-off.

Figuring if he won, the man might get a tad violent, Rick picked up Chief, who had been perched on the back of a barstool by the pool table. He handed his keys and Chief to Gary and whispered for him to go outside and start his truck halfway through the game. Chief's travel cage was on the front seat, he told him, and suggested they might all need to get away fast.

Since it was such a high-stakes game, they flipped a coin to see who would break. Rick called heads but it was tails, so he racked the balls.

The big man broke and sank two stripes. If he sank all the balls on the table, Rick would be basically broke. He did just that but missed the eight ball in the side pocket by a quarter of an inch. It seemed to just float on the edge. Rick's heart jumped out of his throat. It was his turn. He'd have to run the table and make sure not to touch that eight ball teetering on the felt. It would be no easy task.

On Rick's first shot, he sank the six and set up the three perfectly, which led him to a nice, short side pocket of the one ball. He sank the rest of the solids and lined up the eight ball. With one eye on the eight ball and the other on the big man, he took his shot and won the game.

The man slammed his stick against the table, cracking it.

"Son of a bitch!" he yelled.

"Whoa buddy, calm down!" Rick began to back away with the cash in his fist. "We played, I won, that's it," he said.

The big man laughed as he walked toward him. He outweighed him by a hundred pounds easily and Rick had only a second to make a move. He was about to sweep the guy's legs when the fellow stuck out his hand for a shake.

Rick let out a sigh of relief. The man reached into his pocket and handed Rick a card.

Southeast Texas Harley Davidson. Jason Allan, owner.

"Give me a chance to get my money back sometime. Come in and buy a Harley from me. I'll call my loss your five-hundred-dollar discount."

Rick laughed. "If I'm ever in need of a scooter, I'll look you up."

He was about to pay his tab when he heard a ruckus on the other side of the bar. Two guys were arguing, and it looked like it might get violent.

A hefty guy in a wife-beater tank top was cussing at a much smaller man in a denim jacket. Ordinarily, Rick stayed out of situations like this, but when a woman grabbed the big guy's arm, trying to pull him away from the guy in the jacket, he backhanded her and she fell against the table, knocking beer bottles onto the ground. She almost went down as well but caught her balance, then held her face, crying. That was Rick's cue. Two guys hitting each other was one thing, but hitting a woman went too far.

"Hey man, what's your problem?" yelled Rick.

The big guy turned to look at Rick.

"Mind your own business, pal, if you know what's good for you."

"I normally would, but you just hit a woman, so now it *is* my business," replied Rick, moving closer to the guy with the intention of breaking up the fight before it started. Listen, say you're sorry to the lady and buy her a beer, and we can all just relax," Rick suggested.

The woman interrupted.

"Chuck let's just go, let's get out of here."

"You should listen to her, Chuck," said Rick.

"The hell I will. She's my old lady and she was flirting with this punk." He pointed to the other guy, who shrugged his shoulders and shook his head in disagreement.

"I don't care about you or your lady's problems, but I clearly saw you slap her and that's not ok in my book," said Rick.

"I told you to mind your own business. She's my girl, so piss off."

"Well, Chuck, based on your lack of manners, your choice of attire, and your general way with words, maybe she needs a real man—like your buddy over there in the jean jacket."

That fired him up. He moved toward Rick and swung, but Rick leaned to his left and grabbed the man's fist in one motion, spinning him around and putting his arm behind his back. Then he grabbed Chuck's hair and slammed his face against the table, bending his arm to the breaking point.

"Now, say you're sorry!"

Chuck just grunted and tried to break free from Rick's grip, to no avail.

"Say you're sorry!" Rick demanded, bending his arm higher.

"I'm sorry!" he said begrudgingly.

"What kind of beer are you drinking?" Rick asked the tearful woman.

"Miller High Life," she whimpered.

"Oh, 'The Champagne of Beers.' Can I get two Miller High Lifes over here?" he called. A crowd had circled the entire scene at this point. A waitress rushed back with the two beers and set them beside Rick, who offered one to the woman.

"I don't drink that crap," murmured the man, whose face was still sideways against the table.

"Oh, the other one's for me. I haven't had a High Life in ages. Thought I'd give it a try."

The man huffed.

"I'm gonna release your arm and we can all play nice now, ok?" said Rick.

"Ok, fine!" grunted Chuck.

Rick slowly let his arm go and lifted him up from the table. Chuck was breathing heavily and still very angry. He gave his girl an ugly look and then suddenly spun around. Rick had the beer in his left hand and was about to take a sip when the guy pulled out a butterfly knife from his front pocket and spun it in circles, ninja style, into the locked position. He came at Rick, slicing in the air.

With his free right hand, Rick whipped the .38 snub-nose from inside the waistband behind his back and pointed it at the man sideways, like in the movies. The guy froze.

"Drop the knife. You just never learn, do you?"

He dropped it.

"Now kick it over here."

When he did, Rick put his foot on top of it, then slid it toward the waitress and motioned for her to take it.

"Now lie down on the ground." Rick gestured with the gun toward the floor. Again, the big guy complied.

"Turn your head and count to a hundred."

Chuck reluctantly counted, breathing heavily. Rick slowly backed toward the exit, sliding his gun back into his waistband. The woman put her hands together in prayer fashion and mouthed a thank you to Rick.

He acknowledged her with a kind smile, jumped in the passenger side of his truck and told Gary to floor it. Gary peeled out and headed toward his house, just a few miles from the Boudain Hut.

"Did the man you beat at pool come after you?"

"Same problem, different guy."

"What happened?"

Gary stopped in his driveway, Rick pulled out the cash and put it and the pistol in the glovebox.

"Let's just say, never bring a knife to a gunfight."

CHAPTER THREE

Rick awoke to a pounding on the door.
"Housekeeping," a woman's voice called.
It was only 9:30 a.m. and checkout wasn't until noon.
"Can you come back, ma'am?"
"No problem," she replied.
He had done well the previous night and was up several hundred dollars, so he had checked into Port Arthur's finest motel, the Port Arthur Motor Inn. He rubbed his eyes and climbed out of bed to feed Chief breakfast. He really needed a shower but he wanted to get going.
"Ok, Chief, let's go to the library, buddy. Can you be quiet for a while?"
"Cracker, cracker," said the bird as Rick stuck a couple of grapes in Chief's cage and patted him on the head, laughing.
"It's not a cracker, buddy, but that'll do."
Chief looked back at him and raised his crown high. Then Rick grabbed the bird's backpack and travel cage and stepped out of the room.

He had cut two large squares behind the zippers on an oversized JanSport backpack and then sewed in stainless-steel mesh inserts for breathing holes. He'd affixed a piece of half-inch PVC pipe across the middle to create a perch and then spray-painted the outside of the stainless-steel mesh the same color as the backpack. To anyone glancing at it, the backpack looked just like any other JanSport, but it worked perfectly as an undercover home for Chief during their expeditions. Often, Rick would feed him grapes through a small opening between the zippers, and the little guy stayed content. He hoped he'd stay quiet at the library, since no pets were allowed.

After setting Chief on the front seat of the truck, Rick dropped the room key off at the front desk, bound for the Beaumont Public Library. He was hoping to do some research about the treasures hidden in Jasper County.

Rick was at home in the library, and loved to devour books about famous legends and unsolved mysteries. His fascination with treasure hunting was one of the first things that had gotten him interested in travel, and it was the main reason he had gone to Florida in the first place.

Treasure could be found anywhere, and stories abounded. Rick always carried with him a reprinted 1979 newspaper article about buried treasure from the Beaumont Enterprise sourced from an 1898 article from the Galveston Daily News. He'd printed it from the library archives and laminated it. This keepsake sat in his Garrett Camo Digger's Satchel along with the necessary tools he needed for treasure hunting: mechanics' gloves, a foldable shovel, a garden trowel, Buck knife, notepad, pint and gallon-sized resealable plastic bags bound with a rubber band, and a dry box containing kitchen matches.

The most interesting part of the article was a letter written by John E. Fletcher. It read:

Nolan's Trail, Nov. 17, 1816

On the trail a deposit was made in the year 1813 by a company of twelve of us, who were captured by a hundred of Jackson's Cavalry. Nine of our squad were killed dead on the ground. There were three of us left who were carried to New Orleans and put in prison. One man died in prison. The fight (Battle of New Orleans) coming off, we were given our choice to go into the fight, and if we survived, we were to go free, or else stay in prison for life.

We chose to go in the fight, and Nathan Perkins, the eleventh man, was killed in battle, which left me the only living man who knew where the deposit was made in 1813 on Nolan's Trail, leading from Natchitoches on Red River to San Antonio, running in a southwest direction from Red River.

The deposit is in a small, clear-running little creek, which runs the year round, 15 or 20 miles west of the Sabine River. It was taken down the creek 160 yards and put under a waterfall. We could pass through the water and it would fall clear over us, a high backbone ridge headed right up to the bank on the east side.

The first capture was made on April 7, 1813, twelve mule-loads of silver, and on the 26th of October, we captured thirty mule-loads of Spanish gold, and between these, we captured five other small lots which we put in the same place just about where the ridge points up to the creek at the lower end.

We were very careful not to mark the site. We always passed down to the place through the water so as to leave no sign. We never stayed around the place but would pass there once in a while to see that all was all right.

John E. Fletcher

Rick's plan today was to research more about Fletcher's Treasure. Once he arrived at the library, he began his microfilm search for people with the last name mentioned in the article he always carried. He reviewed obituaries and then looked for surviving relatives of John E. Fletcher. The name Mildred Fletcher came up as John's only daughter, and she had a son named Fred Young, whose obituary turned up the name Marcy Hinkley. After a search for Marcy, he found she was still alive in the town of Jasper. Finally, a living relative he could interview.

With the new information in hand, he left the library and decided to call the sheriff's office to see if any progress had been made on Cara's murder case. Deputy LeBlanc sounded frustrated as he told Rick they had no leads yet.

"We don't have a lot to go on, and the autopsy is not complete yet, but as you saw at the crime scene, there were obviously three bullet wounds to the back of the skull. It may be mob-related."

Rick knew the case might never be solved, but he felt connected to it since he was the one who'd found the body.

"I'll keep you posted. The sheriff's department is doing everything in its power to solve this one. It's a big priority here. I'll let you know if anything new develops, and make sure to call me if something you forgot pops into your head."

"Will do, deputy. Thanks for keeping me in the loop."

Rick had a little money in his pocket and a lot of time on his hands, so he decided to head up to Jasper County, hoping to talk to Marcy Hinkley, *if* he could find her, and see if she might have any undiscovered information on the John E. Fletcher treasure. But to do that, he figured he'd somehow need to gain her trust.

He thought long and hard about it as he drove north toward Jasper. While refueling the Ford in Lumberton, he Googled the rules on sharing found treasure.

> *The treasure trove rule dictates that a treasure trove belongs to the finder. Courts distinguish a treasure trove from other mislaid property as refined gold and silver, or paper money buried or otherwise hidden or concealed.*

Even so, maybe he could persuade Marcy, who was the rightful heir to the treasure, to work out some sort of sharing arrangement. In exchange for some information that she might have, he would do the physical searching. She deserved some of the treasure, even if Rick was the finder. It was only fair.

After arriving in Jasper and realizing his own smell was starting to offend him, he pulled into the Deluxe Inn and got a room.

With his most valuable gear stowed safely under the bed, he was ready for a long shower. Chief joined him, using a bird shower perch made from PVC pipes and suction cups.

Once they were both dried off, Rick put Chief in the cage and filled his water and food bowls. He needed to go to the local Jasper library. It was much smaller than the one in Beaumont, but it would have to do.

A rather attractive, thirty-something librarian greeted him.

"Good afternoon, sir. How can I help you today?"

"I wanted to look through some of your old microfilm. I'm trying to track down some descendants of John E. Fletcher."

The librarian rolled her eyes.

"Oh, you're a treasure hunter, huh? You're not the first one searching for that and won't be the last, I'm sure," she said a little haughtily. "But I'll be happy to get you all set up. Do you have a library card?"

"I don't live here but I have a Beaumont Public Library card. Will that do?"

Satisfied, she escorted him to the microfilm machine and gave him some quick instructions. He was already familiar with it, as it was exactly like the one in Beaumont.

Two hours of searching, and he came up with nothing. Finally, out of frustration—and a little hope—he asked the librarian if she knew Marcy Hinkley.

She thought for a minute.

"You must mean Marcy Nobles. She married Lester Nobles many years ago, and I'm pretty sure Hinkley was her maiden name. The only reason I know that is because she used to play bridge at my mom's place—before Lester died.

"After Lester's death, she became quite a hermit, I hear, and rarely leaves her house. I haven't seen her in years. She lives at the edge of town, past the fire station, in an old, asphalt-shingle-covered shotgun house. Why the interest? Are you related to her?"

"No, no, nothing like that," Rick told her. "But I think she has ties to the Fletcher treasure."

The librarian chuckled under her breath.

"Would it be possible to print something?" asked Rick.

"Sure. It's only ten cents a copy."

He printed a copy of a standard search and salvage contract he'd found, then followed the librarian's directions to the Nobles house.

It was exactly as the librarian had described it: shingle-covered, shotgun-style, aptly named because a shot fired from one end of the narrow, rectangular house would go all the way through to the other end.

Rick pulled up to her place and parked. As he approached the entrance, he noticed that the eaves were rotted. There hadn't been any maintenance done to the place in years, and the bare spots and weeds in the yard outnumbered the blades of grass. It hadn't been watered in ages, and there was no sprinkler in sight.

He stepped up to the front door cautiously and knocked twice. Almost immediately, he heard some rustling around and then a crash, as if something had fallen.

"Who's there?" a raspy voice asked. He thought the woman must be smoking five packs a day.

"Ma'am, my name is Rick Waters. Could I come in and speak with you a moment?

She coughed. "You're who?"

My name is Waters, ma'am, and I believe you're a descendant of John E. Fletcher? If you are, I have a proposition for you. Can you just open the door? I believe we can help each other out if you'll just sit down and talk to me."

The lady shuffled to the door and cracked it open just enough for Rick to see her weathered face and a double-barreled shotgun, in plain view, leaning against the couch behind her.

Marcy was short, maybe five foot one. She peered through the door opening with a frown and kept the safety chain on.

"I ain't buying anything, so if you're selling, you can just get."

"No, ma'am, I'm actually here to *give* you something."

Rick explained that she might be entitled to a legal share of John E. Fletcher's treasure if she could prove she was a direct descendant of his. He told her that her house might also be considered a historic site. Her frown slowly faded and turned into an inquisitive look.

As he continued explaining the process, she interrupted him.

"Hell, yeah, I'm related to John. He was my great-great-grandfather, and I got pictures to prove it."

She unlatched the chain on the door and let him in. The house was a pigsty, inhabited by a hoarder. It wasn't easy to even move around inside.

Rick was thirsty, but the pile of dishes in the sink and the smell coming from them quickly changed his mind about asking for a glass of water. It was all he could do to keep the contents of his breakfast down.

She rummaged through an open keepsake box and laid out a few photos on the edge of a coffee table, although the term *coffee table* was a bit of a misnomer; it was more like a coffee stain with a table under it. She pushed a pile of empty beer cans to the floor and made room for more photos. The stench from an overflowing ashtray stung his senses, but he refrained from pinching his nose.

It'll all be worth it if I can get her to agree to the contract for the treasure trove.

"Ah-ha!"

She shoved a photo in Rick's face, and he pulled back to focus.

"There he is. That's my great Mee-Maw on the red wagon next to Pop-Pops."

"Pop-Pops?"

"That's what my great Mee-Maw called him."

Rick looked carefully at the photo and then pulled out a magnifying glass from his backpack. He examined the photo and compared it to the newspaper article. It certainly looked like a resemblance.

"Can I take a picture of this for the East Texas Treasure Hunters Association?"

She nodded and sipped on a beer, then took a long drag from her Pall Mall cigarette.

Rick snapped a couple of shots with his cell phone.

"Well, this certainly looks promising."

For the first time, a smile crept across her leathery face. She dug through the box; one eye squinted as the cigarette smoke wafted in her eyes. As she got near the bottom of the stack, she stopped before quickly closing the box.

"What is it?" Rick asked, trying to conceal his watering eyes. "Is there something wrong?"

"No!" she told him in a harsh tone, and then gathered the pics and put them back in the box.

I need to see whatever it is she came across.

"Mrs. Nobles, if the treasure is real and it's found, you could use part of the money for the restoration of your home, if that interests you, and it may be considered as the next historic home the Society sees fit to put in Texas's National Register of Historic Places. That would give you future tax credits and make you eligible for grant money."

Rick pulled out the search and salvage contract and explained to Marcy that under the law, the finder was entitled to nine-tenths of the find. The state would keep ten percent, but if she would help him, he would sign over fifty percent of the find, minus the state's ten percent to her.

Marcy's eyes widened as soon as he said that. She puffed on her cigarette and pondered awhile.

"Well, fifty percent of something is better than a hundred percent of nothing," she said as she reached for the pen to sign the contract.

She reopened the box and took out a yellowed and tattered piece of paper. Carefully, she unfolded it and laid it down on the table.

"You can take a picture of the map, but I'm keeping the original," she said with a wicked, child-like grin.

Rick took a picture with his phone. He snapped several more photos as she watched him carefully.

"Well, that looks like all I need, Mrs. Nobles. I guess we are now officially partners. I'll send you an official, notarized copy in the mail in a few days."

He stood and put the contract in his backpack.

"Do you really think you can find it?" she asked.

"Well, it's a process. Nothing's fast and nothing's guaranteed, but you never know unless you try," said Rick.

"One thing you need to know about Pop-pops. Mee-Maw told me he loved to play pranks on his grand kids growing up. They'd often play hide and seek with him and sometimes do scavenger hunts. Sometimes he left a clue hidden under a rock that would lead them to the next clue before they'd find something he had hidden. Things weren't always as they seemed with him. Easter egg hunts in my family were never ordinary, and the tradition was passed down from generation to generation from him all the way down to my great Mee-Maw and my mom."

"That's really helpful. Thank you for all the insight, Mrs. Nobles. I'll do my best to find his treasure. I'll stay in touch if something develops."

She nodded and turned away, so he let himself out, and she quickly closed and locked the door behind him. Rick climbed up in his truck, feeling as if he needed another shower.

Anxious to print the picture, he headed back into town to find a Walgreens. A photo-printing kiosk in the corner of the store was self-serve, so he plugged in his phone and selected three of the map images. After manipulating the colors, he enlarged them to eight by tens, and printed nine different versions.

With the enlarged photos spread across the steering wheel, a major clue came into focus. Rick grabbed a pen and paper and squinted as he scrolled over each letter, writing down one at a time.

A half day's horse ride west from Nolan's Trail is a clear creek with a waterfall. To the right inside of the W is the stash.

To the right inside of the W? To the right inside of the W. He repeated this in his mind. *Could that mean to the right inside of the waterfall? That had to be it.*

The Ford almost drove itself back to the library. He needed to do more research and get some local maps, but the library was closing soon, so he'd return the next day.

CHAPTER FOUR

Rick's phone rang at 6:00 a.m. and startled him out of a dream. He fumbled with the phone and tried to clear his throat before answering.

"Did I wake you?" asked an unfamiliar voice on the other line.

"Uh, no. I've been up for a while. Who is this? I don't recognize the number."

"It's Benjamin Johnson. We met in Destin a while back at A.J.'s. You gave me your business card, and I didn't think a lot about it at the time, but I was talking to one of the deputy sheriffs yesterday, James LeBlanc, and he told me you found... my daughter's body."

"I'm so sorry for your loss. What can I do for you?"

"I'd like to hire you to find the killer—or killers."

Rick was snapped fully awake by his statement. "I'd be glad to help, sir. It was horrible what happened, and whoever did that needs to pay for their crime."

"Look, I called around to find the going rate for private eyes, and they range from fifty to a hundred and fifty dollars an hour," Benjamin said. "I don't wanna dick around, and I want you to take this case seriously. What do you need to get started on this? I've put up a $250,000 reward to find out who did this. I don't care who I give it to, so it may as well be you if you solve it. If you can't solve it after a few months and prove to me you've looked at every possible suspect and clue, I'll pay you for your time." His voice quivered. "I have a lot of money, but it means nothing to me if I can't find the son of a bitch who did this to my daughter."

Rick didn't hesitate to take Johnson's offer. The money was one thing, but being given the chance to solve such an appalling murder and to bring closure to a grieving father would give him a good deal of satisfaction. His gut told him to take the gig.

"Ok, sir. I'll do it. I'm more than glad to help in any way."

"Look, I'll draw up the contract, and we can meet somewhere. I'll get you some travel money to start. I want to make sure you have anything you need to find my daughter's murderer. I just want to know I'm getting one hundred and ten percent from you. You are the closest one to the case, and so far, the sheriff's department hasn't made any progress. I'll be in Tyler in a couple of days for business. Where are you?"

"I'm in Jasper, but I'm... but I might be heading to Houston in a day or so."

"Ok. Send me the address, and I'll have my lawyer FedEx you the contract."

"I was planning on heading back north after," Rick said. "Maybe I can meet you in Tyler in a couple of days, and you can give me the contract there. I can start right away."

"Perfect. When can I expect you?"

"It's a three-and-a-half-hour drive from Houston. I'll leave in the morning the same day you arrive. Just let me know exactly which day that will be. See you around noon?"

"Perfect, we can grab lunch at my favorite BBQ joint, Stanley's. You know where that is?" asked Johnson.

"I'll find it."

Rick poured himself a cup of motel coffee and mulled over the surprising phone call and his future plans, still a little stunned that he was now officially working on such a high-profile murder case.

So much was running through Rick's mind, but he had a few days to kill before meeting Mr. Johnson. He wanted to find Nolan's Trail on an old map or microfilm. He wasn't even sure it still existed. For all he knew, there could be a housing development in the way now.

He shrugged off the negative thoughts and entered the library. The librarian he'd met the day before gave him a broad smile as he approached her desk.

"Hello again. How are you today?" she asked cheerfully.

"Better than I deserve."

She laughed. "How can I help you?"

"Well, I need to see as many old maps of Jasper County as you have. I won't be checking anything out but I will need a desk so I can spread them out."

She walked him over to the cartography section and showed him how everything was labeled.

For two hours, he searched for Nolan's Trail. He looked through old atlases and roadmaps, as well as some microfilm maps of the same era as when Fletcher claimed the treasure was buried. He wasn't getting anywhere though, and Nolan's Trail didn't seem to have ever existed. After hours of searching dozens of maps with no sign of the trail, he collapsed into his chair and kicked the table leg. But as he massaged his temples, an idea came to him.

The library was full of books and maps, but searching through them was no easy task. He gathered his papers and moved to the corner of the library where there were computers for public use. There, he began a methodical internet search. As if he were out in the field, he made a list of reference names:

1. *Nolan's Trail*
2. *John E. Fletcher*
3. *Sabine River Gold*
4. *Fletcher Treasure*
5. *Red River Gold*
6. *Buried Treasure*
7. *Texas Waterfalls*
8. *Ancient Texas Maps*

After scrolling past the ads selling old maps and other bogus timewasters, he came across a website called Texas Treasure Hunting. There he found a message board full of discussions from likeminded people, so he scanned through several topics until one called "Fletcher's Gold" popped up. A thread between an avid treasure hunter and the admin monitoring the website interested him.

Debo,
I want to tell you exactly how I came to believe the site I found was the place where John Fletcher buried

his treasure. The note he wrote (because he was the only robber left out of a band of twelve) said they had buried the cache under a waterfall about 120 yards up a clear-running creek just off the trail from Natchitoches, LA to Nacogdoches, TX (Nolan's trail) about 15–20 miles west of the Sabine river.

I found a website that said Nolan's trail is also called El Camino Real or King's Highway. It also showed several supposed routes, but they all started in the same place in Texas—Highway 21. I followed Hwy 21 on Google Maps about 15-20 miles west, and when I zoomed in several times, an obscure little road popped up that connected a curve in Hwy 21. It was called King's Road.

There was only one creek on the road, so when I convinced my husband to take me there for a "fishing trip," that was the one place I wanted to check out.

John Fletcher mentioned that there was a horseback ridge to the east. I pictured in my mind a swayback horse, but when we finally got there, the mountain looked like a horse's rump.

I talked my husband into hiking up the muddy hillside, then crossed over to the creek and found the hole. When I found King's Road, I also noticed Fletcher's trail farther south. I figured if his family was from that area, it all made sense.

I know there has got to be evidence around there somewhere, but I have limited time and resources, and a husband uninterested in treasure hunting.

But my husband was there. He saw the hole and read the corroborative history on all the historical markers in the area. He still doubts it was anything special and says it was a badger hole, but badgers don't dig rectangular holes in creek beds that flood.

How did I know exactly where it was? How did we walk right to it? It was all in the note!

That was the clue Rick was looking for: Nolan's Trail was also King's Highway—or El Camino Real. He printed the message, opened Google Maps, and zoomed in to the described location. Highway 21 was only an hour and forty-five minutes away, and the area was smackdab in the center of Davy Crockett National Forest.

As he looked at the topography on the satellite image, a memory from his childhood brought him back to the banks of a lake he'd visited many times growing up. He instantly knew that the area they were referring to was not the Sabine River anymore. Time and the Army Corp of Engineers had changed it. It had since been dammed and renamed Toledo Bend Reservoir.

"Holy shit. They're all looking in the wrong spot," he muttered under his breath.

"The trail doesn't start on the Sabine River; it starts from the center of the lake."

It was due west of South Lake Toledo Bend—the same lake where he'd spent so many hours bass fishing with his grandpa, who'd raised him after his mom and dad had died in a tragic car crash when he was two years old. He couldn't remember anything about them.

Heated adrenaline surged through him, and his face flushed. Rick knew he was onto something. He printed out the Google maps and copied the GPS coordinates into his phone, his mind racing. Could it be the Hog Creek

Falls waterfall? He had visited and hiked the area a few times when he was in Boy Scouts, and the irony was too much to believe. Could that waterfall be the hiding place of Fletcher's treasure? A place he'd been to at least a half dozen times before?

Hog Creek was thirty-one miles west of where the Sabine River used to be. The distance was right, but Nolan's Trail, or Highway 21, was farther north. He remembered Nolan's Trail wasn't one trail with one name; it was a combination of Indian trails with several names: Camino Real de los Tejas, Camino Pita, Camino Arriba, Camino de en Medio, King's Highway, and Old San Antonio Road.

It was late in the day, and his brain was fried, so he decided to head back to the motel to check on Chief. He stopped at Brookshire Brothers Grocery and grabbed a six-pack of Shiner Bock and a bag of fresh grapes for Chief. It was time to celebrate his findings and blow off a little steam. All that research had made his head hurt but his heart yearn, and he couldn't wait to start treasure hunting—first thing in the morning.

A knock on the door and someone muttering something in Spanish on the other side woke him. For a few seconds, he couldn't figure out where he was. His eyes were still crusty from the night's dreams.

"Hello? Is someone there?" His voice sounded husky, and mouth felt stuffed full of cotton.

"Housekeeping," replied the lady on the other side of the door.

He had once again forgotten to put the *Do Not Disturb* sign on the door. It was 8:30 a.m.

Oh, well. He'd wanted to get an early start anyway.

"Can you please come back later?" yelled Rick.

Rick washed the night off of his face and packed up the necessities for the trip to Hog Creek. He put Chief in his travel cage, dropped the key in the quick checkout box, then hopped in the truck and headed north.

Just the thought of smoked boudin from Smitty's Smokehouse made his mouth water, so he pulled over when he saw the restaurant. It didn't open until 11:00 a.m. He was forty minutes early, but smoke was pouring out the back side of the building.

Smitty, the original owner, had recently sold the place, and the new owner was incredibly friendly.

As Rick walked around back, a heavyset man in denim overalls set down a shiny pair of stainless-steel tongs and wiped his hands on his chest.

"Howdy. We ain't quite open yet, but I can probably put something together for ya real quick if you got cash."

Rick pulled a twenty from his shirt pocket and handed it to the pit master, who pulled out a large Styrofoam container. He loaded up a generous helping of ribs, chicken, and smoked boudin, then put some beans in a small container.

"I sure appreciate the fine vittles. Please keep the change."

He headed back to the truck, then pulled off a rib and took a bite. The smoky smell of barbecue permeated Rick's senses, and his mind drifted to a time when he'd grilled with his grandfather, who would tell him stories of bronc riding in the rodeo. His "Paw-Paw" was a gentle man with a huge heart: a true cowboy and lawman. They often grilled ribs on the back deck of Paw-Paw's lake cabin on Toledo Bend Reservoir, and Rick would spend hours listening to tales of West Texas rodeos and true crimes his grandpa had solved. It made Rick swell with pride to follow in the footsteps of his Paw-Paw. It was the main reason he'd gotten involved in PI work to begin with.

Growing up poor, surrounded by affluent Texas families, made Rick long for the good life. He'd never had a big boat. His jon boat was the only yacht he could afford, but he knew that one day all of his dreams would come true. If he could find the treasure, he'd be able to get that sport fisher he'd always dreamed of, become a boat captain, and run charters. He had always felt less-than-accepted by the wealthy neighbors he grew up with, and longed for the acceptance and status that money would bring. There always seemed to be a financial and cultural gap between the haves and have-nots.

A woman on the side of the road had her thumb out, begging for a ride, and he immediately thought of the girl in the barrel. The murder of Cara gnawed at his insides. How someone could commit such a terrible crime was inconceivable to him, and he wondered if they'd made any progress on the case. He would wait a few days and touch base with the sheriff's department to get an update.

He continued north until a clearing appeared past the woods near Hog Creek. Just as he parked, *Fifty Dollar Treasure Map*, a song by Joe Bennett, a buddy of his from Louisiana, came on his playlist. It was ironic and appropriate. Taking the song as a positive sign, Rick sang along until the end before turning off the truck.

He grabbed his digging bag and transferred Chief to his backpack cage. With a note of his latitude and longitude, Rick looked at his compass and started walking toward Hog Creek.

Rick carried two guns with him at all times—a .38 Special that held incredible sentimental value since his Paw-Paw had given it to him before he passed away, and a Smith & Wesson .44 Magnum he kept under the seat in the Ford. The .44 Magnum was tucked inside his shoulder holster. It was the same gun used in all the Dirty Harry movies: a straight-up hand cannon. Rick had bought it a few years back when hiking near Yellowstone. It was a big gun for hiking, but grizzlies are big bears, and it took a lot of stopping power to bring one down if it was attacking. He would rather use bear spray, but sometimes it wasn't enough, so he was prepared.

There weren't any grizzlies near Hog Creek, but the gun offered plenty of personal protection. Just the sight of the massive handgun would send most wannabe gangsters scurrying away like squirrels on crystal meth.

The sounds of red-bellied woodpeckers echoed through the pine trees, and the occasional nine-banded armadillo scampered through pine needles. As always, he loved being in the woods. The smell of pine filled his nostrils and gave him a feeling of belonging. The only thing that ever concerned him in the wild was other people. Although he thought most meant no harm, he knew it only took one idiot to ruin a perfectly good day.

It was 2:00 p.m. by the time he reached the Hog Creek waterfall. Perched on a large rock near the creek, he ate his lunch and some of the boudin as Chief munched on his seeds and grapes. Chief could be pretty finicky but would sometimes take something new from Rick and then drop it. He liked boudin, so Rick gave him a small piece.

"You are one crazy bird."

"Rawwwwwk," replied Chief as he munched on his snack.

After finishing his lunch, Rick followed the Google map directions along the bank and upstream toward where he thought the waterfall would be. An hour later, like the water he heard rushing in the distance, his adrenaline began to flow.

There it was—a beautiful, fifteen-foot waterfall with large, rocky outcroppings on either side. It was time to explore. He threw a rope over a tall limb and hung Chief's travel cage eight feet up in a tree—far too high for any critter or black bear to get to.

After putting on his rain jacket, he began his trek toward the waterfall, but suddenly stopped to reconsider the plan for his bird. He decided to lower the cage, and took Chief out for a quick stretch and the bird's own safety. Then he tucked him inside his jacket, knowing they would both get a little wet, but that it was safer than leaving the bird alone.

As they approached the waterfall, a gap between the water and the back of the rocks became visible. Could this be it?

He ducked his head inside the waterfall and opened his eyes. The cave, which only went back a few feet, was glistening from the water's reflection and the sun gleaming through. The rocks were shiny and wet, and it was loud inside—almost deafening. The water slamming against the bottom of the creek roared, reminding him of the rapids he'd seen out west in Utah.

With his metal detector and his tactical headlamp, he started scanning, but he didn't get any readings for the entire area—not a single beep.

"Damn!" he muttered aloud. Maybe this was the wrong waterfall.

He made three more sweeps, then stepped out of the watery cavern with Chief still tucked in his jacket. He began to think he was on the wrong path, but he wasn't ready to give up so easily. After all, it had only been one day.

Returning to his flat boulder near the creek, he studied the enlarged photos from Marcy Nobles's place. *"To the right inside of the W,"* he read again.

On the map, an arrow was drawn from inside the crudely sketched waterfall and a line pointed to the W. From what he could see, it had to be inside the waterfall and to the right side.

Back under the cascading water, his sweeps focused more on the right side, and he moved his metal detector in small circles, not missing a single inch. He pulled away loose rocks and dug with his shovel, but still, not a single beep.

After several disappointing hours, it was time to quit.

CHAPTER FIVE

Rick and Chief made it back to the truck late in the afternoon, and Rick saved the spot on his GPS as "GOLD."

After picking up a couple of ninety-nine-cent heart attack burgers and fries, he drove into the nearby town of Brookland and got a room at the Rayburn Inn. There, he put his bag on the bed, then spread out the maps, photos, and documents on the desk. Chief sat on his shoulder, munching on a fry and dropping more on Rick than down his own throat.

After both he and Chief finished lunch, Rick took a break from treasure hunting and switched gears as he went over all the info he could find on the Cara Johnson case. Once online, he logged into NEXUS and did a background search on Cara and her family. Benjamin was clean as a whistle; the search showed a long history of him being self-employed as a contractor and developer.

There wasn't a whole lot on Cara. She had held a few odd jobs as a waitress and a secretary, her credit was clean and she didn't have much outstanding debt. Neither she nor her father had any aliases and seemed at least on paper to be upstanding citizens with no criminal records. He hoped he'd gain more insight once he met with Benjamin.

After he'd closed his laptop, he turned his attention back to Fletcher's treasure. As he studied the maps, he continued to wonder why there were no hits on his metal detector, which he had plugged into the wall to charge. And that was when he remembered a conversation he'd overheard at a scuba diving convention. Two guys were talking about treasure hunting and diving, so naturally he'd eavesdropped.

They had argued about which metal detector was better, and one of them insisted that the Fisher Pulse 8X was awesome for diving but not worth a damn when it came to finding gold on land because it wasn't adjustable enough and used a different technology than very low-frequency detectors did. His model used a pulse signal that traveled well in water, but not so well on land.

Could that be the problem?

He pulled out his laptop and searched for the best metal detector for finding gold. Several blogs mentioned the Garrett 250. It was a land detector but also had a waterproof coil. It sounded like the best of both worlds. Although he was a little low on cash, the detector seemed like a necessity, so he put in an order. He used overnight shipping so he could have it the next day.

But now he was down to a couple hundred bucks and needed to make some money.

Time to hit the pool hall.

Chief was fed and covered up for the night, so Rick got online and looked for the nearest honky-tonk. The Black Sheep Saloon was the only one nearby and was open until 2:00 a.m.

It was Thursday. Biker's night. Perfect, since the only thing larger than a biker's ego was his wallet on a chain.

It was a quarter 'til midnight when Rick pulled up to the Black Sheep. With only a few beers in him, his wits were still sharp. Winning money playing pool might not be considered a career, but it was an easy source of income and he was good at concentration games.

The routine played the same way every time. He parked down the street, facing away from the Black Sheep in case he needed to make a fast getaway. Sore losers were the only downside to pool-hall gambling.

Bikers usually came in two different breeds: the wannabes—doctors and lawyers who had enough money to drop thirty grand on a new Harley—and the hardcore bikers who would rip your eyeballs out if they didn't like you. Rick never knew which ones he'd encounter, but he'd played them both many times.

Rubbing the rabbit foot on his keychain for luck, he headed for the door, approached the bar and ordered two shots of Jack Daniels and a can of Coke with a glass of ice on the side. He downed the Jack and then laughed.

"Oops. I forgot to put it in the glass," he said aloud, to no one in particular.

He ordered another shot, poured Coke into the glass, and when he was sure no one was watching, drank it down to calm his nerves before playing. He ordered another couple of shots and hollered, "Down the hatch!" which got the attention of a couple bikers playing pool in the corner.

Rick could read the lips on one of them as he muttered, "Drunk-ass prick."

The game was on. To pay for his drinks, Rick pulled out a hundred-dollar bill and handed it to the bartender, who was wearing an Ozzy T-shirt and tight jeans. She was friendly, but rough around the edges, and she seemed eager to feed Rick as many shots as she could to get a good tip. But by her body language and frequent glances at the pool table, Rick got a sense that she was in cahoots with the bikers to hustle out-of-towners. He hated being scammed. It was time to turn the tables.

When she turned around to make change, he saw that the bikers were watching him in the reflection of the mirror on the back of the bar.

"Do you want another shot?" she asked, as she turned back to face him.

"Sure, why not? It's only money, right?"

She nodded and gave him two more. As he hunched over his drink, the mirror on the back wall reflected the bartender nodding to one of the bikers, who nodded back.

Rick downed the last two shots and made his way toward the pool tables. As he checked out the various beer signs on the wall, he bumped backwards into the pool table, and then into one of the bikers.

"Watch it, fuckhead!"

"Oh, I'm sorry," Rick said. "I didn't see you there."

"What are you, fucking blind?"

"No, I'm fucking drunk!" Rick declared with a laugh. "Let me make it up you." He pulled out a ten-dollar bill and handed it to the biker. "Let me pay for your pool games."

The biker snatched the money from Rick's hand faster than the strike of a diamondback rattlesnake, causing Rick to almost fall backward.

"I've got an idea," said the biker. "How about I play you at pool for twenty dollars, and we can use this ten for quarters?"

"Ok, sounds good. I'm pretty good at pool, though, I have to tell you. Are you sure?"

"Come on." The biker waved the ten-dollar bill back and forth. "It's only money… right?"

"Ok. Let's do it."

Rick grabbed a pool cue and chalked it up. His first attempt to break resulted in him missing the cue ball and leaving a long mark of chalk on the felt.

"Oops. Let me try again." On his second shot, he managed to hit the cue ball and break up the balls, but sank the cue ball in the corner.

The biker took his turn and sank three solids.

"You're good," Rick stammered. "I'm not off to a good start. You're gonna kick my ass in this game!"

The biker didn't respond but missed his next shot. Rick took a shot and missed the stripe completely. The biker ran the table and lined up for the eight ball, sinking it with ease.

"Crap," Rick muttered, "you won." Rick handed him a twenty and started to walk away.

"Wait. Wait! Let me give you chance to win it back. How about one more game? Double or nothing?"

"Hmm. So, I need to put down forty, and if I win, I get my twenty back… plus twenty?"

The biker smirked. "Yeah, that's it."

"Why not? It's only money, right?"

"Riiiight."

Rick knew he was being hustled, and he also knew how the scam would play out. All was fair in love and war, so Rick threw the game on purpose and began to walk away.

"Look. Let's go one more time," the biker said. "Triple or nothing."

"I don't wanna break another hundred tonight."

The biker raised an eyebrow. "I'll tell you what. I feel bad you lost some money, so let's make a deal. If you put up five hundred dollars, I'll match it and throw in an extra five hundred bucks for incentive." He laughed. "It's only money, right?"

"You'd do that?" Rick asked, faking sincere gratitude.

"Sure. Why not?"

"Ok, but that's a lot of money." Rick pointed to the bartender. "How about we let that pretty girl over there hold it?"

The biker's joy was obvious. "That's cool."

Once again, Rick hit the ATM, and then handed the tightly wound cash to the bartender. The biker counted out ten hundred-dollar bills and slid them over to the bartender with a wink.

They flipped a coin to see who'd break, and the biker won the toss. He broke and sank two stripes and a solid. His next shot was at the ten ball but he missed. Rick took his first shot and aggressively slammed the two ball into the corner pocket. The sound of the ball slapping the back of the pocket echoed and took the biker by surprise.

Shot by shot, Rick ran the table with finesse and power. The biker stood dumbfounded with his hand clutched to his Bud bottle as the condensation dripped onto the leg of his jeans. He realized Rick was going to win and was not happy about it one bit.

"You motherfucker!" The biker flipped his stick around to take a swing.

Before he could get the pool cue halfway back, Rick snatched the .44 from his shoulder holster and pointed it at the biker. "Step back, dude!" he yelled.

The biker stared at the nearly empty green felt on the table. "You suckered me!"

"Nah, I'm just a better player, and you, my friend, are a sore loser." Rick grinned, then swung around to the other side of the pool table and nodded at the bartender.

"Hand it over, lady. I saw you wink at him earlier. I came in here looking for a fair game and I know by those sly looks and winks at Mr. Harley Davidson over there that y'all had no intention of paying me if I won."

Rick shoved the money into his jacket pocket and walked backwards with the pool cue in one hand and his gun the other, then kicked the door open with his foot and backed through.

He woke up the next morning with a grin on his face and over a thousand dollars in his pocket. When a light blinked on the motel phone, he suspected his new metal detector had arrived.

Sure enough, he retrieved his Amazon delivery from the motel's front desk and brought it back to the room, familiarizing himself with the new detector's functions. After popping fresh batteries in it, he grabbed a coffee and a couple of muffins from the lobby to share with Chief.

"You like blueberries, don't ya, boy?"

Chief had grabbed a small piece of the muffin in his left foot and was holding it up to his beak to nibble.

"Good boy."

Once the detector was ready and they'd finished breakfast, Rick put Chief in his travel cage and headed back to Hog Creek. During the hike, Rick hummed, and Chief did his best to mimic him as they walked.

"We're gonna find some gold! Today is the day!" he murmured, repeating what Mel Fisher had said to his crew during the Atocha treasure search in Key West.

Mel had used it as motivation and never gave up, even after decades of finding nothing and losing a son in a boating accident. Mel had repeated the phrase until 1985, when they'd found the Atocha mother lode, worth over four hundred fifty million dollars at the time. For years after, they found more treasure during continued operations in Key West.

Yep. Today was going to be the day.

When they approached the waterfall site, Rick set aside his digging bag, tucked Chief under his raincoat, and then, since he didn't want to waste time digging up rusty beer cans or nails, set the new metal detector's sensitivity threshold to show non-ferrous metals. Only gold registered at this setting. He wrapped the head in a resealable plastic bag and taped the ends tight with electrical tape, since the coil was waterproof, but the head was not.

They ducked into the waterfall and moved to the right side of the cavern. Rick started with a small sweep under the falls and worked his way back toward the inside wall. He did this in a narrow sweep, making sure not to leave any area unchecked. On his third sweep, his detector double beeped.

"Hell, yeah!"

His headlamp lit up the area as he looked for anything shiny. He propped the metal detector against the inside of the rock wall and put the coil directly over the location of the ping. Then, when he moved out from under the waterfall, he felt warmth in the air, and noticed how spooky the steam rising up from the creek looked in the morning sun. Chief was behaving well, peeking his head out every now and again.

After grabbing his shovel and a tire iron he'd added to his bag in case he needed to move a stubborn rock out of the way, he and Chief ducked back inside the waterfall and Rick probed around the location of the reading. He would dig awhile in one area, then bring the metal detector back to see if he was still in the right spot. After twenty minutes, and eighteen to twenty inches down though the mixed gravel, rock, and mud, something shiny appeared.

Using his light to get a better look, he reached down and pulled on what he realized was a chain. It was wedged under years of sediment and didn't want to come loose. But he carefully dug around it and after a good tug, it popped free. Attached to the end was a three-inch mound of mud and gravel, which he rinsed under the waterfall. It was an ancient-looking gold pocket watch. The bezel was intact and covered with mud, but it shone. With a cloth from his digging bag and some creek water and elbow grease, it came clean, and he examined it in the sunlight. On the dial, he made out the name "Waltham." On the inside of the lid was an inscription, and although the first letter was mostly worn off, what was left read "/. S. Glenn."

The first letter could be a V, maybe.

Ecstatic, Rick put the watch and chain into a resealable plastic bag, shoved it in his front jeans pocket, and went back into the waterfall. The next two hours were spent scanning the floor and walls of the cave, but he never got another hit.

Back at the Ford, he threw the digging bag behind his seat and loaded Chief into his travel cage. The content bird munched on nuts and seeds as they drove back to the motel. Rick was eager to do some research on this watch.

Once back in his room, he opened his laptop. Based on the documents available online from well-respected Texas treasure-hunting message boards, the Fletcher treasure was supposedly buried in 1812, so for the watch to be connected to the treasure, it had to predate 1812.

He spent several hours reading about the Waltham Watch Company, and with the serial number from inside of the back of the watch, he concluded that the watch was made in 1869.

Dammit. If the watch was made in 1869, and the treasure was buried in 1812, I must be digging in the wrong place.

A sinking feeling fell over Rick, but he finally shook it, deciding the watch was better than nothing, and that he was lucky to have found something of value in the first place. The watch had to be worth at least its gold weight value.

He thoroughly cleaned it in the sink with a toothbrush and examined it again, taking notes, and then pulling out his magnifying glass to see if there was more detail. The motel's blow dryer would hopefully help to dry it out and bring it back to life. It was a mechanical watch and mostly gold with brass parts. If he was lucky, even with it being wet all those years, it could once again work. At least it had been in fresh water.

After about an hour of drying, he wound the watch. To his amazement, the second hand began to move, coming back to life after all those years under the muck and water.

He ran his hand affectionately over his bird's head. "Wow, Chief. They just don't build things like this anymore."

Chief tilted his head and listened to Rick.

"I need to get this thing appraised, but it ain't happening in this Podunk town."

Rick snacked on some potato chips and lay down on the bed, then flipped the watch around and examined every detail with his magnifying glass. The inscription could now be seen clearly: *W. S. Glenn.*

He searched online for W.S. Glenn, and the first link that popped up was to an article in the *Winston-Salem Chronicle*—it was a story about a sports guy. Nothing turned up on the second and third search pages, so he figured Glenn was probably a nobody who'd lost his watch while bathing upstream.

But then he typed "W. S. Glenn and treasure" into the search bar. The third website on the list astonished Rick. The title read, "The Legend of John Fletcher's Buried Treasure."

After clicking it open, one section of the article got his attention.

> *Appointed by Glenn himself he introduced several commissioned officers who in turn, voted to raise $5,000 for operating expenses by selling 100 shares of stock at $50 a share, payable in three monthly installments by May 1, 1898. All shareholders were slated to share the profits, if any treasure were found, after one-fourteenth had been reserved as a royalty for W. S. Glenn. During the summer of 1898, Glenn superintended the*

search for Fletcher's gold, utilizing some of the best treasure-hunting devices that were available as of that year. He hired a gang of laborers who slowly excavated every inch of the high ridge on the creek's east bank. By October 1898, the firm's funds were totally expended, the search was called off, and so far as is known, no one else has continued the search for the forty-two mule-loads of Spanish gold and silver. The exact location of the Glenn family farm and the name of the creek which passed through it are still unknown to this writer. And perhaps it is just as well, for he has no desire to trigger another gold rush; that is, a stampede of fortune hunters, on someone's private property in Jasper County. A check several years ago with Ms. Eulys Hancock of the county clerk's office revealed that there was no record of a grantee deed to W. S. Glenn for any farm in Jasper County during the 1890's. Of course, the family farm may well have been in estate status, or for some other reason, in some other person's name. Likewise, as late as 1914, there was no grantor's deed on file involving any land sale in Jasper County by W. S. Glenn, although there are many deed records on file for other members, near and distant, of the large clan of Glenn relatives.

"Chief, I believe we have the watch owned by *the* W.S. Glenn."

If this really was Glenn's watch, it was definitely a piece of the puzzle, so he wanted to be certain. He would need more information and an appraisal of its value, so he headed to Houston—H-Town—where he knew just the person who could help him verify his find.

CHAPTER SIX

The morning sun snuck through a sliver in the blackout curtains of the motel, piercing Rick's bloodshot eyes. He had been waking up and drifting back to sleep since the clock showed 3:18 a.m. He quickly packed his stuff and rustled Chief from his slumber.

As he drove west on US 190, he pulled up *The Best of George Jones* on iTunes to get in the mood to see his old friend, Possum. Michael—actually, Michael Jackson—was Possum's real name, but he had been given the nickname because of his love of George Jones, who was also nicknamed Possum. The fact that his friends felt weird calling him Michael Jackson didn't help, so he was stuck with Possum forever.

Rick stopped for fuel and coffee in Livingston, texted Possum to let him know he and Chief were coming and grabbed some warm fruit kolaches from Shipley's for the road. Possum had introduced Rick to kolaches—a Texas tradition that originated in the Czech Republic—many years ago.

"He Stopped Loving Her Today" played though the speakers as Rick approached Houston and exited off I-69 to the 610 Loop toward Galena Park, where Possum lived.

His friend had become quite the historian and the go-to guy Rick always relied on when trying to identify a piece of treasure or historical find. Michael—"Professor Possum"—had double-majored in history and anthropology at Rice University and later studied paleontology in Zurich. His passion was digging up bones and tools, like arrowheads and rock-carved knives. The library of identification books in his house rivaled that of most schools.

Rick and Possum often went on digs and hunts together along the creek banks surrounding Houston and other Southeast Texas sites. Rick had learned everything he knew about treasure hunting, bone identification, and metal detecting from his old buddy.

As Rick pulled into the home's circular drive, he rolled down his windows and cranked up "The Race Is On" for his friend's benefit. Possum's front door flew open, and he ran out in a robe and house shoes, pulling Rick in for a huge, sidearm man-hug as soon as he jumped out of the truck. Rick needed to make sure Chief, hiding under his jacket, wasn't crushed in the process.

"Houston, we have a Possum!" Rick declared.

A wide grin spread across Possum's face. He motioned for Rick to follow him inside. "I see you still have that bird with you."

Rick unzipped his jacket, and Chief's head popped out. "I need to show you something, Possum. I need your help identifying the owner."

Rick pushed a mahogany chair with black leather trim closer to Possum's desk. The desk and chairs were Silla Armida style, hand carved from solid mesquite wood. Based on the furniture and colorful Matador velvet paintings on the wall, Rick knew it all came from Mexico. When Rick and Possum were younger, they had made several trips across the border to Matamoros, and Rick remembered seeing pieces like this down there.

As Possum examined the watch, Rick revealed the origin in great detail. "I was underneath a small waterfall on Hog's Creek when my metal detector went off. Do you remember that place we went to as kids?"

"Yeah, in Boy Scouts, right?"

"Yeah, we went there a couple of times. I remember the Brownies were camped on one side of the creek, and we were on the other, and you had a crush on that girl Becky, and got in trouble when you snuck into the girls' camp one night."

"I remember that!"

"Well, I went inside that small waterfall and began to dig. I set my detector to *discrimination mode* to avoid finding Coke or beer cans, but the signal was strong, so I stayed at it. When I finally grabbed hold of the chain, I knew I'd found something good. What era do you think it's from?"

Possum pulled out his magnifying lamp and took a closer look. After studying it in silence for a few minutes, he slowly looked up at Rick. "It's from the late 1800s." In a whisper, as if he didn't want anyone else in the world to hear, Possum asked, "Do you know who W.S. Glenn was?"

Rick nodded. "Only from what I've read. Are you saying this is authentic?"

"Well, we need to take it to a watch guy I know, but unless there were two W. S. Glenn's from the same time period in the same area, known to have searched sites for the treasure you've been hunting for all these years, then I'd have say it's highly likely this is the real deal."

The possibility of getting closer to the treasure was becoming more realistic, and Rick's face warmed with excitement.

Possum changed into jeans and a Rice Owls tee, and they headed into the city. Chief sat quietly between the two old friends and munched on a few grapes as they made their way toward the University of Houston near Houston's Greater Third Ward.

Even though it was near a dangerous neighborhood, Rick wasn't too worried about it, as Possum explained they would park on campus. His watch guy was also a professor who had a PhD in U.S. and military history and was a major Civil War buff. He could identify anything anywhere from the era, from a Confederate uniform button to civilian jewelry.

Once they entered the campus, Possum directed him toward the history building, where Possum's friend had agreed to meet them in room 524. The pay-only parking lot was far from the history building, so he dropped Possum at the front door, made a U-turn and pulled behind a truck with construction material in the bed. He was about to tuck Chief into his jacket when a lanky guy walked up to Rick.

"No pets allowed."

"Do you work here?" Rick was perturbed by this news.

"Well, sort of. It doesn't matter to me, I'm just letting you know," the man replied. "I'm the foreman for the new sidewalk project. I tried to bring my pit bull here the other day.

He was in the back of my truck, and it was the weekend. I figured no one would care since I was only gonna be here a few minutes, but they told me to leave and not return with my dog. They're hardcore about pets on campus."

"Thanks for the info, buddy. Can I park here for a few minutes?"

"That should be fine. They rarely tow vehicles, and your truck looks like it could be with us anyway."

Rick thanked the man and got his stuff together, then slightly cracked the windows for Chief. Even though it was sixty-five degrees out, he wanted to make sure the bird was comfortable. He wasn't too concerned about Security giving him a hard time about Chief. After all, a harmless bird was a different story than a pit bull. He put the old watch in his inside jacket pocket and made his way to room 524.

Possum stood up from one of the student desks. "Rick, I'd like to introduce you to Professor Colby Adams, another one of my dear friends and colleagues."

"Hi, Professor. How long have you known the Poss—Professor Jackson?"

He chuckled. "Please call me Colby. Well, I've known him long enough to know that his real friends call him *Possum*."

That put Rick at ease. He was just a good ol' boy with a degree.

"Ok, Rick. Let's take a look at that watch."

Rick reached into his pocket and slid the watch across the desk, studying Colby as he examined it. He had a peaceful face with bushy eyebrows, and he came across as intelligent but not conceited. Turning over a piece of treasure to someone Rick had just met would've normally made him nervous, but he felt confident Colby was a trustworthy man.

Using a small flashlight from inside his desk, Colby looked at every crevice and took notes. After five minutes, he stopped and looked up at Rick. "I can't be 100 percent sure, but 99.44 percent certain this is the watch lost by W. S. Glenn on the expedition to find Fletcher's treasure. May I hold onto it for a couple of days and go through my research books?"

"Of course."

Rick beamed with delight at the thought of the discovery and proof. As he and Possum made their way back to where Rick had parked, the noise from the construction site grew. Steel girders were driven into the ground with loud thuds that echoed through the buildings. Rick pulled his keys from his pocket, scanned the street, and then stopped in his tracks. His truck was gone. Glass and skid marks covered the ground.

In a rush of emotion, the reality of the situation hit him all at once. "Oh my God! Chief was in the truck!"

His hands shook and fear gripped him. If something happened to Chief, he would never forgive himself. His mind raced.

Who took the truck? How did they start it? Where is it now?

Possum said, "Let's get an Uber and go back to my place and call the police."

Rick couldn't think straight. "Ok. I gotta calm down and think about this logically. Whoever took it could've hotwired it, but we were only in the office for ten minutes."

Then he remembered that the backup set of keys was in the glovebox. After breaking the window, they must've rifled through there and seen the keys.

In frustration and anger at himself, Rick ran his hand down his face and kicked at the dirt. "Idiot!"

"We're not dealing with highly experienced car thieves, but more likely opportunistic tweakers."

UH had a great reputation and was one of the best schools in Texas. The campus was beautifully maintained and felt safe, but it was a far cry from the Third Ward. It always astounded Rick how a huge university could be so close to a neighborhood known for drugs and crime. Alongside beautiful old mansions were small, rundown apartments and meth labs on every corner.

Whoever took the truck could have used the noise camouflage from the construction site to smash the window without being heard.

At that moment, the foreman from earlier walked up to them, looking surprised.

"I looked up and saw your truck peel out. I figured you picked up friends and were in a hurry to get somewhere."

"You saw two people drive off?" Rick asked.

"Well, actually three. I couldn't make out the driver or the person in the middle, but the guy on the passenger side looked right at me. I assumed it was the person you went to see in the building. He was definitely Mexican, and he was all tatted up like a biker, even on his face, which I thought was odd—but I don't know you or your friends. Oh, and he gave me the Hook 'em Horns sign."

Rick made a hornlike gesture. "Like this?"

"Yeah, exactly."

"Fuck! That's not the Hook 'em Horns sign. That's the MS-13 gang sign. They're one of the most violent gangs in

Houston. They've killed and tormented many people in the surrounding area."

He turned to his friend. "Let's get to your place, Possum, and regroup. I'll get us an Uber."

The foreman stepped up. "Geez, I'm sorry, man! I was about to take a break. I can give y'all a lift. Where do you live?"

"I'm in Galena Park," answered Possum.

"Oh, I know that area. I've done a few jobs out there."

The three jumped in the truck, and Possum navigated.

"I feel terrible," said the foreman. "I would have tried to stop them if I had known it wasn't y'all."

"It's a good thing you didn't," said Rick. "Those guys are ruthless and would've shot you in the face without hesitation."

The foreman did a fake shiver and winced.

Back at Possum's place, the foreman shrugged off the twenty Rick tried to hand him. "Good luck," he said, and drove off.

"There's no use calling the cops," said Rick. "Half of them are scared of the gangs and the other half are dirty."

Possum opened his massive gun safe. Rick knew he had quite a gun collection, since they used to hunt deer together many years before and often talked about guns.

"So, what's the plan?" Possum said now.

"Well, those fuckers got lucky when they got my keys so easy, but their luck is about to run out. I've got to track those scumbags down somehow. That's gonna be the hard part."

Rick slammed his hand on the desk, startling Possum.

Possum jumped. "What's wrong?"

"Nothing. It's actually a good break. I left my iPad behind the seat in my go bag. "I synced all my Apple devices together, and luckily I can track them all with my iPhone."

He used the Find My app on his phone and discovered that his iPad, which he had fully charged the previous night, showed offline. He couldn't determine its location unless it was on.

"So, what now?" asked Possum.

Rick spun the chamber on his .44 Magnum and put it in his side holster, then pointed to the short-barrel Mossberg twelve gauge and the Sig P229 nine-millimeter in the gun safe. Possum handed him two extra clips, a box of shells, and binoculars.

"Now we wait," replied Rick. "Those pricks will find the iPad and turn it on. And that will turn me on."

Possum grabbed his Glock 19. "We can take my Bronco."

"No, *I* will take your Bronco. You're staying here. It's too dangerous, and I need you to stay here in case it goes sideways." Rick winked. "And you'll need to identify my body at the morgue."

"Not funny."

"Not *being* funny. These guys are stone-cold killers and have no respect for life. If they hurt my bird, I won't have respect for their lives, either."

They loaded the Bronco, while Rick repeatedly refreshed his Find My app every few seconds. After what seemed like a lifetime, the iPad suddenly popped up online. The tracker map showed a location sixteen miles away at the corner of McGowen and Sauer streets, smackdab in the center of the Greater Third Ward.

"That's my cue." Rick threw the duffel of guns on the seat and fired up the Bronco.

"Be careful, bro."

"Don't worry, man. If this goes well, I'll be back for happy hour."

Outwardly, Rick showed no fear, but on the inside, he was extremely nervous. These guys were lethal, and this was their turf. It wasn't gonna be easy. He needed a way to get the jump on them. As he drove toward the location, he passed a Taco Bell and a Domino's and suddenly an idea hit him like a ton of bricks. He pulled into the Domino's, where a stoner-looking kid stood behind the counter.

"Hey, bud. How'd you like to make a quick fifty bucks?"

"Sure, dude. How?"

"Let me borrow your hat, a Domino's vest, a pizza box, and one of those car top signs."

"I don't know, man. I could get in trouble."

"Look, it's for a prank I'm doing on one of my neighbors. I wanna put dog shit in the pizza box and deliver it to a guy whose dog has been shitting in my yard forever."

The kid looked like he wanted to agree but was still hesitant.

"I'll tell ya what. I'll give you fifty now and fifty when I return the stuff. Deal?" He handed the kid a fifty-dollar bill.

"Deal." The kid pocketed the money. "That's an expensive prank."

"Trust me. It'll be worth it. I can't wait to see the expression on his face when he opens that pizza box."

Rick jumped in the Bronco and pulled behind the building, where the boy affixed the car sign to the SUV and handed him the other items.

"Thanks, kid. I'll be back soon."

"I get off at six. Please try to be back before then."

"No worries. Thirty minutes or it's free, right?"

The kid nodded with a smile, and Rick took off.

He drove up McGowen and stopped a block shy of where the iPad—and hopefully Chief and the Ford—was. With a pair of tactical binoculars, he scanned the house. Only two cars were there. The house was run down and had a large yard overgrown with weeds, enclosed with a chain-link fence and a huge gate. A ratty porta-garage sat in the side yard, but there was no sign of the Ford.

Rick was still scanning the yard when a small gust of wind suddenly blew, and the bottom corner of the porta-garage flew up just enough to see tire rims. He recognized them immediately.

He slowly pulled the Bronco past the house, out of sight, turned the corner and parked by the curb. After he'd put the Sig with the barrel pointing forward in the pizza box and slung the strap of the sawed-off combat shotgun around his neck, he made his way toward the house.

This was definitely an MS-13 crib. The two Impalas with ridiculously oversized rims and low-profile tires that cost way more than the car itself were a dead giveaway. Ranchero Mexican music sounded from inside as he cautiously approached the front door. After stepping up on the porch, he peered through a crack in the curtain. On a coffee table that was covered in Modelo beer cans and cigarettes sat Chief in his travel cage. Heat and adrenaline flowed though him as if he'd just stepped into an oven. Chief was visibly shaking, but Rick was beyond relieved to see him alive.

He composed himself and pressed the doorbell. No sound. He took a deep breath and knocked twice. "Domino's!"

He heard rustling and whispers, and a tatted gangbanger peeped through the crack in the curtain. Most of his face was covered in MS-13 tattoos, including a couple of teardrops indicating he'd killed before.

The man slowly opened the door, and Rick could plainly see the butt of a pistol bulging from under his shirt.

"We ain't order no fucking pizza, *vato*."

Rick scanned the living room.

"Are you sure?"

Chief was to the left, and another gang member was sitting on the couch to the right, with a cigarette dangling from his lips. He had black ink around his eyes, skull-like, and "MS" tattooed on his temple. A Glock was sitting on the end table to the left of him.

Hopefully he's right-handed, Rick thought.

"I'm pretty sure I have the right address. We have a program where friends can order a pizza for their other friends through Facebook. It's called the Domino's Dinner Bell."

Rick could see the gangbanger relax a little.

He squinted and nodded. "Cool, *esé*."

"Here, let me show you the pizza."

With the pizza box turned sideways and his hand behind the back of the box, he slowly lifted the top.

"Cool bird," said Rick.

The gangbanger glanced toward Chief, and in one move, Rick grabbed the nine-millimeter with his left hand, dropped the pizza box, and with his right hand, aimed the twelve gauge at the other gang member. Before either one of them could move, Rick had the pistol pointed inches from the man's forehead, and the shotgun's sights squarely set on the one on the couch.

With eyes wide open, both gangbangers slowly raised their hands.

Rick pushed the barrel of the pistol against the man's forehead and cocked it.

"What do you want, *vato*?"

"Well, I want to beat your asses, but I'll settle for taking my bird and truck back for now, as well as my iPad and dig bag. You should have never turned it on, *esé*. Now, you, over there. Slowly get off the couch and put your face on the floor," he said, doing his best Clint Eastwood impression.

The gangbanger glanced at the Glock.

"Don't even think of reaching for that Glock. I have the jump on you and a hair trigger. Now *you* back up and put your face on the floor, too."

The guy slowly did as he was told. Rick walked toward the end table and picked up the Glock, releasing the twelve gauge to hang by his side. His Ford keys were also on the table, and he hooked them around his pinky, never taking his eyes off the gang members. As he walked sideways around them toward Chief, one of the punks kept glancing up toward Rick with a look of pure evil.

"Stop eyeballing me and put your face on the floor. Both of you close your eyes now!"

The guy put his face back down and looked the opposite way, toward the wall. Rick pulled out his Leatherman, unplugged the lamp and cut off the electrical cord. There was nothing else he could see in the house to tie them both up with.

"Ok. We can play this two ways. You can cooperate and no one gets hurt or… well, you don't want to know, I promise."

With the pistols tucked away and the shotgun hanging from his shoulder, Rick tied up the first guy's hands to the foot of the couch and then tied the hands of the other guy behind his back and his feet to his hands, hog style. "You seem like the smart one here," Rick said, as he finished tying him up.

"I'm gonna ask you a question, and you better not lie to me, you understand?"

"Ok, I got it."

"There were three of you. Where's the other guy?"

"That was my cousin, and we dropped him off on the way here."

"So, there's no one else in this house?"

"Noooo!"

"Sit tight. I'm gonna clear the house."

It was a small house and only had two bedrooms. The door was missing from one room, and the other one down the hall had the door closed. In the first room, he crouched down at the corner, seeing it was empty except for a table with drug paraphernalia on it—scales, a bowl of meth, and a roll of plastic baggies.

Scumbag drug dealers.

Being church-mouse quiet, he made his way toward the back bedroom, where the ranchero music was coming from. With his Sig now in the front of his pants with the grip exposed, his .44 Magnum in his shoulder holster, and the Glock in his rear waistband, he pointed the shotgun toward the door, crouched down low, and reached up to the door handle. He turned it slowly.

Bam! Bam! Bam!

Three shots came though the center of the door above his head. With the barrel of the shotgun he shoved the door open which knocked the gun out of the gangbanger's hand, then swung the shotgun as hard as he could toward his face, landing it squarely on his nose. The punk slammed to the floor, and his baseball cap shifted, letting the tucked-in hair fall out the side. He was out cold and bleeding from his nose like a stuck pig.

Knowing there was no one left after a final scan, Rick kicked the gun the guy had dropped away from his body and into the hallway. He quietly stepped toward the living room, tucked away the sig and unholstered his .44 Magnum.

Back in the living room, he put the massive gun against the back of the closest gangbanger's head and cocked it.

"I told you not to lie to me, didn't I?"

The gangbanger shook and breathed hard.

"I'm gonna get my stuff and get out of here. I want you to count to a hundred before you even try and untie yourselves, ok? All I can say is, you guys are both very lucky you didn't hurt my bird."

His iPad sat on the dirty kitchen table next to his dig bag. With those both in hand, he snatched up Chief and ran out the back door.

Rick fired up the Ford and peeled out of the porta-garage, tearing down the sidewall as he plowed across the overgrown yard toward the double gate. He slammed through it and took a hard left around the corner, then stopped by Possum's Bronco and grabbed the Domino's car sign.

The Bronco would have to wait until after the place cooled off. He headed toward the campus and pulled into an open parking spot. After punching in *67 to block his number, he dialed 911.

"I just heard gunshots on the corner of McGowen and Sauer Street," Rick said to the operator. "I think they're MS-13 drug dealers." He hung up, took Chief out of his cage, and tucked him inside his jacket to calm him down.

After making his way back to Domino's, Rick knocked on the back door. When the kid opened it, he handed him the vest, the hat, the car sign, and another fifty-dollar bill.

The kid smiled. "Wow, thanks! Did you surprise them?"

Rick smiled. "I doubt they'll ever forget it."

He climbed back into the Ford just as three Houston PD cars and a SWAT van, lights blazing, flew past the building in the direction of the gangbangers' house.

Happy hour. Perfect timing.

CHAPTER SEVEN

"Hey, Possum. Open the garage."

Rick clicked the phone off, then pulled up the driveway; Possum closed the garage door behind him. Chief still had a tight grip on Rick's jacket, and Rick kissed his beak.

Possum just shook his head. "Well, what happened?"

In Possum's man cave, Rick told him everything over a couple of Cruzan and club sodas. They turned on the TV to see if there was anything about the gangbangers, and not surprisingly, it was breaking news.

The reporter, holding a mic, stood in front of the house Rick had just left. "Three MS-13 gang members were taken into custody today for allegedly running a meth lab in this house in the Greater Third Ward. One was treated for minor injuries from a suspected rival gang."

Rick laughed; sure, he'd never be suspected. He knew those guys would be too proud to say that one man had done this to them. It would ruin their street cred.

Early the next morning, using another of Possum's cars, they picked up the Bronco.

Rick hopped in the Bronco and rolled down the window.

"Do you mind if I keep my Ford in your garage for a while?" he yelled over to Possum. "I need to lay low for a few days and recharge my batteries."

"No problem, *amigo*. By the way, I called a buddy who owns a junkyard. He has a replacement window for your truck. I can get it here in a few days. You want it?"

"Yeah, go ahead and order it. I'll give you my credit card."

"Shall we retire to the man cave for some 'ha-ha, clink-clink?'" asked Possum, after they'd returned from retrieving the Bronco.

Rick raised an eyebrow. "Ha-ha, clink-clink?"

"You know, laughs and drinks."

"I love it. I'm gonna remember that one."

They stayed up until the wee hours, sipping rum and reminiscing about old times before they finally called it a night. Rick realized he must've been running on adrenaline because when he pulled back the sheets on the guest bed, an overwhelming sense of exhaustion came over him. By the time his head was an inch from hitting the pillow, he was asleep, with Chief snuggled under his arm.

The next day Rick called the station back in Jefferson County to see if there had been any developments on the case, but when he asked for Deputy LeBlanc, he was told he was in the field, so he left a message on LeBlanc's cell phone and asked him to return the call.

Afterward, Rick and Possum spent the next few days studying the case notes together and planned future treasure hunting trips. It was some nice down time that Rick needed.

"I have a friend, Carson Peters, who I was thinking might be able to help you with your case, if you're cool with that," Possum told him, on the morning he was scheduled to end his visit.

"I'll take all the help I can get."

"He used to work as a profiler for the FBI but he's retired now. I'll call him up and see if he's around. I'm sure he'll jump at the chance to practice his old trade again."

"Great idea, but I need to get that window on the Ford replaced first."

"Already done."

"Wait. It's 7:00 a.m., you've already got biscuits and gravy going, *and* you replaced my window before I woke up?"

"You know what they say about idle hands?"

"You're amazing, Possum." Rick jabbed his friend in the ribs. "You'd make a great husband."

After Possum called his FBI buddy, he reported to Rick that Peters was game.

"It's just across town—I'll drive. Let's take my Honda." said Possum.

"Ok, let me grab my notes."

They arrived at the profiler's place just after 10:00 a.m., and Carson greeted them at the door before they could ring the bell.

"Hey Possum, good to see you!"

"You too, Carson. This is my friend Rick Waters that I told you about. He's working on the murder case over near Beaumont."

"Yeah, I read all about that case. Horrible. I'm glad to help," Carson said, as he and Rick shook hands.

They all sat down in Carson's study. There were hundreds of books on the shelves about forensics and profiling, as well as some fiction and true crime.

Carson pulled out a large yellow note pad and pen.

"I assume Possum told you I've been hired by the victim's father to help solve the case?"

"Yes, he told me. I already know a few things I've read, but let's start at the beginning, as if I know nothing, ok?" asked Carson.

"Sounds good," said Rick, as he began. "The victim's name was Cara Johnson. She was a very popular cowgirl who competed in barrel racing regionally."

"Would you say that was her occupation?" asked Carson.

"I'm not sure. Her father Benjamin Johnson is very wealthy, so I don't think she really needed an occupation, but she worked a few odd jobs. I know she waited tables for a while."

"Ok, then. Daddy's little girl. I'm familiar with Benjamin Johnson."

"Yeah, I think she competed for fun, but she wasn't on the national circuit," Rick told him.

"So, rodeo was a hobby?"

"I guess you could say that."

"Do you think she had any enemies?"

"I have no idea. Maybe a jealous competitor. I know she dated one of the bull riders for a while, but it ended, and he tours all over now. I don't know too much about him," said Rick.

"So how was she killed?"

"The detective I was speaking to basically confirmed what I saw with my own eyes, which was three gunshots to the back of the head."

"Execution style, huh? I'm looking for motive. Was her body covered or in the open?"

"Her body was burned and wrapped in a burlap rice sack, then placed in a fifty-five-gallon drum and buried."

"Someone going through such an elaborate process makes me feel that whoever killed her had close ties to her. It was personal."

"That's what I was thinking," agreed Rick.

"When I profiled for the FBI, it usually involved multiple murders, serial killers and the like. It's not as easy to create a profile based on one murder, but let's keep going. What else can you tell me about the crime scene?"

"There seemed to be a voodoo connection. I found a gris-gris bag filled with some creepy items. Let me text you some photos."

Rick put Carson's number in his phone and forwarded all the photos he had taken from the crime scene. Carson studied them, then carefully synced them with his computer for a better look.

"So, we have a gangland-type murder with a voodoo connection. The voodoo thing could just be a diversion to send the cops on the wrong path. Since we don't know if she had any enemies and do know she was popular, maybe it was someone who hated her father. As a wealthy man, he's bound to have enemies. Anything else you can tell me? Think really hard. Any other ties to her?"

"Well, one of the deputies, James LeBlanc, said he knew her and danced with her once, but I don't think that's important. Everyone knew Cara, from what I'm told."

"You never know. I just want as clear a picture as I can possibly get."

Rick closed his eyes and tried to put himself back in the bayou where he found the buried body.

"Possum also told you I was the one who discovered the body, right? I found the drum with my metal detector under an old campfire."

"What was in the ashes of the fire? Just old burnt wood or what?"

"I never thought about that. Now that you mention it, there were no burnt aluminum cans or anything else metal, which is usually what I find in old campfires."

"Do you think that's where the murderer burned the body?" asked Carson.

"No, I think the body was burned somewhere else, then put in the barrel."

"Why do you think that?"

"Because there were no bone fragments or anything other than old embers on the fire."

"So, it's possible that whoever killed her buried her, then made a fire above the earth she was buried in. Why?"

"So someone would find her more easily!" Rick exclaimed.

"Exactly!"

"I also have these," said Rick, as he passed his notes and case files to Carson.

"Can I make copies of these?"

"Sure, anything you need," replied Rick.

Carson took the stack of notes and scanned them into his computer.

"I think these files will help. My first instinct was to think that she was assassinated in a hit, but the more info you've given me, the more I'm beginning to think it was personal.

Maybe a payback of some sort, either to her or to hurt someone close to her. Like her father."

"I agree. That thought has crossed my mind many times. Just because Johnson hired me doesn't automatically excuse him. I'll be investigating him as well. But I don't think he would do it. He loved her too much, from all accounts, but I think someone who had a grudge against him could commit this crime, knowing Cara was his soft spot," said Rick.

"Johnson is a well-known public figure, so I'll be doing some research of my own about his business dealings, partners, et cetera."

"How much do you need to make a profile?" asked Rick.

"You mean money? You can't afford me," Carson told him. "I'm doing this for you as a favor to my friend, Possum. And to be honest, I love this stuff. I never really wanted to retire, but the FBI gave me no choice. They still use me from time to time, but it's not as often as it used to be, and I miss it."

"Where did you work?" asked Rick.

"So many crimes were solved because of advances in profiling and forensics that the FBI created a complete profiling division over in Quantico. That's where I got my start. They call it the Behavioral Analysis Unit—BAU for short. I worked directly under Howard Teten, the founding father of the BAU, and I was lucky enough to get in on the ground floor. I'm proud to say I was involved in some pretty high-profile cases."

"Really? Would I have heard of any of them?" Rick was fascinated. This was right up his alley.

"Well, have you heard of Ted Bundy, David Berkowitz or Dennis Rader, the BTK killer?"

Rick was impressed. "Wow! Those were major! Well, I can't thank you enough. I know with experience like that, you can help me."

"It's my pleasure and I'm happy to be back at it. If you think of anything else, call me. Anytime. You have my cell number now, so don't hesitate to use it," said Carson.

As Rick turned to go, Carson stopped him.

"There's one more thing," the profiler told him. "This may sound strange and many people don't believe in it, but you may also want to consider hiring a psychic. I hired one out of my own pocket for a case, and she was instrumental in helping me profile and eventually catch Richard Ramirez, aka. the Night Stalker."

"Oh, I remember him. A sick bastard that killed a dozen or so people, right?" asked Rick.

"Yep. Fourteen, that we know of for sure. The original profile was that he was a thirty-something white male with a mommy complex. I never felt confident with that analysis, so I found a psychic. She went into a dream-like trance and when she came out of it, she drew an upside-down pentagram and a Day of the Dead skull."

"That's freaky," said Rick.

"No doubt. With her help I came up with a profile of a man of Mexican descent with ties to the occult. It turned out that Richard was the son of Mexican immigrants, living in El Paso, and he actively pursued Satanism. Her sketches were right on the money."

"That's amazing," said Rick.

"Let me call and set up something. She lives in Austin and I keep in touch with her."

"Ok, thanks."

Carson called her and brought her up to speed on Rick's case. After a few minutes, he handed the phone to Rick.

"She wants to read you."

"Now?"

"Yes."

Rick hesitantly took the phone.

"Hi, this is Rick."

"Hi Rick, my name is Mariam Albright," she told him, "and Carson filled me in on the case. I'd like to help you in person, but I'm leaving tomorrow for a job in California for two weeks. If you can concentrate, I may be able to help from here," said Mariam.

"Ok, I'll do my best."

"Do you believe in psychics?" she asked.

"Well I never really thought about it until today, but I'm willing to try."

"Ok. I want you to close your eyes and whisper the name of the victim to me, three times. Put yourself at the crime scene and just say her name softly."

Carson and Possum, who'd been sitting quietly in a corner all this time leafing through one of Carson's books, left the room. As they did, Carson lowered the lights and closed the door behind them, as Mariam had instructed him to do.

"Ok, let's begin," said Mariam.

"Cara Johnson, Cara Johnson, Cara Johnson," whispered Rick.

"Again," said Mariam.

"Cara Johnson, Cara Johnson, Cara Johnson,"

Rick repeated the process several times.

"Ok, I see a fire. I also see a ritual. It's unholy. There's a man and a woman standing over the victim. The woman is evil. She has a power over the man. She has power over all men."

Rick listened, chills running down his spine and the hairs on the back of his neck standing at attention.

"I see a lot of hatred and occult symbols. I see three x's."

Her voice sounded different and Rick wasn't sure if she was in a trance and talking or just talking.

Suddenly she stopped and her voice came back to normal.

"Rick, I got a strong reading. The person or persons involved in this murder have ties to the dark side. The occult. I can't tell if the beliefs are sincere or if the rituals were practiced just to create more fear in the victim. And whoever did this has studied black magic."

"Are you sure? How much of this did Carson tell you?"

"He only told me a young girl was murdered and buried and that you found her body and were later hired to find her killer," she replied.

"You said you saw two standing people over the body, does that mean there are two killers?" asked Rick.

"That's unclear, it could be symbolic. There could be one murderer and one witness. All I know is that the unholy one is somehow tied to your case."

"Wow, I'm blown away. Can I pay you?"

"No need. I'm leaving for California, as I told you, and I will be getting paid handsomely for my expertise. You just concentrate on the case. Get my number from Carson if you need any more help. Keep God close to you on this one. I don't know if you are religious or not, but you need to surround yourself with goodness and love to stay safe."

"Thank you, Mariam. I will. Did you need to speak with Carson before I let you go?"

"No, that's fine. Just remember to pray, and good luck. I hope you find the murderer."

Mariam hung up and Rick shuddered in his seat. That whole conversation felt surreal and gave him the creeps.

"Hey, guys, you can come back in," he finally hollered.

"Did she help?" asked Carson as he sat back down at his desk.

"I think so. I hope so. It was the most unusual phone call I've ever been on."

"I can imagine," said Carson.

"You ready, *padre*?" asked Possum.

"Yeah, I guess so. Thanks once again, Carson, for all your help. I look forward to seeing your profile. Do you need details of what Mariam said?"

"No, I don't want to cloud the facts yet. If I need them, I'll call her. Give me a couple of days and I'll try and come up with something for you."

Possum drove Rick back to his house and gave him an extra garage door opener for when he returned. That Ford would stand out, and he was sure the gangbangers would want revenge if they ever spotted it. Leaving fairly early in the day and heading north would lessen his chance of seeing any of the infamous MS-13 members, but just in case, he laid his revolver on the seat and set his GPS for Stanley's in Tyler.

The traffic was bad, just like every other day in Houston, but once he got past Spring on I-45 North, it thinned out. He was excited and anxious for his meeting with Benjamin Johnson. If he could solve the case, it would be the most money he'd ever had at one time, but it was more than just the money. He was honored Benjamin had asked him to help solve his daughter's murder, and this would be the most high-profile case he'd ever worked on. It got his blood flowing. He was determined to find out who'd committed this gruesome crime.

That poor girl didn't deserve this. Hell, no one did.

He was making good time and got to The Woodlands in less than an hour, so he pulled off and grabbed kolaches in the little town of Shenandoah. He and Chief were early, so Rick drove down to Kilo Landing on Lake Palestine to eat his kolaches and kill a little time next to the water. He backed the Ford right up to the bank and sat on the tailgate with Chief on his lap, munching and listening to the bird's chirp. They watched a few bass boats on the lake and soaked up the peaceful morning rays before getting back on the road.

CHAPTER EIGHT

It was 11:55 a.m. when Rick pulled into Stanley's Famous Pit BBQ. He gave Chief a few grapes and almonds and stepped into the building where he would be meeting Benjamin. The sign out front read, "Open for Dinner — Live Music and Covered Patio."

It was an unassuming place and smelled like heaven. Inside to the left was an order counter. To the right in a booth beside an old jukebox sat Benjamin Johnson. He waved Rick over. Although they had only met once, Rick knew his face from newspaper articles and had recently seen him on the cover of Texas Monthly Magazine, where they did a story about his new development in Rusk, Texas. Apparently, Benjamin recognized him as well.

That development was controversial. Benjamin had planned to build an open-air shopping center across the street from the Texas State Mental Hospital. Most people back home called Rusk "Crazy Town," and for good reason. The facility had opened in 1919, and in 1967, a maximum-security unit, known as Skyview, was opened for the criminally insane. The people of Rusk were against putting a mall for families and children right next to a mental facility, and the Skyview Unit housed many of Texas's most dangerous men and women, criminals who had committed horrible crimes.

Benjamin stood to shake Rick's hand. "I took the liberty of ordering for us. I hope you don't mind."

"Nah, I'm not picky. What'd ya get?"

"A couple rib and brisket combos with all the fixin's. These ribs have won awards," he said. He slid two envelopes, one large and one small, over to Rick. "But let's get down to business. I hope you don't mind cash."

The smaller envelope was stuffed full of bills. Rick picked it up and tucked it inside his jacket.

Benjamin then instructed Rick to open the other one and sign a few documents. There was a contract for $25,000 plus expenses if he didn't solve the case. It also specified a $250,000 bonus, the reward fee, if he did solve it. Rick signed the documents and handed them back to him. Other papers were inside the envelope, held together by a paper clip.

Rick tapped the envelope. "What are those?"

In a shaky voice, he explained, "That's all I could get from the sheriff's department, plus there's more information about the night my daughter went missing. I personally collected it from her friends. It also includes the most recent picture I had of her before she was killed." He took a deep breath. "I also included a list of anyone who had contact with her the month before she went missing."

Rick moved the paperwork down to his seat just as the barbecue arrived. They ate but didn't speak much. The food was amazing, but eating was uncomfortable for Rick, considering the circumstances. He finished half of his food and asked for a to-go box. Benjamin slid his untouched brisket over and told him to take his, as well.

Benjamin grabbed the check as soon as the waitress placed it on the table.

"Listen, Mr. Johnson, I—"

"Please, call me Benjamin. No formalities here. We're on the same team now."

"Ok, Benjamin. I want to reiterate that I'll do everything in my power, within the law, and maybe alongside it at times, to find out who did this. I didn't know Cara, but I feel like I did."

"I have a good feeling about you, Rick. I don't know you that well, but you come across as a stand-up guy. I hope you can do me proud on this case. I'm counting on you. I have to run. Keep me updated."

Benjamin walked out the door, and as Rick finished his sweet tea, he decided that his first stop once he was back on the road was going to be to the nearest Bank of America.

But first, he began sorting through the various new information he'd found inside the larger envelope. There was the entire list of names Benjamin had mentioned and a short history of Cara that he had typed up. Apparently, Cara had a twin brother named Darren.

Strange, I've never heard a thing about him.

In bright red ink, Benjamin had scribbled,

> *Top Secret.*
> *Only a few people know about Darren these days, and I want to keep it that way. Having a mentally*

unstable son isn't good for my reputation. Darren is a guest of the Rusk State Hospital. He is out of the picture and not important.

Rick's respect for Benjamin took a dip, but he didn't know the whole story, so he decided to reserve judgment, and after he finished his tea, he grabbed the paperwork and headed out the door.

Once back in his truck, he typed "Bank of America" into his GPS. A few popped up, including one on US 69 on the way to Rusk. Next, he did a search on his phone's browser for Darren Johnson. Nothing. It was as if he didn't exist.

There were only two people in front of him inside the bank. As he waited, he fiddled with his phone, searching again for Cara's twin brother.

"Next, please," said the young Latina teller.

"I need to make a deposit."

"Please swipe your card," she said. "Do you have a deposit slip?"

"Crap. I forgot to fill one out." Rick swiped his debit card and typed in his PIN.

"No problem, Mr. Waters. I have some here, and I can fill out most of it."

She filled out everything but the amount and pushed it toward Rick. "How much are you depositing today, Mr. Waters?"

"Umm, twenty-five... no, make that twenty-four thousand dollars." Rick pulled back ten hundred-dollar bills and shoved them into his wallet.

Her eyebrows rose, as if she was surprised an ol' country boy had that kind of money. Rick would've been surprised himself.

She put the cash in an electronic bill counter, then handed him back a receipt with his new balance circled.

$24,021.32

Rick shook his head and smiled to himself. *Wow. Yesterday I was down to $21.32 in my account. Today's a new day.*
He thanked the girl politely and walked out the door.

His route took him down US 69 and straight to the Texas State Mental Hospital. He made his way to the reception desk.
"Hi, I'm Rick Waters. I need to get some information about one of your patients."
The heavyset black lady cocked an eyebrow and swung her head indignantly.
"I'd like to win the lottery, but that ain't happening either, honey. All the patients' info here is confidential unless you is family. Is you family? Unless you is family, I can't help you."
Rick squinted his eyes. "Well, you have a good day."
How was he going to get those files?
Just then, he noticed a help wanted sign posted on a door of the building he was exiting. "Need CSAs, Janitorial, and RNs."
Janitorial. Now even I can do that.
He memorized the website to apply online, walked back to his truck, and pulled out his iPad. It took no time at all to fill in the form and hit Send, but he was anxious to know how long it would take to get an interview after he'd sub-

mitted the application, so he decided to call the number at the bottom.

"Texas State Hospital Human Resources. How can I help you?"

"Hi. I recently filled out an online application and was wondering how long it'll be until I hear something."

"What is your name, and what position did you apply for?"

"Janitorial, ma'am. And my name is Rick Waters."

He could hear her typing on a computer keyboard.

"Oh, you just sent this now, is that right?"

"Yes, ma'am. I'm extremely motivated to get some work."

"Well, we are short-staffed. How soon could you come in for an interview?"

"Right away."

"Ok. Come to the H.R. building, room 124. Ask for Mrs. Gina Landry."

"Well, thank you, Mrs. Landry. I'll be there shortly."

He grabbed his bag from the back of the truck and shook out his suit. Then he put on the clear faux reading glasses he kept in his bag as well, in case he had a chance encounter with the receptionist again. She probably wouldn't recognize him anyway, as he had been wearing a hat and jeans. Then he pulled into a nearby gas station, stepped into the men's room, and exited wearing a suit and tie.

Back at the hospital, he found the H.R. building. A modest-looking, middle-aged woman sat behind a desk in room 124, wearing a nametag with Gina printed on it.

"Hi. Are you Mrs. Landry?"

"Why, yes, I am," she replied in an upbeat voice.

"Hi, I'm Rick Waters. I spoke to you earlier about a job interview for a janitorial position."

"Wow, you are fast. Have a seat."

"I do my best. I could really use a job. I'm a hard worker and very dependable," said Rick.

"Well, you're off to a good start, Mr. Waters. So, let's begin. Can you push a mop?"

"Yes."

"Ok, you're hired. I'll have to do a background check, which can take up to forty-eight hours, but barring anything on your record that would disqualify you, you can start this week. Will that work?"

Rick was rather stunned but kind of understood.

The turnover at the facility must have been high. They paid eleven dollars an hour to mop floors. The building had the mixed aroma of Clorox and urine, and the combination of the awful smell, drab colors, white lab coats, and downright depressing overall aura gave off a disturbing vibe.

Rick stood up and shook her hand. "Thank you. See ya Wednesday."

Back in the hallway, Rick eyeballed a guy talking to himself. He realized it was just a worker talking to someone on his wireless earpiece, and chuckled.

I'm getting paranoid already.

Back at his truck, he searched on his phone for a nearby hotel.

It was going to be a hotel this time—not a motel. He was sick of sleazy motels full of bedbugs and with micro-thin walls where he could hear a whisper in the room next to him. This time, he was staying in luxury.

The Westin popped up on the website on his phone. Pleased, he took Chief out of his cage, rubbed his head, and scratched under his wings. The bird nuzzled up to him.

"Wow, Chief, a Westin. I've heard great things about those. We're staying in style, boy," he told him, clicking on his phone to complete his reservation.

Chief cocked his head and let out a little happy whimper.

As Rick pulled into the parking lot, he was unpleasantly surprised. It wasn't a Westin; it was a Weston with an O. He hadn't noticed it on the small screen of his phone. Close to the state hospital, and with no four-star hotels around period, it would have to do for the next three days.

"Welcome to the Weston," said the guy behind the counter.

"Uh-huh," Rick murmured. "I have a reservation for three nights." He pushed his driver's license and a credit card toward the clerk.

"Thank you, Mr. Waters," he said as he typed on his keyboard. "I'm not finding your reservation. When did you make it?"

Rick pulled out his phone and read the reservation number to him.

"Thank you, sir. I see you made it on Priceline. Sometimes it takes a while for it to show up in our system."

"Do you have anything on the first floor? In the back?"

"Let me check."

He got on his walkie-talkie and asked the housekeeping staff if anything was ready.

"We just got one cleaned. It's all yours. One key or two?"

"One is fine."

Rick drove around to back of the building and spotted his room number. Once inside, he placed Chief's cage on the desk, then brought in his metal detector and digging bag, placed them under the bed, and put his pistols in the nightstand.

As Chief hung out on top of his cage, Rick turned on the Discovery Channel and then spent hours reviewing the papers Benjamin had given him and getting a start checking out some of the people on the list that had been provided. It was close to midnight, and Chief had long been asleep. Rick's eyes felt like sandpaper and the pounding in his head wasn't helping matters. Although his mind was racing, and he was sure he'd never fall asleep, he decided to call it a night.

His brain was awash with thoughts of the new job. The challenges he would face as a janitor. He needed to fit in, be liked, but not be too memorable. His main objective was to find out more about Darren, whatever it took.

The next day was spent making phone calls and researching other people from Benjamin's list. He accounted for every name, and none seemed to have anything about them that really stuck out to Rick. They were mostly just good ol' boys and a few debutantes from the rodeo. He decided to call Benjamin to ask if he had remembered anything further he wanted to tell him about.

"I was going over the same papers I gave you," Johnson told him, "and I can't recall anything new about Cara. She didn't really share her love life with me. She didn't have a lot of boyfriends and her only long-term relationship I can think of was in high school. They got into different colleges and ended up drifting apart, I believe the break-up was amicable. She did date a rodeo bull rider named Tuck Wilson, but he was always on the road, and it didn't last long. Cara didn't barrel race the national circuit, only regional, so they only saw each other when he was in town. Cara was popular, sweet and kind and would do anything for anyone."

Why would anyone want to kill such a sweet girl, Rick thought to himself once again, but to his new client, he responded, "There's no doubt, based on all the accounts I have about Cara, that she was well-liked. I'm truly sorry for your loss. I'm working hard to get to the bottom of this."

"Thanks, Rick, I appreciate it. It sometimes feels like just a bad dream."

"I can understand that, Benjamin. Hang in there and I'll keep you updated as I make progress. Talk to you soon."

The case was intriguing, Rick thought as he made his way to the lobby, where he synced his laptop with the house printer. After printing a rodeo photo of Cara, along with all the photos of persons of interest, he went back to his room and taped Cara's photo to the center of a large piece of paper, pinned it to the wall, then drew lines from her photo to those of persons of interest pics. He then drew more lines from each person tied to any other person via school, work, or just friendship. Last, one line went to a question mark, which represented the killer. The person-of-interest map gave Rick a visual look at Cara's known associates and friends, which helped create a better picture in his head.

This was a tried-and-true tactic used by law enforcement. Rick had studied books on crime solving, like *Mapping the Trail of a Crime*, and he'd also found that true crime books weren't only interesting and entertaining, but also informative. But as he studied his newly created person-of-interest map, he knew he needed more intel on the ones closest to Cara, including her dad and brother.

He worked all day and late into the night, ordered Chinese food to his room, and never left once, except to take a short walk to clear his mind. What bothered him most was that he couldn't find photos of Cara's brother anywhere. It was as if his slate had been wiped clean and he'd never been born. But somewhere in that hospital, where he'd just landed himself a position, there was a records room, and his gut told him that getting inside that room was going to be his best shot at getting information on Darren.

It made perfect sense to Rick that having a son in a mental facility could be a little uncomfortable for a prominent businessman like Benjamin Johnson. But wanting to keep his son's existence a secret did not give Rick a very warm feeling about Benjamin. It seemed a total contradiction in his character that he cared so much for Cara and took such good care of her, but let Darren sit in a facility like Rusk and just rot away. There had to be more to the story. One way or another he was going to find it.

He needed sleep, but his mind was still going a million miles a minute, so he decided to read something to distract himself and searched in his Kindle Unlimited account for true crime. But the book he found about profiling and the career of John E. Douglas of the FBI was so riveting that he still couldn't sleep. Finally, he put it down, turned off the light and concentrated on his breathing.

Suddenly someone knocked on the door of his motel room. It was 3:10 a.m.

He stepped to the door and peered through the peephole. He could see a girl with a hood on but couldn't make out her face.

"Who's there?"

"Can you help me? I need some help," said the girl.

"What do you need?"

"Please open the door, I'm in danger."

Rick walked back to the bed and grabbed his .38 from the nightstand. He cracked open the door but left the chain latched. The girl had turned around and her back was facing the door.

"What do you need? It's 3:00 a.m."

"I need you to find someone for me."

"Who are you?"

She slowly pulled back her hood. The back of her head was shattered. She spun around to reveal a face that was burnt and charred.

"I'm Cara! Find who killed me!"

She lunged toward Rick and he bolted up in shock, covered in sweat, his hands shaking from his nightmare. The case was getting to him, and it was going to be a long night. He finally fell asleep a little after five.

CHAPTER NINE

The next morning, barely awake, Rick stared at the ceiling as he ran though the list of possible killers again. What was the motive? Was someone trying to make a point? Was it revenge?

He suddenly sprang from bed and made his way to the person-of-interest map. He drew another line, made a circle, and inside it, wrote "Benjamin." Although he had considered it, and even discussed it with Carson, he'd tried to quash the idea since Benjamin had hired him. But that could be a cover, he reasoned, so now, reluctantly, he decided he had to follow up on his hunch.

Then another lightbulb went off.

The barrel could represent the barrels from barrel-racing in the rodeo.

The barrels they used nowadays were called flex barrels, and they were soft so they wouldn't bruise the horses or riders. But in the early days, and still in some smaller rodeos, fifty-five-gallon drums like the one Cara's body was found in were still in use.

He jotted a quick note but realized it would be better to follow up with the sheriff's department. He had a feeling they had put all of their forensic efforts into what was inside the barrel, but none on the outside.

He'd never heard back from Deputy LeBlanc, and thought he'd try him again. Two rings, three rings, four. He was about to give up.

"Hello?" said a voice, clearly out of breath.

"Is this James LeBlanc?"

"Yeah, hang on. Let me turn off this treadmill."

"Hi, deputy. It's Rick Waters. The guy who found Cara Johnson's body."

"Oh, yeah. How are you doing?"

"I'm great. Listen, I won't keep you long. Do you know if forensics found anything unusual or interesting on the outside of the barrel?"

"On the outside? Well, I'm sure they dusted it for prints and looked for hair or blood. I'm heading into the station after my workout. Why are you asking?"

"Cara's father Benjamin has hired me to help with the investigation. We all want to solve this case, and I hope we can work together and not step on each other's toes," replied Rick.

"That's for sure. I'll pull the case file when I get to the office and ask forensics to get back to me."

"Thanks, deputy. I really appreciate it. Please call me when you have something. Talk to ya later."

Rick set his phone down, but it rang as soon as it touched the desk. It was Possum.

"Rick, I have great news—two pieces of great news, actually. First, congratulations. The watch you found was authentic. It's from the correct time period and definitely belonged to *the* W.S. Glenn. My buddy over at U of H used the serial number to track down where it was sold, and low and behold, there was a record of it being purchased by W.S. Glenn. The address listed on the sales invoice and warranty card is our beloved treasure hunter of the same name."

"That's incredible! What's the second piece of news?"

"You will be getting a text from Carson soon. He has a profile for you. He called me thinking you might still be here, and to ask my opinion on another matter. He said he has your number and will text you in a bit. I just wanted to give you a heads-up."

"That's great, Possum. I can't wait to hear from him. What else is happening?"

"Same ol' same ol', *padre*. You?"

"I'm in Rusk. Long story."

"You getting committed?" Possum asked with a chuckle.

"Something like that."

"Ok, well keep me posted, I'll hold down the fort here in Houston."

"Sounds good. Catch ya on the flipside."

His phone whistled shortly after the call with Possum. It was a text from Carson with the profile details he needed:

Single White Male
Age 28-35
Lives alone
Works with his hands
Is fascinated with the occult or Voodoo
Traumatic Childhood
Delusional
Wet bed past age 12
Possibly sexually abused

Rick committed the profile details to memory but knew they were general and could be incorrect. Profiles usually changed over time once new evidence was brought into a crime.

A few minutes later, just as he'd turned on the shower to start his day, the phone rang again. He quickly turned the water off and answered.

A pleasant female voice said, "Hi, is this Rick? It's Gina from the Texas State Mental Hospital. I got your background check back quicker than I expected. Is there any way you can come in today for your orientation?"

"Sure, no problem. What time?"

"Can you be here by ten-thirty?"

"I'll be there."

Rick put on his suit and glasses and realized he'd have to wear the glasses the entire time he worked there to make sure the receptionist never recognized him. Chief got an extra helping of seeds, and Rick put the *Do Not Disturb* sign on the door.

He parked in the back by the H.R. building when he arrived and stepped into the office. Gina was on the phone as he sat down.

She handed him an employee handbook and told him to read it over. Then she asked him what size pants, shirt, and shoes he wore, and disappeared into a back room. Minutes later, she came out and handed him a white duffel bag and shoebox. Inside were five pairs of plain white pants and shirts, and white, slip-resistant shoes.

"If you would like to purchase additional items, we have them here at a fair price," she said.

"These should be fine to start."

She handed him a schedule. "You can work five eight-hour days or two doubles and a single shift. Fill out your preference, and I'll try to accommodate you. We're so understaffed at the moment, you can pick up as many shifts as you want, really—up to twenty hours overtime." Gina winked at him, as if she'd just given him a winning lotto ticket.

Rick scanned the shift choices and put down two doubles, starting with a single midday shift that day. Noon to eight. She told him where the lockers were.

"Good luck, and congratulations."

Rick nodded and walked out the door toward the locker room. The building was barren, with walls all painted the same drab color; the overwhelming smell of urine reminded him of Sunday morning on Bourbon Street. But he was on a mission and had to shrug it off.

An older black man named Frank Byrd came in and introduced himself as the shift leader. Frank was a likable guy and told Rick that if he liked it there, it could become a long-term job with great benefits. Rick thanked him, knowing he would leave the hellhole as soon as he'd found the information he needed. On his first day of work at the hospital, though, he was hoping he could gain the confidence of some of the longer-term employees and get info on Darren Johnson.

"How long have you been working here?" Rick asked Frank, who stood in front of his locker, changing his shirt.

"Twenty-seven-and-a-half years, I reckon," replied Frank with a sense of pride.

"Wow, that's a long time. I bet you've met some interesting people over the years."

"Interesting? More like nuttier than a squirrel turd."

He covered his mouth.

"I'm not supposed to say things like that."

"When I said interesting, I meant colorful people. Maybe famous?"

"Well, the most famous residents we have are over in the Skyview Unit." He scowled. "That's where the guy who shot up all those people at a gas station in Channelview was before they moved him to Kerrville."

"Oh, yeah. I remember that guy."

Frank led Rick out to where the equipment was stored, handed him a mop and bucket and showed him a map of the building where he'd be working. It was the main building, which contained the reception area he'd been in the day before.

Oh, man. I'm sure she's gonna recognize me.

Rick walked through the halls to the main building, steering clear of the patients, who often seemed to look right through him.

After he made his way toward the front entrance and unfolded the yellow "Caution Wet Floor" sign affixed to his bucket, he started mopping. No one was behind the desk when he started, but after a few minutes, she walked in—the same black lady he'd met a few days before.

Here we go.

She looked directly at Rick, turning her head slightly, as if she recognized him.

"You're new here, ain't ya? I don't think we met."

Rick breathed a sigh of relief.

"Name's Richard, ma'am."

"Well, nice to meet you, Richard."

Rick mopped the entire hallway, and as he got his bearings, went around the corner to study the map. He did a combination of work and recon until his scheduled lunch hour at 3:30 p.m.

It took a while to familiarize himself with the layout, but he finally found the cafeteria, walked down the line, and studied his options. The food was as drab as the room, but with the addition of quite a bit of salt and pepper on his Salisbury steak, mashed potatoes, creamed corn, and cornbread, he managed to get some of it down.

Frank sat down across from him as he ate his own lunch.

"How's your first day going?"

"Not bad. I'm getting the swing of things here. I was going over the map, and I was gonna clean the records room, but it was locked."

"You need a higher security clearance to clean that room." Proudly, Frank displayed his keychain, which held a large, square key. "Only management has access to that room."

Big mistake, Frank.

Rick now knew which key opened that door and who had it.

"My shift is over soon. I'm gonna finish lunch and head to the house," Frank said. "If you need anything, ask for Kevin. He's the redheaded shift leader coming in at four. You can't miss him."

After lunch, Rick mopped for another thirty minutes to make sure Frank had left the building, and then walked back to the locker room, confident no one had seen him go in. Since people changed clothes there, no cameras were around.

On the tool cart sitting just inside the locker room were a pair of needle-nose pliers and two paper clips used on the daily duty sheets. Using the pliers, he bent one of the paperclips in half and created a tension tool. The other one he straightened flat, then, with the pliers, bent the end about an eighth of an inch in a forty-five-degree angle to make a feeler pick. Once he located Frank's locker, whose number he'd carefully noted earlier, he placed the newly formed tension tool in the bottom of the lock, inserted the pick inside, turned it slightly, and put pressure on it as he moved it to the left. The lock popped up, and he was in.

He snatched the keys off the hook inside and grabbed a baseball cap from an unlocked locker. After stashing the hat in a garbage bag on the supply cart, he closed Frank's locker without locking it.

The records room was near the locker room, so he rolled his mop and bucket down the hall. A nurse walked past him, but she was too busy looking at her phone to notice.

With the hat he'd quickly snatched from the cart pulled down low over his eyes, he put the square key in the keyhole and held his breath. The door unlocked, and he pushed his mop and bucket in, then quickly shut the door behind him. Knowing there were cameras everywhere, he kept his eyes to the floor and never looked up. As he mopped, he occasionally glanced at the file cabinets, trying to locate the J drawer.

In the corner of the room was a file cabinet labeled J–L. He pulled on the handle. "Locked, dammit! But there's more than one way to skin a cat."

The Leatherman toolkit he carried held a flat-head screwdriver. He had to work fast, and quickly stuck the screwdriver in the slot at the top of the cabinet, pushing upwards as hard as he could. With a loud pop, it came open, barely leaving a mark on the cabinet. He shuffled through the files. Jackson, Jennings, Jimenez… Johnson. He thumbed through until he found the file labeled "Johnson, D," then tucked it inside his shirt.

In a bathroom in the back of the office, he laid the file open across the sink counter and snapped pictures of each page. He was going as fast as possible but being careful to get each sheet in focus. The last page shocked him. Stamped across the top in big red letters was the single word "DECEASED." Rick's jaw dropped. Benjamin hadn't said anything about his son being dead.

Rick returned the file to the cabinet, remembering to never look up at the cameras. Through a small crack in the door, he peered down the hallway. It was clear, so he walked out and locked it behind him. He pushed his mop and bucket back to the locker room, shoved the hat back where he'd found it and put the keys back in Frank's locker.

It was after five. He knew H.R. would be closed, so he put on his street clothes and shoved his work clothes and shoes in the duffel and into his locker. On the back of a checklist taken from the parts cart, he wrote:

Hi Gina, I appreciate the opportunity to work here. I just can't take the smell. Thanks anyway. Don't bother paying me. We'll call it even.

Sincerely,
Rick Waters

He slid his note under the door of the H.R. office and left the building. On his way to his truck, he spotted a red-headed man in a white suit like Rick's, speaking with a couple of female residents in the yard. He figured it had to be Kevin, the shift leader.

Rick got in his truck and tilted the mirror back so Kevin was in view. Suddenly, the guy slapped one of the women and knocked her to her knees. Rick didn't see what instigated the blow but a split second later—bam! He hit the other woman.

Rick jumped out of his truck and ran toward the action.

"Hey, what's going on here?" Rick shouted.

"A couple of crazies tried to attack me, so I enforced the rules."

He began to pull out a night stick and was clearly going to wail on the woman. As he brought the baton back to strike, Rick caught it in his palm and ripped it from the man.

"What the hell is your problem? Who are you?" yelled the redheaded jerk.

"Who I am is not the issue, what you're doing *is*."

"These women were out of line and tried to jump me."

"No, we didn't!" shouted one of the women on the ground.

"He beats us all the time."

"You like to beat women, Kevin?"

"How do you know my name?"

"Let's just say, a little *Byrd* told me. Now, you keep quiet while I talk to the ladies."

Rick whacked the nightstick in his palm and Kevin got the message.

"How often has Kevin hit you?"

"Almost every day," they said in unison.

"Almost every day, huh? Does it make you feel like a big man, Kevin? How long have you been working here?"

"Nine years."

"How long have you ladies been here?" asked Rick.

"I've been here twelve years and she's been here seven," said one, as she pointed to the first woman who'd been hit.

"That's a lot of hitting!" said Rick, clenching his jaw. Do you ladies by any chance know of a room that's private, I suspect a room Kevin makes you go into from time to time?"

The second woman piped up.

"Yes, the old shock therapy room. He makes us go there sometimes, and he makes us, he makes us…"

"So, hitting isn't enough? Kevin? You force these ladies to have sex with you? You make me sick! Can you ladies show me this room?"

They looked up sheepishly and glanced at Kevin with fear in their eyes. They were clearly terrified of him.

"Don't worry, I'll be right behind you, and Kevin is gonna make up for what he has been doing to y'all. Right, Kevin?"

Kevin shrugged his shoulders defiantly. Rick shoved the stick in Kevin's ribs.

"Walk!"

The ladies scurried ahead and opened the door, then led Kevin down to the basement. It was musty and dark. Behind a curtain was a set of double doors.

Rick pushed on them, but they were locked. He held out his hand and Kevin reluctantly handed him the keys.

"Which one is it?" asked Rick.

"The brown one!"

Rick unlocked the door and shoved Kevin inside.

"Ok, ladies, you both stay here and keep a look out. I need to speak with Kevin for a few minutes."

He closed the door behind him.

In the center of the room was a stainless-steel bed that tilted down, with leather straps for the neck, arms and ankles.

"Is that where you defile the women, Kevin?"

Rick shoved the baton into his back, which pushed him closer to the table.

"It's not like that. They're crazy bitches. You can't believe them," he said.

"We'll see. I'm gonna ask you some questions and if you're honest, you may come out of this all right. Ready?"

Kevin just glared at Rick and nodded.

"Do you remember a patient here named Darren Johnson?"

Kevin said nothing.

"Answer me!" shouted Rick.

Kevin was startled and jumped.

"Yeah, yeah, I remember him."

"What happened to him?"

"He died."

"How?"

"I don't remember. Wait... I think he overdosed."

"Overdosed? How did he get drugs?"

"Man, don't be so naïve. You can get anything you want in here for a price," replied Kevin.

"Do you have anything to do with it? You seem to have a way with the patients."

"Nah, man, you got it all wrong, I'm a fair guy. I occasionally sell cigarettes here but I'm not as bad as those girls say."

"Yeah, right. What else can you tell me about him?"

"Man, I didn't know him. You know how many patients are in here?"

"Well, you seem to be quite friendly with some of them. Now, lean against that table."

"What?"

"You heard me. Put your back against the table and be still."

"You're crazy man. What are you gonna do?"

"Nothing. I just wanna restrain you and get out of here."

Kevin put his back against the table and Rick tightened the straps around his neck, wrists and ankles.

"You can't leave me down here alone!"

"Oh, you won't be alone."

Rick grinned, then walked out of the double doors and handed the night stick to the oldest woman.

"He's all yours, ladies."

As he walked up the stairwell, he heard the sound of nine years of payback.

CHAPTER TEN

It was only a little past 6:00 p.m. when Rick arrived back at the motel. He began to go over the files he'd photographed and learned a lot about Darren, who had been troubled since childhood. The complete opposite of Cara, he did poorly in school, although his IQ was quite high. He was involved in drugs and quit school before graduating, living mostly on his daddy's money, but still managed to stay on the wrong side of the law.

Rick was confused as to why he couldn't find out any of this information about Darren through normal channels. The hospital files said he was involved in an accident that caused the death of a prostitute he had picked up. His car had caught fire, and the hooker's body was burned beyond recognition. Darren was thrown from the car and sustained some brain damage, along with minor injuries. The state charged him with felony manslaughter, his lawyer pled insanity and Darren was convicted and sentenced to Rusk State Hospital because of his mental condition before and after the crash.

According to the doctor's notes, his brain returned to ninety percent of normal function and left him with a small speech impediment, but no other problems. He overdosed in the hospital after stealing a bottle of Oxycontin, his street drug of choice before the crash.

Something about this smelled even worse than the hospital, Rick thought, quickly punching in Benjamin's number.

"Benjamin, we need to talk," he began, trying to tamp down the fury that had risen in his throat.

"Go ahead, Rick. I've got a few minutes before I have to meet someone for dinner."

"I know it's personal, and I'm sure it still hurts, but why didn't you tell me your son was dead?"

There was a long silence on the other end.

"I'm sorry, Rick. I had my reasons. You have to understand."

"Look, if you want to me to work for you, then you need to be honest with me. I need to know everything."

"Well, I don't see how this has anything to do with my daughter's death."

"Dammit, Benjamin!" Rick said before he could catch himself. He didn't want to talk to his new boss that way, but he was upset. "I need to know everything. You never can tell which leads will help or not. What aren't you telling me?"

"Ok, ok. Is this phone safe?"

"Yes, I'm in my motel room."

"What I'm about to tell you, no one—except for a few people I paid off—knows. You understand?"

"Go on."

Benjamin went on to tell Rick that he'd never given Darren the attention he gave his sweet Cara. She was his pride and joy, and he felt guilty about neglecting Darren, who became more and more defiant as he entered high school. He was an embarrassment to Benjamin and often got in trouble.

Cara was an overachiever, and Darren was a burnout.

After the accident, Darren began to improve, and Benjamin visited him at the hospital, though Darren was miserable and begged his dad to get him out. He was on a long-term stay and wouldn't see the light of day for years, if ever. Benjamin finally admitted to his son that he felt guilty about the way he'd treated him over the years.

"I had a confidant in New Orleans who said he knew a guy from Haiti who had the ability to turn people into zombies," Benjamin went on. "Not zombies like you see in movies, but in a zombie-like state where breathing and heart rate are virtually undetectable. I paid him fifty thousand dollars to fake my son's death."

Rick listened in utter disbelief as Benjamin continued.

"I paid an orderly to steal a bottle of Oxy for me. I visited my son, gave him a couple of the pills, and told him the plan. I explained that a man with a Haitian accent would be visiting him later that night, and he would soon know freedom. So, that night, the Haitian guy came and did whatever he does, and Darren slipped into a sort of trance-like coma. The man poured a few pills on the floor beside Darren's bed and put the half-empty bottle on the nightstand. He slipped out of Darren's room. Darren was pronounced dead by the coroner that night and moved to the morgue. I told them I was having him cremated, but I hired a guy from the medical research clinic to swap Darren's body with a research cadaver and transport Darren to my house.

Darren really looked dead. I put him in his bedroom, and the Haitian guy returned and did his thing. He wouldn't let me watch. After a few hours, Darren was awake and alert like it never happened."

Rick listened intently, making mental notes as Benjamin continued.

"I bought him a house in the mountains in St. Croix and opened an account at Banco Popular for him under a new name—Laney Smith. I arranged to have a new passport and identity set up for him and flew him there in my Gulfstream. I had to.

"I also paid the hospital administrator to erase him from the computer system, but they obviously kept a printed record that you found. Finally, I paid off a judge in Austin to expunge Darren's record. That's where the wreck happened. I basically made him vanish."

"That is the most insane story I have ever heard," said Rick. "I'm having a very hard time swallowing this pill."

"I know, Rick. It does sound crazy and unbelievable but it's true. You have to believe me." Benjamin was almost pleading with him.

"Listen, I need to stop you for a minute. I don't believe in vampires, werewolves and creatures in the night. That goes for voodoo as well. What you're telling me sounds like something out of a bad B-movie," said Rick.

"I know, I know. I would feel the same way, if you told it to me, but you have to understand, it's not like the voodoo in bad B-movies, it's more like science. I researched it and gurus in India have been able to lower their heart rates and breathing through deep meditation to the point that they are virtually undetectable. Look it up if you don't believe me. I think it's the same concept."

"Where's Darren now?"

"Well, that's the thing. He was doing quite well under his assumed identity since I moved him to St. Croix. He had started a garden at the property I bought for him and was working as a bartender near Christiansted just to keep busy. He seemed happy. I checked on him regularly, but I haven't heard from him in a couple weeks. I didn't think too much about it, because last time I had talked to him, he said he had purchased a thirty-six-foot Catalina sailboat from a guy who was also teaching him how to sail. He planned to go on a trip to Barbados, so I figured he'd been sailing. I was eventually going to tell you about Darren and ask if you could follow up on him, but I wanted you to focus on Cara's case first. I was also embarrassed about keeping it a secret from you, but I hope you understand why I did. I promise to fully disclose everything from now on. You're obviously a good detective, since you managed to find out about Darren on your own, and so quickly. Again, I'm sorry. I hope this doesn't affect our working together."

"I accept your apology, and I'm counting on you to be straight with me from now on." Rick said. "But I think it's important that I go to St. Croix."

"Do you think there's a connection?" Benjamin asked.

"I don't know, but I'm going to try and find out. The only way to know firsthand is to talk to Darren. Also, I want to visit that voodoo guy in Haiti. Do you still have his info?"

"No info for the voodoo guy," said Benjamin, "but I do have the name of the man who found him for me. Only a name, though. Emmanuel Deveraux. He's originally from

Haiti. I met him on a trip to the Dominican Republic. He worked for me for a while as a project manager in St. Croix and now works odd jobs down there. He seems to know a little about everyone and everything. He also used to drive me around as a tour guide, and told me if I needed anything at all, he was the guy to get it. I made up some story about wanting to throw a voodoo party in Texas and needed an authentic voodoo priest to perform at the party. That's when Emmanuel gave me the number of the guy who came to the hospital."

"How did you come up with the idea to fake Darren's death in the first place?" asked Rick.

"I Googled *how to appear dead* and that's when I learned about the gurus in India. When I continued to research, I found out that voodoo priests from Haiti also did something similar. I never told Emmanuel about my plans with Darren, though. I just got the number of the priest from him. After the fake death was done, I called back the number, but the phone was disconnected. It must've been a burner phone. So, do you want me to call my pilot and arrange my plane?"

"No, I'll fly commercial. I have to take care of a few things first."

Rick disconnected from Johnson and opened his laptop. The voodoo nonsense was hard to believe but it was a lead. He typed voodoo into Google and began to read. He was vaguely familiar with voodoo and gris-gris bags, having visited New Orleans several times, but he'd never delved into the subject in depth. Now, he felt it was important to know more, since the crime scene had displayed telltale signs of voodoo symbolism.

Voodoo practiced chiefly in Haiti and the Haitian diaspora. Practitioners are called Vodouists. In Haiti, some Catholics combine aspects of Catholicism with aspects of Vodou, a practice forbidden by the Church, and denounced as diabolical by Haitian Protestants.

He then typed *zombies* into Google. All sorts of zombie movies popped up on the screen, so he changed his search to "authentic Haitian zombies."

On the first page, he found a website describing an actual event in Haiti that supposedly proved the existence of zombies. It was similar to the experience Benjamin had recounted about Darren:

At 1:15 a.m. On May 2, 1962, a Haitian man called Clairvius Narcisse was pronounced dead by two doctors after weeks of an excruciating, mystery fever. His two sisters, Marie-Clare and Angelina, identified his corpse.

Narcisse's family buried him in a small cemetery near the dusty town of l'Estere the next day in what should have been the end of his story.

Eighteen years later, in 1980, a heavy-footed, vacant-eyed man approached Angelina at the village market and introduced himself as her brother, the man she buried in 1962.

Narcisse explained to her that he had been resurrected by a witch doctor who had enslaved him on a sugar plantation.

Local villagers, like most Haitians who believe in the magical power of Voodoo, accepted the story -

but Western scientists were obviously skeptical of his apparent resurrection.

"Chief, that gives me the creeps."

The bird flapped his wings and raised his crown in agreement.

Other websites described similar events in detail, but they all had one thing in common: the use of a white powder, often referred to as zombie powder. Rick certainly didn't believe in zombies the way movies depicted them, but there was one movie that seemed to be a little closer to reality that he had seen when he was younger. It was called *The Serpent and the Rainbow* and was based on a book of the same name written by Harvard Professor Wade Davis.

Rick was so fascinated that he had looked up the professor. Davis was the foremost authority on Haitian voodoo, he discovered, and was so convinced by the power of the wonder powder that he had written the cult book, which spawned a blockbuster movie, that in turn sparked a new genre of zombie movies, myths and horror stories.

Rick sat up on the bed with Chief on his lap and began to read a downloaded version of the book on his Kindle. If he wasn't disturbed by anyone, he could probably finish the book in one night. Rick loved to read, and this zombie material, although farfetched, was interesting to him.

Close to 9:00pm, he finally put down the book. Now, more than ever, he believed that what Benjamin told him could actually have happened.

Rick ordered Chinese food for the second time in as many days and stretched his legs as he searched for a flight. There were none out of Tyler, and he needed a place for Chief to stay while he was gone, so he looked for one in Dallas. There was a bird-boarding hotel called the Kookaburra Bird Shop just outside of town.

"Wow, it even has an Australian name, Chief."

The bird squawked and rustled his feathers.

Rick pulled out his pad and made some notations about the weird voodoo connection of Darren's fake death and Cara's real death. The obvious link was the gris-gris bag found at the crime scene, along with other voodoo symbols and the fact that Darren was rendered comatose by some Haitian voodoo guy. It was either a genuine link or just an odd coincidence. The only way to find out was to talk to Darren.

Rick was still upset with Benjamin for keeping him in the dark about the Darren story, but felt it was important to follow up on it. He would do his best to keep an open mind about all the otherworldly narrative that Johnson had presented.

Rick wasn't born a skeptic, but he'd become one. It started with Santa Claus. Like most kids, he'd believed in Santa Claus until he reached a certain age and realized things just didn't add up.

The same went for Bigfoot. Growing up in Southeast Texas near the Big Thicket, Rick was exposed to many stories about Bigfoot. As a child, he was a believer. Even as an adult, he wanted to believe, but there just wasn't any evidence to prove it. In all the years of all the sightings all over the world, not a single strand of hair, DNA or bone had ever been found.

The voodoo thing was somewhat different. It was partially based in science, and the white powder that was used to put people into a zombie-like state had been proven to exist. So at least there was a shred of evidence.

But as any good detective would, he needed to follow up the lead.

The next morning, Rick opened his laptop and looked again for flights out of DFW. Chief was still asleep on his perch, with one foot propped under his chest. After a few minutes of searching, Rick closed his laptop, tucked it under his arm, and stepped outside into the crisp air. Dew covered the hood of his truck as he walked past it to the lobby of the motel, looking for a change of scenery.

After grabbing a fresh cup of coffee, he opened his laptop back up and continued his search. The Wi-Fi signal in the lobby was oddly weaker than in his room and after a few frustrating minutes, he decided to call American Airlines.

Eventually, he was transferred to a human named Cindy, who politely took his required information and came back with a suggestion of a flight out of Dallas that departed at 10:30 a.m. on Thursday, with one stop in San Juan. He asked for a seat in coach, mindful that he was travelling on Benjamin's dime, gave her his Visa number, confirmed all the flight information, and headed back to his room.

As he approached his door, which was partially open, he heard Chief squawking and barking. He had forgotten to put the *Do Not Disturb* sign on the room and the maid was inside.

"Oh, excuse me sir," she said. "Your bird doesn't seem to like me."

"He's ok. He thinks he's a guard dog, that's all. He grew up with dogs and picked up their barks. He even growls sometimes."

"I know, I know. When I first knocked on the door, I heard a yappy *ruff, ruff, ruff,* and then a *woof, woof.* I thought there were two dogs in the room. I was a little nervous, so I opened the door slowly at first, but when I saw the cage and the bird barking at me, I laughed so hard!"

"Well, thank you for cleaning the room. The bird's name is Chief and I'm sure he won't bark at you again. Right, Chief?"

Chief cocked his head and whimpered.

"Oh my God, that is precious. He whimpers like a puppy," said the maid.

"Yeah, he's a very confused bird," said Rick.

The maid let herself out and Rick fed Chief his breakfast of nuts, fruit-flavored pellets and a couple of grapes. Chief sat on his perch and munched.

Rick patted him on the head, murmuring, "Good dog!"

CHAPTER ELEVEN

Rick hated to leave Chief behind as he pulled into the birdie hotel outside of Dallas, but knew it was for the best. The paperwork and time it would take to get Chief into St. Croix was not feasible.

Chief was a big hit, as usual, with the workers in the kennel. Chief wasn't your average cockatoo. He was animated, like most, but had a personality that was more human, and sometimes canine, than any other cockatoo Rick had ever encountered. He was a ball of joy that made everyone who met him smile.

"Ok, Chief, now you be a good boy and I'll be back to pick you up soon," he told him.

The bird raised his crown, jumped up and down on his perch in protest, and mimicked a crow with a loud *"Caw, caw, caw"* as Rick walked out of the Kookaburra Bird Shop.

At the Dallas airport, Rick sat in the boarding area and waited for his group to be called. He already missed Chief, but knowing his friend was cozy and safe at the boarding shop made him feel better.

Rick leaned back in his seat as the Airbus pushed back early from the gate at 10:15 a.m. It was a half-empty flight, and he had the row to himself. It felt weird paying for tickets, since he'd flown stand-by all the time when he worked for Delta, but this trip was full fare, and Benjamin Johnson was footing the bill.

Before the flight left, Rick had called Phillip Semenuk and asked him about Laney. Benjamin had given Rick Phillip's name and told him he might be a good contact.

The man's voice had sounded shaky and anxious, as if he was worried someone might overhear him talking. Phillip was the guy Darren, aka Laney, had purchased the Catalina sailboat from in St. Croix, and Rick wanted to speak with him in person. Face-to-face was always better for reading body language, and Rick could easily see if the guy was full of it or being sincere.

They planned to meet at the Divi Carina Bay Resort and Casino, where Rick had booked a room for two nights.

During the stopover, he grabbed coffee and a beef patty, which kind of reminded him of a kolache, but a little different and much spicier. Rick had never been to St. Croix, or to San Juan, for that matter. As he waited for his connecting flight, he familiarized himself with St. Croix from a book he'd picked up in the gift shop.

It was one of the three main U.S. Virgin Islands, the least populated, and the farthest south—about forty miles south of St. Thomas.

St. Croix had suffered a downturn, with little work available. As a result, crime had risen sharply. He was sorry he'd had to leave his gun behind.

As the plane lifted off from San Juan, it flew right over the beautiful Spanish Virgin Islands of Culebra and Vieques. The water was spectacular, and the sun brought out all its shades of blue. Blue water always amazed Rick. Growing up in Southeast Texas, he was used to fishing and surfing in the greenish-brown mudflats of Gilchrist and Galveston. It was a vastly different experience from the sight of the crystal-clear water he saw below. It made him smile. Sailboats and pangas dotted the bays around the islands, and as they moved over open water, the dark blues seemed almost black.

It wasn't long until St. Croix, mountainous and green, came into view. Rick almost forgot he was there to do a job—not to be a tourist.

But then he thought, why can't I do both?

The plane touched down softly, and several people clapped. Rick always found it funny that passengers applauded a safe landing, but the alternative wasn't good, so he joined in on the clapping.

As he walked into the baggage claim area, a smiling, young, local girl giving out samples of Cruzan Rum greeted him.

"I'll have a Croo-Zan," Rick said.

She handed him a plastic shot glass. "It's pronounced Crucian, sir." said the girl. "After the people of the island—we are all Crucians. Drinking too much *KRU-źhun* might cause some *confusion*," she said with a smile.

"Thanks for the tip, miss," Rick said. "I'll remember that. I'll be a local before you know it. A born-again Crucian."

She laughed and handed him a brochure that described a Cruzan Rum factory tour.

"Oh, I gotta do that!" he exclaimed.

He tried one more shot of coconut rum and then headed to the car rental area. There was no line at the Hertz desk.

"Y'all got any cars?" he asked.

In a snotty tone, the man behind the counter responded, "Good aftanoon. Where you from, mista?"

"Born and raised in Texas," Rick said proudly.

"Well, in St. Croix—and all de Virgin Islands, for dat matter—it's respect to greet someone depending on the time of day with a good morning, good afternoon, or good night first," said the man.

"Oh, I was unaware. No offense! Well, good afternoon?" offered Rick tentatively.

The man's frown turned into a grin.

"Good aftanoon, sir. Where you be staying?"

"The Divi Carina Bay Resort," replied Rick.

"Ok. Da Divi is at di end of di island. I suggest you get a Jeep and take da mountain pass back to da Divi."

"Sounds like a plan," said Rick.

"If you take da main road out di airport, you could take Centerline Road, and a left on Hwy 705 to Mahogany, and visit da beer-drinking pigs."

"Beer-drinking pigs?" asked Rick, amused.

"Yeah, mon. Dem pigs is a must-see." He pulled out a map and drew the route with his pen. "Don't forget to drive on da left side."

Rick grinned. "Best tip of the day," he told him.

After paying for his rental and finishing the paperwork, Rick shook the clerk's hand and put the map in his pocket. In the parking lot, he matched his keys to a bright yellow, four-door Jeep Unlimited X. He threw his backpack into the front passenger seat and the duffel into the back.

The Jeep drove stiff and was built like a beast, but the straight-six engine had a surprising amount of power.

"It ain't my Ford, but it'll do." Rick murmured to himself.

He soon pulled the Jeep into a dirt parking lot where an open-air bar was set up next to a wooden fence, but there were no pigs in sight. A heavyset black lady was behind the bar, looking at her phone.

"Good afternoon, ma'am. Can I get a Cruzan and soda?" asked Rick.

She perked right up. "Good aftanoon, mista. I mix one up for ya."

She filled a tall plastic cup way more than halfway, then topped it with soda.

"Wanna buy da pigs a beer or tree?" she asked.

"What's their beer of choice?" asked Rick.

He thought she'd hand him a Carib or Presidente.

She handed him two cans and pointed toward the fence. "Dey only drink O'Doul's. Someone reported us for animal cruelty," she said, "so we had to switch to non-alcoholic beer. Da pigs don't care, really. Dey just like anyting cold."

"Do I open it?" asked Rick.

"Nah, just hand one to dem."

As soon as he stood by the fence, a huge, four-hundred-pound hog stood up and plopped his legs over the fence in anticipation. Rick jumped back in surprise, then scooted closer. He slowly reached toward the pig with the beer. The swilling swine snatched it out of his hands, crushed it in his teeth, and then slurped down the ice-cold beverage.

"Wow. That's impressive!" said Rick.

He took the other beer can and repeated the process. The pig demolished it in a split second.

The lady hadn't moved from behind the bar.

"How much do I owe you?" Rick asked.

"Six bucks. Two bucks for da rum, and two bucks each for da pig's beers."

Above the bar hung a beautiful, three-foot long tree branch with the words *Beer Drinking Pigs, USVI*, and several signatures written in a permanent marker.

"What kind of wood is that?" asked Rick.

"Dat's a manzanita branch, very hard wood. I used it as a perch for my parrot. But she die, so I hung it up der."

"I have a parrot, too—well, a cockatoo—named Chief," Rick replied.

"Aw, I miss my bird. Her name was Bella," said the woman.

She reached up and handed Rick the branch.

"Here, take dis for Chief as a souvenir from da pig lady."

"Really?" asked Rick.

"Fo sho, mista." replied the woman with a smile.

Rick handed her a twenty and said, "Keep the change and thank you very much for the perch. My bird will love it."

She took the money and tucked it into her bra.

"Tank you, mista."

"No, thank you." said Rick. "That was worth twice the cost of admission."

Rick backtracked toward where he'd started, finding a route that ran south around the edge of the island toward the Divi Carina Bay Resort. The route gave him the best of both worlds. Through his left window were mountains and through his right was the ocean. The drive was peaceful, and he was surprised how quickly he got used to driving on the "wrong" side of the road.

A side road appeared in his view that headed down to the water, just past Pinham Point. He realized he still hadn't set foot on the sand of a real beach yet, so he turned down the little road that dead-ended on a secluded stretch of sand.

Rick backed the Jeep up so it faced the way he'd come in, then slipped off his shoes and walked down to the shore. The warm sand felt amazing between his toes as he stood at the edge of the water.

Where the water met the sand, he sat down and enjoyed the view. There wasn't another soul on the beach, nor any houses nearby. But the tranquility of the waves lapping on the shore was soon disrupted by some rustling back near where he had parked.

Rick flipped onto his stomach and scanned the underside of the Jeep. Someone was trying to break in.

"Hey! What are you doing back there?" he yelled.

Someone peered around the side. Rick hopped up and ran toward him as the man moved out of view. When Rick got closer, he saw the guy wasn't alone. There were three of them. One had a crowbar, the biggest guy had a machete, and another, with dreadlocks, was holding a knife.

Rick didn't have any weapons on him, so he tried to reason with them. They wanted whatever Rick had and planned to take it, period. Without a weapon, he didn't stand much of a chance.

"Listen guys, I don't want any trouble. I'm here on company business and I have cash in my backpack."

Rick pointed to the passenger door.

"It's sitting on my front seat. You can have everything in it. My company will pay me back anyway and you obviously need it more than me."

The big one shook his head and said, "Open it and hand it over, muddascunt."

Rick didn't know what a muddascunt was but assumed it wasn't good. He slowly walked around the group with his keys in his hand, reached for the handle with his right hand and pulled open the door. Once he got closer to the seat, he reached in with his left hand to grab the backpack, then turned his body to block the guy's view for a second. With his right hand, he snatched the heavy branch off the floorboard, threw the backpack back in and jumped away from the Jeep, slamming the door as he pivoted.

"All right, punks, now it's an even fight."

"How yo figure? Dere's tree of wi an one of yuh."

"English?" said Rick.

"Tree of wi!"

"Tree of wi? Oh, you mean three of us! Well, de tree of wi just picked the wrong guy to rob today."

The guy with the crowbar rushed at Rick and swung, but missed Rick's head by an inch. His forward momentum pushed his upper body close to Rick. Out of instinct, Rick head-butted him. The guy's forehead exploded with blood and he hit the sand like a sack of potatoes.

"One down, two to go," said Rick aloud. Odds are getting better, boys!"

The biggest one ran directly at Rick, swinging the machete wildly. Rick ducked and did a backswing, nailing the big guy across the shins with the heavy branch. He screamed in agony and went down. Rick swung the branch hard at his head, at an angle hitting him against the temple and deeply ripping into his ear. The big guy shrieked and grabbed at the side of his head. Blood was gushing through his fingers.

The dreadlock dude looked down at the bleeding man, dropped his knife, and took off running down the beach. Rick grabbed the machete from the ground and threw it, along with his lucky souvenir manzanita perch, back in the

Jeep. He fired it up and spun out, throwing sand on the two remaining wannabe thieves, still on the ground moaning.

As Rick drove, he clenched the steering wheel in a death grip. Then, after releasing his right hand and putting it on the armrest, he realized his hands were shaking; he took some deep breaths and tried to calm down. His first few hours on the island had been a mix of excitement and danger. Not what he was expecting.

He wanted to go directly to Darren's place but needed the address from Benjamin. While sitting on the plane, he had emailed him from his phone but didn't have any Wi-Fi service yet to check for a response.

The sun was setting anyway, he'd had a long day and thought it might be best to start fresh in the morning.

The winding road was tranquil and the beautiful scenery slowly calmed his nerves. Rick glanced at the coast and stopped from time to time to take in the panorama.

As he made the final turn of his drive, he stopped at another beachside spot to take it all in. The crashing of the waves on the rocky beach was soothing and the gentle trade winds made the palm trees sway in the breeze.

It was about as beautiful as a postcard. Sandpipers ran back and forth on the beach as the waves came in and once again retreated. A few black-headed gulls soared overhead, making their distinctive laughs as pelicans dove into the water, feasting on schools of silversides.

All those birds made Rick miss Chief. He wondered what he was doing and if he was being boisterous and amusing with the girls at the kennel, or pouting because Rick had left him there. Knowing Chief, he'd already captured all their hearts and was taking full advantage of the special birdie treats he was probably getting.

"I'll bet he's gonna be fat when I pick him up," Rick said aloud.

Reluctantly, he climbed back into the Jeep and continued his journey toward the resort.

The road straightened out a little as he neared his destination, which made him hopeful he might arrive before sunset, maybe grab a drink at the pool bar and possibly get a glimpse of the green flash as the sun dipped below the horizon. He was making good time now.

Hungry and tired of being behind the wheel, he was excited about finally arriving at the resort and being able to get settled in. But just as he thought he'd be there in no time at all, he spotted something ahead of him in the road. It looked like a huge shadow at first, but then he realized what it was—a giant herd of goats, with a few sheep mixed in.

They took up the entire road, both sides. Rick slowly approached them, thinking they'd quickly move out of the way once the Jeep was in their midst. He was wrong.

He needed goats like a hole in the head. He honked, but they glared at him with no reaction. With no other option, he inched forward through the herd of lazy livestock. They gradually moved out of the way, in no hurry whatsoever.

Man, even the animals here are on island time, he thought.

CHAPTER TWELVE

As Rick pulled up to the Divi Carina Bay Resort and Casino, the sun was just starting to set on the Caribbean Sea. Although he was on the east end of the island, the sky still displayed a spectacular orange and red hue. His forehead was a tad sore from head-butting his would-be thief, but a few aspirin and a stiff drink could fix that. He bypassed checking in right away so he could catch the sunset, and walked down to the pool bar, which was to the right of the expansive infinity pool and directly adjacent to the beach.

The girl behind the bar was blending a frozen drink.

"Good night, mistah," she said in greeting. "Can I get ya a pain killah or a bushwhackah?"

"Good night. Those are interesting-sounding drinks, but I think I'll have a Cruzan Single Barrel with one cube of ice."

"Comin' right up," she replied over the racket of the daiquiri machine.

She poured Rick's drink and wasn't stingy with the liquor. The sun was beyond the horizon, hidden by the mountains as he sipped on his aged rum.

The air had cooled off and the humidity seemed to drop some. He finished his drink and paid his tab as the folks who had been swimming in the pool toweled off and headed to their rooms to change for dinner or gambling. Rick liked to gamble but liked to win more, though. Losing wasn't fun. He'd learned a long time ago that the longer a person played, the more chance the house had of taking it all back, and then some.

With his backpack and duffel bag, he stood in line at the front desk. There was just one person in front of him. A young girl checked in as Rick eyeballed the menu from the Starlite Grill. One dish in particular stood out from the Rock Dinner Menu—a dry-aged filet or ribeye, covered in fresh grilled shrimp in garlic and served over a steaming hot lava rock, which continued to cook the steak as it sizzled, ensuring every tasty morsel was warm until the end.

The desk clerk waved Rick to the counter.

"G'night, sir. How I help ya?"

"Good night. I have a reservation—name's Rick Waters," he said, as he slid his driver's license and credit card across the counter to the man.

"Welcome to paradise, mon. I see you be staying two days wif us, is dat correct?"

"That's right."

"One key or two?"

"Just one."

The clerk typed methodically in his computer, made Rick's key and put together a folder with a few brochures in it.

"I see you is scopin' out da Starlite Restaurant menu," he noted, since Rick had set it on the counter. "I suggest da steak and shrimp on de lava rock. It's to die fo'." He pumped his fist to his heart twice.

"I'm way ahead of you, my man."

"Can I make a reservation for ya, sir?"

"Do I need one?"

"Sometimes when you get to dinner, the steak is finish?"

"Finish?"

"No mo', all gone."

Rick glanced down at his phone. It was 4:45 p.m.

"Ok. Can you order me a large filet, medium, with shrimp for 7:30?"

The clerk picked up his phone and told the dining room to put aside one for... Suddenly, he hesitated, then put his hand over the receiver.

"Are you dining alone, or is someone joining you?"

"Alone, but thanks," said Rick.

"They's lots of honeys here, especially in the casino. I'll have dem set aside two for you. It's no worries. If you go alone, dey sell it."

Rick smiled, thanked him and took his key card. His room was clean and spacious, with a king bed, as he'd requested when he made the reservation. The room was nicely adorned with hardwood floors, sea-foam green paint, and matching abstracts on the walls. Pleasant and comfortable.

Beyond the sliding glass doors, he could see a glass table and two chairs, so he dropped his bags and walked out to enjoy the cool breeze. Since the humidity wasn't that bad, he turned off the air conditioning and kept the terrace doors open to let in the fresh air.

It had been a long day, but he wanted to play some craps in the casino before dinner. He grabbed a pair of khakis and a long-sleeved white shirt from his bag and hung them in the bathroom, cranked the hot water up all the way, and closed the door to let the steam get rid of some of the wrinkles in his clothes. After a few minutes, he lowered the temperature and hopped in the shower. The water felt good on his skin, so good that he didn't want to get out. But it was 6:15 p.m. now, so he stepped out and dried off. His clothes looked almost as if they had been ironed.

It was 6:30 by the time he entered the casino, but he still had an hour to kill before dinner. Although craps was his game of choice, the table was dead. So, he made his way around the room and started to notice that the majority of people in the room were female. Most were Asian or black, but there were a few white girls.

Then he spotted the Five-Dollar Three-Card Poker table and decided to play that until the action at the craps table heated up.

He sat down and laid out a hundred-dollar bill on the table. The dealer gave him his chips, he put down a bet on all three spots, known as playing blind. Playing all three spots meant the player would bet regardless if the dealer qualified or not. Playing blind could be risky but could save an ante many times, as he would push instead of just fold, when the dealer didn't qualify. A cocktail waitress suddenly appeared.

"Drinks?" she said.

"I'll have a Cruzan Single Barrel on the rocks."

Rick was the only one on the table playing blind. The Asian gentleman to his right was playing twenty-five dollars on ante and Pair Plus and waiting for his cards. The older woman to his right was playing five dollars the same way. Both of them folded before the dealer flopped out a ten of diamonds and a four of clubs, and the dealer didn't qualify. She turned over Rick's hand, and his high card was a king, but no pairs, so he pushed.

She took all the money from the other two players who had folded. The woman lost ten and the Asian gentleman lost fifty.

This scenario repeated three hands in a row. Now the Asian guy was down a hundred and fifty and the woman on his left was down thirty. Rick still had exactly what he started with and was already working on his second drink.

On his fourth hand, the dealer qualified with an ace of hearts. She also had a jack of spades and a four of spades.

Both of the other players folded again. She took their money, then turned over Rick's first card. It was a three of clubs. She slowly turned over his second card and exposed another three—a three of hearts.

"Ooh, a pair," said Rick, as he took a big swig of rum.

The suspense was building, and Rick had his right fingers crossed. Then, with the flick of her wrist, the dealer flipped over his last card, suddenly revealing a three of diamonds.

"Yes!" shouted Rick, slapping the table with both hands and bouncing his chips up a few inches.

The dealer began to pay him out, putting down $150 on the Pair Plus spot, five on the ante spot, and twenty on the play spot, which paid a bonus of four-to-one for three of a kind. He was now up $170, after only four hands. Noting it was now 7:25 p.m., he tipped the dealer ten bucks, collected his money, and headed to the cashier window.

As he pushed the chips to the girl behind the window, he did the rough math in his head. After tip-out, he was way up.

With the house's cash in his pocket, he pulled his cell phone out and noticed a missed call and voicemail. It was a message from Benjamin, so he returned the call immediately.

"Benjamin, it's Rick. What's up?"

"There's been a break in the case, sort of. I got a call from the lead detective, and he told me the crime lab thinks my daughter's murder was a mob hit."

"A mob hit? In Texas?"

"That's why I said 'sort of.' It makes no sense to me, but I wanted you to know, so you could follow up. A few years back, I built a condo on spec in Baytown for some Italian guys from Houston. They were late on their construction draw payments and failed to make their final payment, so I sued. I was awarded the property and they lost their original deposit due to breach of contract. After that, they made several threats against me, but it was so long ago and because nothing ever happened, I had forgotten all about it. Do you think there's a connection?"

"It's possible. Can you email me their names and the name of their company?"

"I'll look through my files, but it was over ten years ago and I've done so many projects since then, it's all kind of a blur. But I'll try," said Benjamin.

"It sounds like the sheriff's department is grasping at straws, but you never know."

They hung up and Rick headed to the restaurant.

The steak was as tender and flavorful as it looked on the brochure. A glass of Caymus cabernet sauvignon paired perfectly with his meal, which he wolfed down quickly, as he was eager to get back to the casino. He tipped the waiter thirty percent, kept the receipt for expenses, and headed back to the tables, hopefully to roll some bones.

It was almost 9:00 p.m., and the casino was hopping now. There appeared to be a fresh batch of working girls milling around the table games looking for johns, but Rick wasn't the kind of guy to pay for sex, so he had no interest.

The craps table was busy. There were only a couple of open spots, so Rick grabbed one on the end of the left side of the table. He always started with even money so it would be easier to keep up his wins or losses. Since he was starting out with mostly casino winnings from earlier, he decided to pull out two hundred-dollar bills and set them on the table. The puck was on the six, and the dealer was paying out all the players. Whoever threw the dice last hit the six before the dreaded seven-out.

The table had a five-dollar minimum but since Rick was up, he decided to start with ten bucks on the pass line instead of five. The dealer placed the puck back in the off position to indicate it was the come-out roll.

The stick man in the center, in this case, stick girl, pushed the dice toward a cute, young, redheaded woman standing beside a smiling young man.

The redhead chose two dice as the stick girl pulled back the other three dice and wished the girl good luck.

"The newlywed has a hot hand tonight!" the stick girl said.

Rick loved it when new players threw the dice, especially women. They had very good luck.

The girl picked up the dice, shook them a few times, blew on them, then threw them against the back wall of the table. It was a four and a three.

"Seven, winner!" said one of the dealers.

Seven or eleven always won on the come-out roll when betting on the pass line. The dealers paid all the pass-line winners, and Rick picked up his ten bucks and put it in the chip rack above his other chips to keep them separate.

The young redhead repeated her dice-throwing process and threw an eleven.

"Yo, winner!" yelled another one of the dealers.

Rick liked this shooter. Everyone at the table did. She was winning them money.

She threw again—a ten. The dealer turned over the puck and placed it on the ten. Now all she had to do was throw a ten before a seven and everyone playing the pass line would win.

Her next throw bounced one of the dice off the table. The stick girl examined the dice and then gave them back to the newlywed, making Rick happy. It was bad luck to change the dice in the middle of a hot roll, but the house had the right to do so if they wanted.

Rick winked at the hot little stick girl. She was gorgeous, about twenty-five, with dark eyes and long, dark hair in a ponytail. With her petite, toned body and golden almond skin, she looked like a surfer girl. Rick couldn't take his eyes off her and when she smiled back at Rick, he sensed she was letting him know that she was aware he was checking her out. He needed to focus, and she was definitely distracting him.

The redhead's next roll was a ten. The table erupted with excitement as she threw the winning number.

Winner, winner, chicken dinner.

The newlywed rolled one winner after another and held the dice for almost forty-five minutes before the dreaded seven-out. All the players applauded her. It was a terrific roll; people were congratulating her and patting her on the back.

Rick was up over $750 now and was about to play one more session, but the stick girl was replaced by an overweight local guy, so Rick colored up his chips. He knew when to quit and that was his sign to cash in.

After he cashed in his winnings and realized it wasn't even 10:00 p.m. yet, his adrenaline was still flowing from the win. Since his meeting in the morning with Phillip wasn't super early and he felt like a change of scenery, he asked the front desk guy where he could go to get a nightcap.

"Der's a new place called Sharkey's Bait Stand in Christiansted. It only about fifteen-minute drive."

"Thanks, buddy."

After Rick returned to his room and put all but a few hundred bucks of his winnings into the room safe, he was ready to scope out Sharkey's.

The route to the bar was an even more treacherous drive than the one to the resort from the airport. The winding roads abounded in cutbacks and sharp curves on the edges of cliffs.

Suddenly, on a hairpin turn, Rick was blinded by headlights and veered to the right. Luckily, there was a bit of a shoulder, so he slammed on his brakes, then realized the lights in his face were coming from a car that had flipped over and was facing the oncoming traffic at an angle.

The accident must have just happened, as there were no other vehicles around and steam was pouring from under the hood of the flipped car. Rick jumped out quickly and ran over to the accident scene. Broken glass was strewn all over the road and the smell of gasoline was strong.

A man and a woman inside the vehicle were dangling from their seatbelts.

The driver was groggy and had blood dripping from his face and arm. On the other side of the car, the woman was moaning and pulling at her seatbelt, trying to free herself.

"Are you hurt?" asked Rick.

She glanced at Rick with glazed eyes. "I'm not sure," she muttered.

"Let me try and get you free."

Rick pulled out his Leatherman and started to cut through the seatbelt. He held the woman's shoulder and eased her down once his cut was complete. With her head lying sideways, he coaxed her out.

With every move, she moaned in agony. She wasn't bleeding, but in pain nevertheless. Supporting her by the arms, Rick slowly dragged her to the edge of the road, where he propped her against a rock.

"Just be still. You're going to be ok. I'll get some help. Is that your husband in the driver's seat?" asked Rick.

"Yes, it's Tom. Is he ok?" she asked, panic-stricken.

"Yeah, he'll be fine. You just relax and stay calm and I'll get him out."

Since there was nothing in his Jeep to keep the woman warm, and she was clearly in shock, he unbuttoned his shirt and draped it across her. It was still warm out and he was wearing an undershirt.

The man had lost a lot of blood and was responsive but sounded drunk.

"Tom, I'm gonna get you out of there, ok?"

Tom looked over at Rick and nodded. Once again, Rick cut the seatbelt, slowly lowered the driver to the roof of the overturned car, and wriggled him free. His face and chest were covered in blood, and pulling back the man's hair revealed a gash on the top of his forehead.

"You're gonna be ok. It's just a small cut on your head."

The man nodded in agreement and he and Rick made their way over to his wife at the side of the road. The couple embraced, both trembling badly.

"What happened?" asked Rick. It was then that he recognized the woman. She was the redhead from the craps table.

"We were heading to town to grab a drink and when Tom turned on the curve his wheels hit gravel. I guess he overcorrected, and we spun around the opposite way. The tires hit the ledge and caused the car to topple. We rolled a couple of times and ended up upside down."

"You guys are very lucky," Rick told them, pointing to the drop-off two feet from the car.

"One more roll and you might have ended up off of the cliff," said Rick. "You really are a lucky one. You won me all that money at the casino."

She squinted up at Rick, trying to get a better look at him.

"Oh yeah, you were at the craps table," she said.

"Yep, lady luck shines again," said Rick with a wink.

Rick got a sweater from the man's car and with his permission cut it and made a tourniquet for his forehead. After they'd calmed down a bit, he helped them to his Jeep and drove toward town.

Once at Sharkey's, he ran inside and asked the hostess to call an ambulance. She did and Rick waited at the Jeep until it arrived. He insisted the redhead keep his shirt, made sure the couple were safely dispatched to the hospital, and, in his undershirt, headed into the bar for a different sort of excitement.

CHAPTER THIRTEEN

Inside Sharkey's, most of the people who had come outside to gawk at the excitement from the ambulance had returned to their perches. It was a typical sports bar—a mix of locals and tourists watched the giant TVs, and some people played pool or foosball.

Rick went straight to the bar and ordered a Carib. He was all rummed out for the night. A blond-haired guy in a Philadelphia Eagles jersey was bartending.

"What'll you have?"

"I'll take a Carib. Do y'all sell Sharkey's T's?" asked Rick, not wanting to sit in the bar in his undershirt.

"Yeah, we have those over there," he said, pointing to the far-left wall.

Rick walked over to have a look and then returned.

"Can I get the tan one in XL?" he asked.

"No worries, be right back," he said, pushing the beer toward Rick.

In no time, Rick was pulling his new Sharkey's tee on over his undershirt.

In all the excitement, he hadn't even noticed the stick girl from the casino walk in. She must've passed him while he was looking at the shirts.

Rick called the bartender back, nodded in the girl's direction and asked, "Can you send her another of whatever she's drinking, on me?"

The guy behind the bar obliged, whipped her up a martini, and delivered it, with a glance back at Rick to indicate who her benefactor was. In response, she wiggled her index finger seductively at Rick to gesture him over.

He didn't have to think twice, grabbed his beer and walked over to her.

"Hi, my name's Rick," he said, as he stuck out his hand to shake hers.

"Juliana, but my friends call me Jules. Thanks for the drink."

"Well, it's nice to officially meet you, Juliana. I hope to get to know you better so one day I can call you Jules."

He had to lean in to hear her, partly because it was loud in the sports bar, and partly because she almost whispered it. She sounded and smelled damned sexy.

"Have a seat," she said.

"Thanks, Juliana. You want something else?"

"Nah, I'm good. Thanks again for the martini."

"My pleasure."

Rick told her all about the wreck he had encountered on the way to Sharkey's as she listened, wide-eyed. It was kind of tough to talk with the volume of noise in the sports bar, but every time he leaned in to hear her, he took in her fragrance. Her perfume lingered in the air like a sweet spring morning.

After a few more martinis and chitchat, Rick took a swing.

"You wanna go somewhere quieter?"

"That would be nice," she said.

Rick paid the tab and they walked out.

"There's not a lot to do here and I took a cab from my apartment downtown, because I knew I might have too many drinks to drive home. I live close to the boardwalk, and it's nice at night for a walk." she suggested.

"I have a Jeep. Hop in, and you can show me the way."

"Cool."

She climbed into the Jeep and Rick closed her door behind her. By the time he had walked from her side to the other and opened his door, her perfume had filled the interior.

"I have to know. What are you are wearing?" asked Rick.

"This dress?"

"No, your perfume. It's lovely."

"Oh, I don't know, Shalimar, I think."

"It smells like vanilla almost," said Rick.

"You have a good nose. That's how it was described when I bought it."

"Well I ain't gonna lie to you, it's driving me crazy, in a good way," he said.

She blushed, put her hand over the top of Rick's on the steering wheel and smiled at him sweetly. Rick drove toward downtown as she navigated. He parked next to the boardwalk and spotted a street cart.

"It ain't a dirty martini, but can I get you a beer?" asked Rick.

"I'm a beer girl actually, but I like a crisp martini once in a while. I've had enough to drink tonight, though, so I'll take a Ting."

"Two Tings," said Rick to the vendor, "whatever that is."

"Ting is a soda with a slight grapefruit flavor, you will like it," said Juliana.

"Ju got it," the guy said, reaching into his cooler.

"The stars looked like God's little lanterns, twinkling on and off in the heavens," said Rick, borrowing a line from a Jimmy Buffett song. "So, tell me a little more about yourself."

"Well, I moved to St. Croix from Colombia, where most of my family still is. My dad was in the military, and my mom runs a little convenience store in a small town called Ciénaga, on the northern coast that sits adjacent to the Parque Nacional Sierra Nevada de Santa Marta."

"That sounds amazing! Although I do speak some Spanish, I can't pronounce most of those words." Rick commented with a laugh.

"That's ok. You would love it if you ever saw it, I promise."

"I'm sure I would."

They finished their Tings as they strolled down the boardwalk, taking in the moon's reflection on the calm water. Rick told her how he was raised in Texas and did pretty much anything to make a living, and how he had come to St. Croix to find his friend, Laney. He didn't tell her why though, just that Laney hadn't returned any phone calls or messages and was probably just out sailing.

"Oh, I know Laney," replied Juliana. "He slings drinks over at The Bombay Club, but come to think of it, I haven't seen him for a while myself. The place is here in downtown. We could walk over there, but they're closed this time of night."

"You know him? That's great news! Thanks for the info. I'll swing by there tomorrow and see what's up," said Rick.

They strolled leisurely a while more, until she said, "This is me," pointing up to the second-floor condo above a place called Rum Runners.

"I'd invite you up for a nightcap but I'm going windsurfing early tomorrow morning, and I don't know you that well," she said with a wink.

"I understand. I have an early meeting tomorrow anyway. Can I see you again?"

"Why?"

"Why?" repeated Rick.

"*Sólo estoy bromeando*. I'm just busting your balls. Yes, of course. I'm off tomorrow. Can you pick me up at four? I wanna show you something beautiful, and then I'll let you buy me dinner."

"Sounds like a plan," said Rick. "See you at four. Can I walk you up?"

"I'm a big girl," she told him, as she leaned in and gave him a soft kiss on the cheek. "*Hasta mañana.*"

"Good night."

Rick headed back to the Jeep, feeling on top of the world.

When he pulled into the resort, the casino was dead. He decided to call it a night and headed up to his room, where, still stoked about his lucky encounter with Juliana, he opened his door and high-fived an invisible person in the air. He was asleep before his head hit the pillow.

The next morning, he could still smell Juliana's perfume on his cheek. He didn't even want to shower, so he just lay there in bed, thinking about her and enjoying her scent. His meeting with Phillip was at 9:30 a.m. so he ordered some *huevos rancheros* from room service, drank four cups of coffee while waiting, and when it finally arrived, scarfed it down like a yard dog.

His room phone rang at 9:25 a.m.

"Mistah Waters, dey is a Mistah Semenuk in the lobby to see you."

"I'll be right down."

After hitting record on his iPhone voice memo app, he made his way down to the lobby and knew who Phillip Semenuk was right away. He was wearing Sperry Topsiders, quick-dry shorts, and a red Mount Gay hat, a dead giveaway of a sailor. Rick moseyed up next to him and stuck out his hand.

"Phillip Semenuk, I presume?"

"How did you know?" asked Phillip.

"Well, first, you're wearing all the typical garb of a sailor, and second, you're the only one in the lobby, besides me."

"Oh, yeah. Of course."

"You mind if we talk in my room? It'll be more private."

"I'd prefer it."

Once back in Rick's room, he pulled out the chair for Phillip at the desk and then sat down on the sofa.

"So, I understand you sold a Catalina 36 to Laney?"

"Yeah, he gave me half down and had been making regular payments, sometimes double payments right on time up until a couple of months ago. Then he just stopped."

"Did he go sailing?"

"No, that's just the thing. The boat's still sitting in the slip and I just haven't seen him. He always used to come down to the marina and pay me, so I'm not even sure where he lives. I know it's up on the mountain somewhere on the way to Christiansted, but I'm not sure which house is his. I went to The Bombay Club where he works, but they said he just quit coming in to work."

"I see. Anything else you can think of?"

"Is he in some sort of trouble?" asked Phillip, rubbing his hands together nervously.

"Not that I know of. I just need to find him."

"How well do you know him?"

"Extremely well. He's one of my best friends," Rick lied.

"Ok, then, I'll level with you. Laney had been dealing coke at The Bombay Club, where he was bartending. I think he was also using pretty heavily. A few days before the last time I saw him, a couple of rough-looking black guys were talking to him at the marina. They were being aggressive, and I heard them speaking French to each other when they were heading toward the parking lot. Haitian, I think."

"Haitian, huh? Interesting."

"I'm sorry if I was acting a little nervous when you called, but Laney gave me a baggy with an ounce of coke in it in lieu of a payment, and I was worried you were with the DEA or something. I really just wanted him to pay me cash, but he said it was all he had, and that he needed to re-up with his supplier before he could pay me cash. He told me the coke was worth three times more than the monthly payment.

"I like to party as much as the next guy, so one night I did a line. The coke was uncut, freaking pure as the driven snow, and I got so high and paranoid that when I saw cop lights near the marina, I thought they were coming after me. I flushed the rest of it down the head. Laney came to my boat a few days later looking rattled and a bit frazzled, and wanted to swap the baggy back for his monthly payment. When I told him I'd flushed it, I thought he was gonna have a coronary. He just bolted off, murmuring how fucked he was. That's the last time I saw him."

Rick listened to the whole story, which rang true to him. He was convinced Phillip must have been trying to protect Laney or himself when they spoke initially, but was speaking candidly now that he knew Rick wasn't a threat.

"Can you show me the boat?" asked Rick.

"Sure. Now?"

"Yeah. How far is it?"

"It's just five minutes up the road at the St. Croix Yacht Club. You can follow me. I'm driving the Super Beetle."

Rick followed Phillip to the parking lot, and then north to the yacht club. It wasn't fancy by any means, and only had one pier for boats, a mix of blow-boats and stinkpots. As they walked down the pier, Phillip pointed out his own boat as they passed it—a forty-one-foot Morgan Out Island.

Rick was quick to compliment him. "I love your sailboat, Phillip. Beautiful lines."

"Thanks," he said with a smile. "She's my pride and joy."

"I like sailboats, but I fell in love with a sport fisher a little while ago in Destin, Florida. I've always owned a little jon boat, but my dream is to one day own a big sport fisher like that fifty-five-foot Viking I saw in Destin, and start a charter business."

"Go for it, man," said Phillip.

"Well, I can't pay for it with my looks," replied Rick.

"True dat!" Phillip declared with a laugh, as they continued to slowly stroll down the dock.

About five slip spaces down from Phillip's boat was Laney's boat. On the stern in blue letters was the name, *Silent Dream*.

"Why *Silent Dream*?" asked Rick.

"I'm not sure, Laney renamed her a few days after I sold her to him," replied Phillip.

Then Rick remembered what Benjamin had told him about having his son put in a zombie-like trance to fake his death at the insane asylum. *Silent Dream, it fits.*

It was covered in bird shit and obviously had been neglected of late. There was blue tape around the side of the teakwood accents, which had been sanded but not stained.

"He was refitting her for cruising," said Phillip. "I helped him from time to time and gave him pointers. I also was giving him sailing lessons and he was really into it. I sure hope nothing bad happened to him."

Rick could tell that Phillip was sincere, and undoubtedly fond of Laney.

"Me, too. Can we go aboard?"

Phillip was hesitant but reached into his pocket and pulled out a set of keys.

"I already checked a few days ago because I was getting worried, but he wasn't on board."

"Maybe we can find something that will give us insight into where he went—a note, or flight reservation, or something," said Rick, trying not to sound too much like a PI.

"That makes sense."

Phillip stepped on board and unlocked the companionway. They both climbed inside. It was musty and smelled a little moldy too. Nothing looked out of the ordinary, though. There were gloves and blue duct tape on the settee, and some unused brushes and unopened varnish sitting on the right side of the stainless-steel sink.

In the master cabin, everything looked normal. Rick dug through the garbage can, looking for something printed, but the only things in there were empty beer cans and dirty shop rags. The v-berth was empty, so he opened the chain locker, but besides the moldy smell, nothing really tweaked his senses.

Rick thanked Phillip and told him that if he found out anything else, he would let him know. Back in his Jeep, he decided to head into Christiansted and The Bombay Club, to see what else he could find out about Laney.

He headed into town, but before he set out, he had texted Benjamin so he could get the address of Laney's house in the mountains. Once he was on route, Benjamin texted him back, saying he had already sent the address via email the previous day.

Rick checked his inbox and sure enough, it was there. With all the excitement of flying and then winning in the casino, he realized he hadn't even checked his email.

He pulled into The Bombay Club right at lunchtime. It was busy and wasn't the best time to be sniffing around, but he did it anyway. His stomach was growling, so he sat down at the bar and asked for a Carib and a menu. The bartender was none too pleasant and seemed uninterested in serving him. He was typing on the bar computer more than he was paying attention to the customers, and was mainly focused on a notebook, where he seemed to be doing an inventory of some kind.

Trying to break the ice after the guy had begrudgingly slid a beer toward him, Rick asked, "How long you been a bartender?"

"As long as I've owned this place!" the guy responded.

Rick could tell by his voice that he was perturbed.

"I guess you gotta do pretty much everything here, when you own a place," said Rick.

"Yeah, especially when you get shit employees who call in sick or just quit coming to work for no reason."

"I'm looking for a friend who works here—Laney Smith?" asked Rick.

"No offense, mister, but I'm not really happy with Laney at the moment. I had high hopes for him, and people liked him. He drew lots of folks to the bar, and then about two months ago, he no-showed on a Saturday night. I haven't seen or heard from him since. He's part of the reason I'm behind the bar instead of in my office placing a food order!"

"Hmmm, I'm sorry to hear that. Well, I hope you have luck getting better employees. Laney was kind of a fuck-up, so I'm not surprised. Excuse me. I have a call to make."

Rick placed a five-dollar bill on the bar and stepped outside, not really wanting to eat lunch there anymore. It seemed that Laney just bailed on everyone and everything all at once.

Rick copied Laney's address from the email into his GPS and started up the road. It was only about a thirty-minute drive from The Bombay Club up toward the rainforest and foothills, to a place called North Central.

It was lush, green and damp as Rick continued up the winding roads. The GPS took him right to it with no problem. It was exactly as Benjamin had described it: a small cottage with a little garden on the side. It was overgrown with weeds and there was an old orange VW Thing parked in the drive.

From the end of the driveway, he texted Benjamin.

"What kind of car did Darren drive?"

Benjamin texted right back, "some kind of VW. I can't recall the name but it's orange."

Rick knew he was at the right place. But if that was his only car, where was he?

After parking, he took a look inside the VW. The ragtop was worn, and the windows were up, so he pulled on the handle, but it was locked. Peering through the glass, he saw only more boat supplies on the back seat.

After slowly observing the surroundings as he walked to the top of the steps, he reached for the front door, but then noticed it had been kicked in. With a bandana wrapped around his fist, he pushed the door open. The place was in shambles. A vase lay smashed on the floor, evidence, among other things, that a serious struggle had taken place. There were dark, round splotches on floor and wall, which Rick recognized immediately as blood splatter from a blunt object, such as a bat, or a brick.

But he detected no smell of death, so he checked the one and only bedroom. It seemed untouched, and the bathroom was clean too. The only disturbance seemed to be in the living room and hallway leading to the back door, where he noticed what appeared to be a small trail of dripping blood on the floor, heading to the back yard. Not good.

He pushed open the back door and noticed a small, wooden shed near the back edge of the property. As he got closer, he began to smell a sweet, pungent scent he was far too familiar with. Pulling the bandana over his mouth and nose, he slowly

pushed on the partially open shed door.

When the sunlight hit the back wall, he almost puked. Hanging on the wall was a severely decomposed body that had been suspended there with square-cut nails through both wrists and feet. A crown of thorns was wrapped around the head.

Telltale signs of a ritualistic murder were everywhere. A pentagram was drawn in a dark substance resembling blood on the floor beneath the body, and chicken feet were laid out like an upside-down cross, which was surrounded by burned-out candles. The smell was intense, causing Rick to gag, but the last thing he wanted to do was leave his own DNA along with his breakfast at a murder site.

Carefully, he examined the body. He slowly lifted the crown of thorns and could clearly see three bullet holes from a small caliber handgun in the back of the head.

The body was so decomposed that he was afraid it would just fall off the wall in pieces, but he wrapped a piece of cloth around a pair of pliers lying on the floor and used it to pull a wallet out of the corpse's back pocket. As he held his breath, he carefully opened the wallet and pulled out a driver's license. He read it, but already knew what it would say. *Laney Smith.*

In the driver's license photo, Laney—aka Darren—was smiling. Rick looked up at the skull and the jaws, which were wide open. Some of the teeth had been pulled out and were lying in a pile by the body's feet. Rick picked them up and wrapped them in his bandana.

After he took a few photos with his phone and made notes, he walked back to the Jeep and sat down. Dropping his head to his chest, he took several long, deep breaths.

Several minutes went by as he stared at his phone, dreading the call he had to make. Finally, he pushed the send button for Benjamin.

"Hello, Rick." said Benjamin. "You got any news on Darren?"

"Benjamin, I have bad news and there's no easy way to say this, so I'm just gonna say it."

There was silence on the other end.

"Darren is dead."

More silence, then a shivering deep breath. "What happened?"

"Well, it looks like Darren was killed in the same manner as Cara. I'm so sorry."

"Why? Why would anyone wanna kill both my son and my daughter?"

"I don't know, but I'm gonna find out. I'll call you in a few days."

"Are you sure it's Darren?"

"I'm pretty sure. I have some of the teeth from the body and I'm gonna FedEx them to you, so you can match them with his dental records."

"Ok, I understand. I'll be standing by."

They both hung up at the same time. Once he got back to the Jeep, he drove around until he found a pay phone, then pulled out the phone book and looked up the local police department office. The phone rang for what must've been ten times.

"VIPD, how can I help you?" said the lady who answered.

Rick disguised his voice; told her he'd like to report a dead body and gave the address.

"What's your name, sir?"

"Never mind," he said, and hung up.

Rick drove back to the resort, headed to the front desk, booked another couple of days and asked the clerk where the nearest FedEx office was. The fellow told him FedEx picked up at the resort daily and handed him a packing envelope.

Back to his room, he wrapped the teeth in several tissues, sealed them in the envelope, which he addressed to Benjamin, and rushed back down to the front desk.

"Can you let me know when they pick it up?" asked Rick, writing his name and cell number on a notepad and sliding it over to the clerk.

"No problem, sir, I will. It's usually around 4:00 p.m."

"Can you text me?"

"Will do, sir.

CHAPTER FOURTEEN

Back in his room, Rick was pacing. He was beside himself with uncertainty and bewilderment.

Why were a brother and sister murdered in a similar manner, thousands of miles apart?

Based on the decomposition and timeline according to when Darren stopped showing up for work and was last seen, he must've been murdered near the same time as Cara. But why? Darren was a burnout drug user and seller who was at least trying to turn his life around. Cara was a grade-A student and rodeo star, and the pride and joy of her dad. Except for being twins, they couldn't have been more different.

The only thing that linked them was their dad, Benjamin Johnson: a wealthy, powerful man with the potential for many enemies. He really couldn't see Benjamin knocking off his disappointing son after going to so much trouble to get him out of the mental hospital and set him up in a new life, or Cara, for that matter, who was the light of his life.

Benjamin just didn't seem like the killing type anyway. What made the most sense was the idea he'd thought of before—that these murders were some kind of payback to Benjamin.

Rick paced and paced and went over again and again every detail of the papers Benjamin had given him. He'd completely lost track of time when Juliana called to ask if they were still on for four o'clock.

He couldn't fake how he was feeling. He really wasn't up for a night on the town.

"Juliana, something has happened. There's been a murder."

"Oh, my God," she gasped.

"It's Laney," said Rick.

He heard another large gasp on the phone.

"Laney? Who would hurt Laney? Everyone seemed to like him."

"I don't know, but I'm damn sure gonna find out. There are some things I want to tell you. Let me get cleaned up and I'll meet you."

"You sound upset, Rick. Let me come to you. Just sit tight and I'll be right over. I need to drop something off for work anyway."

"Ok, see ya soon."

They hung up and Rick did his best to shake off his mood. He didn't even know Laney, but the murder disturbed him greatly, maybe because he had found Cara in similar gruesome circumstances, or maybe because he felt so bad for Benjamin losing both of his kids to murder at approximately the same time. All he knew was that the whole horrible situation made him a little dizzy and nauseous.

There was a knock on the door about twenty minutes later. Through the peephole, he saw Juliana looking stunning in a formfitting little sundress, her long black hair flowing down over her shoulders. Her high-heeled cork sandals really emphasized her perfect calves. On her left shoulder she carried a cloth grocery bag, and under her other arm she held a small purse.

Rick opened the door, and to his surprise she leaped up, wrapped her arms around him and gave him a huge hug.

"I'm so sorry, Rick. I don't know what to say."

"Thank you, Juliana."

"Call me Jules."

A slow smile spread across Rick's face. "Thanks, Jules. I really needed that hug." He paused, and then suggested, "Let's sit on the terrace and talk. I need to tell you a few things before we go any further."

"Sounds serious," said Jules.

"It's not that big a deal, but I really want to get to know you better, and I don't want to keep any secrets."

"Secrets, huh? Sounds like we need some wine. Do you have any glasses?" she asked.

"I believe so." From the cabinet above the mini fridge, he grabbed two wine glasses and a corkscrew.

"It's a twist off," Jules told him.

"Oh, ok."

They moved to the terrace and sat across from each other as Rick poured two glasses of the pinot noir she'd handed him from her bag.

"Jules, I'm a private detective and I was hired to find Laney. I can't tell you a whole lot, but I'm working for Laney's dad."

"Ok, I understand," she said. "Thanks for explaining that to me."

"Good wine!" he murmured appreciatively.

"Yeah, I got it from a friend of mine who is a sommelier here at the resort. The distributors give him free bottles all the time. I think he has a crush on me, but he's never moving beyond friend status. Not my type. He's nice, but just a little too feminine for my taste."

"What is your type?"

She took another sip and looked into Rick's eyes.

"You are."

Rick was a little surprised and slightly embarrassed. "You mean you like the rugged, good ol' boy type, who doesn't care what people think?" he asked.

"No, the honest, caring type, who would do anything for a friend and knows how to treat a lady," she said.

"I guess I was way off because now I have no idea what to say."

She laughed and continued to hold his gaze. "So, tell me what's going on. I didn't know Laney that well, but he was always nice when I saw him at The Bombay Club. He was the go-to guy for an eight ball. I don't touch the stuff, but tourists are always asking me where to score some. So, if I thought they were cool, I'd send them to Laney. He wasn't hurting anyone, just simply supplying the demand."

"Do you think his dealing coke had anything to do with his death?" asked Rick.

"Who knows? I know some of the dealers around here have been investigated for violence and missing persons, but none have been arrested as far as I know. The Haitian guys bring in the coke, from what I understand. I steer clear of those guys." She paused to study his expression. "How are you feeling now, Rick?" she asked.

"I'm ok, I'm just glad you're here."

"Can I ask a favor? Can we go somewhere else for dinner? My sommelier friend is working, and I don't want to ruffle any feathers."

"Of course. I get it. You don't wanna hurt his feelings or make him jealous. Besides, you don't want your wine reservoir to dry up! Tell you what… why don't you head down now, and I'll be down in two minutes and meet you by the Jeep."

"Perfect! Thanks for not making it weird."

She playfully slapped him and laughed as she headed toward the door.

"¡Hasta pronto!"

"¡Sí!" he replied.

He put away the empty wine glasses, grabbed his wallet, and headed out the door in much better spirits. That nagging feeling in his gut had subsided, thanks to Jules.

Rick was grinning ear to ear as he moved down the steps toward the Jeep. In the late afternoon sunlight, Jules's black hair was glistening. The wind blew her sundress up just a little, revealing her silky thighs.

She had a little cooler with her and a blanket under her arm that she had taken out of her car.

Rick opened her door and closed it after her, stowing the cooler and blanket in the back seat as he hopped into the driver's seat.

"Where to?"

"I want to show you a place I love that almost no one knows about. Just head right on East End Road and I'll tell you where to turn."

Rick drove as she directed. The road took them north along the top of the island and then hugged the coast, turning west. The view was stunning. The sun was starting to get close to the ocean; there was probably forty-five minutes to an hour left before sunset.

They stayed on that road for about ten minutes as it veered to the right, then T-boned into Hwy 60. There was only one way to turn so Rick took the left.

"Ok, now pay attention. You're going to turn right shortly, just up from here," she directed.

There were no road signs so Rick was glad she knew where she was going.

"Ok, turn right now."

Rick obeyed. The road wound about, heading more northerly until it dead-ended into The Buccaneer Hotel. She told him to drive around the back toward the beach and pool, and then park.

"This doesn't seem too unknown," said Rick.

"You just wait," she said as she took his hand. "Follow me."

Rick was carrying the cooler and blanket in his left hand and felt he had an angel on his right. They came to a tunnel made of sea grape bushes that they passed under, and then, as they stepped through the end, an expansive, beautiful, completely empty beach opened up in front of them. There was a colorfully painted wooden sign with arrows pointing towards different cities, naming the mileage to each one: New York, Tokyo, New Orleans, Rome and many more.

The sky was on fire from off toward the west, and wispy cirrus clouds lay motionless above them. She pulled him along, almost skipping as a child would heading to a playground.

"Welcome to Romance Cove," she said.

"Oh my God, it's gorgeous!"

"I told you you'd love it!"

She took off her shoes and set them near the end of the botanical cave. Rick did the same. They strolled hand-in-hand for a few hundred feet, making the only footprints on the beach before she asked Rick to spread out the blanket. Then she opened the cooler and pulled out a container of cheeses and a bottle of rosé. After laying out the cheese tray, she pulled out two wine glasses that she'd wrapped in cloth napkins and poured wine into each glass.

For Rick, the evening couldn't have been more perfect when she scooted next to him, taking his hand and leaning her head on his shoulder. They both marveled at the painted sky God had gifted them. Then she gazed up at Rick as he looked back down toward her and kissed him for the first time. Her lips were soft and moist—a kiss Rick would never forget. He put his arm around her and kissed her back.

"I've never brought a guy here before, never brought anyone here, actually. It's my special place," Jules told him.

Rick nodded and thanked her as he squeezed her hand. They finished the bottle of wine and some of the cheese and then suddenly, she hopped up playfully and declared, "Let's eat! The Terrace Restaurant at the Buccaneer has the best scallops on the island. After all, I told you I was going to let you buy me dinner," she announced with a little lilt in her voice.

Rick shook out the blanket as the sun sank even lower beneath the horizon. It would be dark soon. They strolled back to the Jeep, hand-in-hand, and when Rick opened the door for her, she kissed him again.

"I like you, Mr. Rick Waters!"

"The feeling is mutual, Jules."

"The restaurant is in the Great House," she said. "We'd normally need a reservation, but I know the manager."

Rick drove up to the parking area by the main building, but before he'd come to a full stop, Jules jumped out and ran ahead.

"Meet me at the bar. I'm going to find my friend and see if we can get a table."

Rick gave her the ok sign and locked up the Jeep. The grounds were beautiful as he made his way to the Great House. He could see that The Terrace was on the second floor and overlooked the salt pond and the ocean, but he found the bar and was about to sit down when Jules ran up to him.

"I got us a corner table, secluded and private." She seemed almost giddy.

"Sweet. Let's go."

Rick followed her to the table. There was already a bottle of chilled white wine and two glasses waiting for them when they sat down.

"It's good to have friends," said Jules as she winked at Rick. "I'm in the mood for scallops and my buddy said this bottle of old-vine chenin blanc is a perfect accompaniment. I ordered us an appetizer of escargot. I hope you like snails!"

Rick nodded and couldn't stop smiling. Jules noticed.

The escargot arrived steaming hot and were delicious: tender, buttery, and loaded with garlic and herbs. They worked well with the wine too.

They chatted as they nibbled on the snails and sipped wine, touching each other's hands often.

The waiter brought another bottle of the same white wine before the main course arrived. The scallops were lightly seared and golden brown around the edges, dusted with Caribbean spice and finished with a creamy white drizzle.

They ate slowly and ordered a third bottle of wine. Rick was really buzzed by this point. They talked so easily about everything, that before they knew it, the restaurant was closing. Rick paid the bill and they stumbled, slightly unsteady, back to the Jeep.

She held his hand all the way back to the resort and looked at him with her big doe eyes as he drove.

As they pulled into the parking lot of the Divi Carina Bay, Rick could tell she was really drunk. She was slurring her words a little and her playfulness was really obvious.

"You really shouldn't drive. You can stay here in my room."

"I really shouldn't. I want to, but it's too soon. I'm a three-date kinda girl."

"Look, I like you a lot, and I'm not pressuring you at all. I just don't want you to drive and hurt yourself or someone else. I'll take the couch and you can have the bed," Rick suggested.

"I knew you were the type of guy I liked! Ok, you're right. I'll stay."

Rick handed her the room key and told her he'd meet her there in a few minutes, then went to the front desk to get her an extra toothbrush.

"Do you have a late-night dessert menu?" he asked the desk clerk.

"We do indeed, sir." He handed it across the counter and Rick gave it a quick glance.

"Ok, could you send up a molten chocolate cake with a couple of forks?" Rick gave him his room number and headed up. When he got to the room, the door latch was propping open the door. She was in the bathroom and the water was running.

"I'll be right out!" she called.

He told her not to rush, took off his boots and set them in the corner. Then he unbuttoned his shirt, laid it across the chair, grabbed a T-shirt out of the drawer and threw on a pair of jogging shorts.

She walked out of the bathroom wearing one of Rick's fishing shirts.

"I hope you don't mind. I wanted to get out of that dress, and I didn't have anything else to wear."

"Not at all," said Rick with a grin.

Her tanned legs looked amazing against Rick's white shirt as she walked toward him, then tiptoed up to give him a kiss. He kissed her back deeply. Her breasts, rubbing against his body, felt firm and supple, even though her bra was in the bathroom. She rubbed his back as they kissed, pressing hard against him.

A knock at the door tore them out of their embrace. Jules stepped out of sight onto the terrace, while Rick opened the door to the room service delivery.

"Molten chocolate cake," announced the bellhop as he rolled in his cart.

Rick signed the receipt and gave the guy a tip.

"Thank you, thank you, sir. Is der anyting else I can get for you?"

"Nah, just put the *Do Not Disturb* hanger on the door on your way out."

"Yes sir. Have a good evening.

When Jules came out from her hiding spot, her eyes lit up at the sight of the dessert.

"I love that cake. It's my favorite. How did you know?"

"You're a girl, right? All girls love chocolate."

"I guess you're right."

Rick carried the treat out to the terrace and lit the candle on the table. Then he poured a little rum over ice for each of them and offered one of the glasses to Jules.

"I'm not much of a rum girl. I've had some bad experiences with rum."

"That's ok, this is sipping rum—goes great with chocolate."

"In Colombia, we didn't drink much rum, mostly aguardiente. It's an anise-flavored liquor made from sugar cane. You probably wouldn't like it, but I was raised on it."

They sipped the rum as they nibbled on the cake and talked on the terrace. The trade winds were providing a nice cool breeze, but Jules was getting a little chilly, so Rick grabbed an extra blanket from the closet and pulled his chair up close to hers. He slid his arm around her, she laid her head on his shoulder, and they stared at the stars until they almost drifted off to sleep.

"We better hit the hay," said Rick.

"Yeah. I think I dozed off for a second."

"I think we both did."

Rick pulled back the comforter on the bed for her and laid the blanket down on the couch with one of the pillows for himself.

"You want me to tuck you in?" asked Rick as she slid under the covers.

"You are so sweet."

Rick drew the covers up and ran his fingers through her long hair. She circled his neck for a goodnight kiss, which led to another and another as she pulled Rick into the bed. Rick could feel her firm breasts pressing against him through his shirt while he softly traced his fingers down her waist to her hips and legs. She was perfect. She kissed him deeply over and over and rubbed her hands through the hair on his chest. Finally, he started to unbutton her loose shirt when she gently tugged his hand back and kissed him.

"I really want to, but we're both drunk, or at least I am. I want our first time to be special. I don't want you to sleep on the couch, though. Can you just stay and hold me?"

"I'd love to."

"I really, really like you, Rick. I want to be with you, too. I guess what I'm trying to say is… not no, but not now."

CHAPTER FIFTEEN

The sun was starting to rise, and slivers of light were sneaking into the room through the terrace door. Jules was still sleeping peacefully, a tiny smile on her lips. Rick watched her for a minute and was about to climb out of bed when she reached for him and pulled him toward her.

"I told you I was a three-date girl. If you make me coffee, we can call it three."

Jules slowly unbuttoned the shirt she was wearing.

"Are you sure?"

"Yes, I'm sure, Rick. She put her hand over her mouth to cover her morning breath. "I'll be right back."

In the bathroom, Rick could hear the water running as she brushed her teeth.

He reached into his duffel bag and pulled out a bottle of mouthwash, gargled and then spit it into one of the potted plants on the terrace before rushing back into bed.

Jules slowly undid the last two buttons on the shirt, glanced slyly up to meet his eyes, and handed the garment over.

"Thanks for the loaner."

"My pleasure."

Once more, she circled his neck with her arms and drew Rick close. He studied her beautiful, sun-kissed face and knew he had found someone special. They made love as the sun began to show its full roundness. It had been a while for Rick, and as appealing as she was, he was afraid it would be over before it started. The lasting effects of alcohol helped, though, and they finished at the same time, with Jules on top. She collapsed into his arms with a deep sigh.

"Let's eat," she finally said.

"Well, you certainly know what you want and when you want it. I'll order room service."

Jules smiled at him with a look of agreement and mischievousness, then headed to the bathroom to clean up. While she showered, he ordered croissants and a pot of coffee to the room, then joined her in the bathroom.

"How's the water?"

"Good. You're next."

When he stepped back into the room a few minutes later, Jules was standing on the terrace in her sundress, her head tilted back and her arms stretching in the air, basking in the warmth of the morning sun. She looked radiant.

"I have to work today. I'm on from 2:00 p.m. to 10:00 p.m.," she told him, as they ate breakfast on the terrace. "Boring shift, but I need to run home and grab fresh undies and my uniform."

"I can take you."

"My car is still in the parking lot. Remember?"

"Oh yeah, that's right."

That's how this whole thing started.

She took a big swig of coffee and stood up, giving Rick a kiss on the head.

"*Tengo que irme ahora, mi amor.*"

Rick replied, "*Hasta luego, hermosa.*"

Jules smiled as she sauntered to the door, then looked back at him and blew him a kiss.

The door closed behind her, and Rick was allowing himself to linger over another cup of coffee when his cell phone rang.

"Rick, you awake? It's Benjamin."

"Yeah, I've been up for a while."

"I wanted to talk to you. You know that reward I put up for info on Cara?"

"Yeah."

"Well, it's paying off. I got a phone call from the guy in the DR who originally hooked me up with the Haitian guy who faked Darren's death. He gave me a name and address to check out."

"The DR?"

"Dominican Republic."

"Oh ok, go on."

"I'm going to text you where he works, because I can't pronounce it— it's French, Spanish or a combo of the two I think. I want you to fly there and check it out."

"Ok, I'm on it."

"I'll text you the details as soon as I hang up."

"Ok, Benjamin. I'll be standing by."

Rick was getting dressed when he heard the text whistle tone from his phone.

Ask for Emmanuel Deveraux at the Hotel Guarocuya de Barahona, Av. Enriquillo No.15 (Malecon de Barahona), 81000 Santa Cruz de Barahona, Dominican Republic, I told him if he gave you a real solid lead, *you'd give him $1000 cash, so make sure you have some money on you.*

His laptop was still on the desk, so he booked a flight leaving at noon and a night at the hotel Benjamin had directed him to, but it totally bummed him out that he wouldn't be able to see Jules before he left.

The clerk at the front desk was the same one who had originally checked him in a few days before, so Rick asked him if there was any way he could avoid being penalized for cancelling the additional day he still had booked.

"No problem, mon."

Rick thanked him and headed to the parking lot, fired up the Jeep, and then called Jules.

"Miss me already?" she asked.

"Jules, I got a lead on the case and I need to fly to the Dominican Republic."

"I understand. When will I see you again?"

"I'm not sure, but I'll make it up to you. I had a great time with you, Jules, and I really enjoyed spending time with you."

Rick could tell she was disappointed and so was he, but the case had to take priority right now.

At the airport, he deposited the Jeep keys in the drop box at Hertz, then found the Jet Blue counter and checked in. All the flights into Santo Domingo were via San Juan, but Rick's was direct, without a plane change.

His trip was uneventful, and he landed in Santo Domingo about 3:00 p.m. He tried to rent a Jeep, but the only cars the agent had available that were even close to his preference were Toyota 4Runners.

He asked to rent a GPS, too, as soon as he realized his phone didn't work there. The agent had Rick sign all the paperwork, then handed him the keys, a Magellan GPS, and a paper map. His rental was a silver 4Runner that looked brand new. He hopped in and when he typed Hotel Guarocuya into the GPS, it popped right up.

Just as he was about to pull out of the parking lot he stopped, turned off the key, parked and walked back into the airport. He found a gift shop and grabbed a tourist guide, an English/Spanish translation book and an English/French phrase book. Since his phone didn't work and everyone there spoke Spanish or French, he figured he'd better get some sort of backup he could use to converse.

Once he got back to the Toyota, he started his journey, which took him along Highway 3, through some roundabouts, and then onto Highway 6, all along the coast. It was dark by the time Rick reached the hotel.

His room was plusher than he expected, with a balcony overlooking the cigar-shaped pool. From there, he could see a long pier with a thatched hut at the end. Another larger thatched hut to the left of the pool swarmed with people chatting and glasses clinking. He didn't feel like socializing but he was hungry.

At the tiki bar and restaurant, the chatter around him was in Spanish and French. He grabbed a seat at the bar, asked for a menu in English, and quickly ordered a blackened fish sandwich and Coca-Cola. He took a huge swig of the Coke before the fizz had even settled.

The fish sandwich came out really fast; the filet, so large it hung out on both sides of the bun, was accompanied by a massive pile of fries big enough to feed an army. He scarfed the sandwich down in no time, barely touching the fries, and then got a refill on his Coke to wash down the heat before pushing his plate toward the back of the bar.

"*Toma esta tina a la cocina, Emmanuel,*" said the bartender as he waved over the busboy.

Emmanuel? Could this be the Emmanuel he was supposed to meet?

Rick waved over the busboy.

"*Señor, ¿Cuál es tu apellido?*"

"*Deveraux, porque?*"

"Do you speak English?"

"Yes, I do."

Rick took out a pen and wrote his room number on a twenty-dollar bill and folded it up.

"You called a friend of mine in the United States and told him you had information about Cara Johnson's murder," whispered Rick as he handed him the twenty.

The man's eyes grew wide as he took the bill.

He quietly told Rick in terrible broken English and Creole that he got off work at 10:30 and would meet him in his room. Rick got the gist of it. He paid his tab and went back upstairs.

At 10:35 p.m. he heard a knock at the door and let Emmanuel in as the man looked nervously over his shoulder.

"*Mwen se fè pè,* I is scared. They always watch."

"Who always watches you?"

"*Bèl fanm vodou!*"

"English, please."

"The woman who does de voodoo. She see evryting."

While Emmanuel scanned the room anxiously, Rick tried to calm him down by pouring him some rum. When he took a big swig, Rick could clearly see that his hands were shaking.

"I can give you money if you tell me everything. My boss said $1000 now and more if we can solve the case."

Either the rum or the mention of money seemed to do the trick. He motioned with his head to walk to the other side of the room, carefully peered out of the balcony door, closed it, and drew the curtain. After he sat down on the couch, he asked Rick for another drink, but almost choked on the large swig from the generous refill Rick had given him. Finally, he gestured for Rick to sit down, leaned in toward him, and began to whisper.

"Dey is a woman named Angelique Beauvoir, she seductive. She practice de black art. She been involved wif many crimes, but never convicted. She run a drug den in Port-au-Prince and lure young men from night clubs into it. Dey always axin' her 'bout lost souls. I tink she involved with Laney's sista's murder.

"Dey say she seduce de boys and lure dem to a room, den she drug dem and dey force dem to be mules to bring coke back to de states. She got curly black hair and she wear a red silk bandana. She always wear di ear loops. She *bèl ti fi*. Um, how you say? Beauty.

"Laney not come here a fo' some time, now no one see him. He stay by di condo down di street and I meet him on beach. He axe me 'bout goin' cross di border to Haiti and I tol' him how ta do it if he don' wanna check in wif immigration. My wife sometime clean de condo where he stay. A guy own it from Texas but he rent it out when he not dere. She say she went to clean di condo and all Laney's bags still in de room after de time he suppose check out. So in de end she put dem in de storage, 'cause new guests comin'. He never come back to get dem. I tink something happen to him in Haiti. He was doin' a lot of coke when I met him an' he coulda got mix up wif bad guys in Haiti trying to score. Haiti is bad place wif little money. Dat why I work here. I always be Haitian, but I need make money fo' my family. Dat why I have many jobs an' my wife she too."

"Is there anything else you can think of? How do I find this Angelique?"

"If you go to Port-au-Prince and ask fo' her, she find you!"

Emmanuel picked up a pen and scribbled down an address on a piece of hotel stationery on the desk—the address to the condo where Laney had last been seen. Then he wrote down a routing number and account number for Banco Popular Dominicano and pushed it toward Rick.

"For de mo' moneys, if you fin' where Laney at."

Rick handed him a hotel envelope he'd prepared earlier with ten hundred-dollar bills inside and thanked him. Emmanuel folded it up and stuffed it in his front pocket, still visibly shaking as he scurried out of the door.

There had to be a way to check out that condo, so Rick pulled out his laptop and typed in the address Emmanuel had written down. It was just a few miles up the coast from the hotel. When it popped up on Airbnb, he booked it, knowing that would give him the perfect opportunity to investigate it.

The next morning, he quickly packed up his stuff, grabbed some eggs and coffee in the thatch-roofed restaurant, and headed to the parking lot. He threw his gear into the Toyota and set the GPS for the condo, which was only ten miles away near Playa Azul.

The drive along the coast only took about fifteen minutes. When Rick pulled into the driveway, he found another car parked there, belonging to the cleaning lady who would also check him in.

He stepped around the back on to the deck, which had a beautiful pool and attached hot tub, situated on a cliff with a breathtaking view overlooking the sea. The woman cleaning inside waved at him through the full-length glass windows at the back of the house, and then stepped out on to the deck.

"*Hola, ¿te llamas Rick?*"

"Yes, I'm Rick. I'm here a little early."

"*Es no problemo*, come in, come in, let me show you de place."

"Do you know who owns this villa?" asked Rick.

"*No se, es some policia.*"

Rick stepped inside the expansive sliding doors and she gave him the grand tour. The place had three bedrooms and an enormous great room with an open-air kitchen. She spoke good enough English for them to understand each other very well.

Once she'd given him the keys and shown him the paperwork he would have to sign, along with helpful instructions on how to leave a review, she finished making up a bed in one of the rooms and left.

Rick grabbed his stuff from the 4Runner, dropped it in the master bedroom, and checked to make sure she'd left the property. Then he began a methodical search through the spotless villa, looking for any clue he could find. He started in the master bedroom, checked all the drawers and looked under them. Every crevice or cubby hole was turned inside out.

He was studying the bookshelf, examining the inside of each book, and was getting discouraged. But as he replaced one of the books, he accidentally knocked a picture frame containing a sunset photo off the shelf. Before he could grab it, it fell and shattered on the tile floor.

"Shit!"

He hustled to the kitchen to snatch up a broom and dustpan. Then he laid the broken frame on the kitchen table and swept up the glass. He had seen similar frames at the gift shop in the airport. They were pretty common and sold in most tourist stores. The frame looked to be about four by six inches, made by means of a clay mold, and displayed a 3D image of a beach scene, with an empty beach chair and sunglasses. The words "Playa Azul" decorated the top.

He knew he could replace it, and no one would be the wiser, so he pulled the photo out slowly, being careful not to damage it. Behind that photo sat another one, and to his astonishment he discovered a picture of someone he recognized: Deputy James LeBlanc. He was posing with his arm around Cara, and as Rick brought the picture closer, he could see she was wearing the CJ belt buckle. The photo was obviously snapped on the deck out back.

Why was she here with the deputy? Why did he lie to me about not knowing her all that well?

Scratching his head, he continued to search every frame on the shelf and counter, and then began to pull down the paintings hanging on the wall. Nothing.

As he tried to lift the third painting in the master bedroom down, he realized it was screwed into the wall. In the garage, he located a Phillips screwdriver, took out the screws and pulled down the frame. Behind it, he found what he'd been hoping for—a wall safe. It was a Giantex brand, recessed wall safe.

He tried to open it, but there were too many code combos to break it.

Back inside the garage, he found a magnet in a toolbox. With any luck the magnet would activate the solenoid in the safe and he would be able open it.

After moving the magnet across the face several times, he heard a click, tugged on the handle and the door unlatched.

Inside was a large envelope. He dumped the contents on the bed, examined each piece and then photographed it. The evidence was compelling and turned the whole case upside down. It also created more questions than answers.

There was clear proof that Cara and Deputy LeBlanc were more than just acquaintances. They were a couple.

He opened his laptop and signed into the house Wi-Fi, then sent an email to Possum. It was short and sweet.

Possum,

I'm mailing you something from the Dominican Republic. It is valuable evidence, so hide it somewhere safe in your house.

Thanks,

Rick.

Although Rick had taken pics of all the documents, he wanted to make sure the hard copies were stored in a secure place with someone he trusted. And Possum was his guy.

CHAPTER SIXTEEN

Rick needed to find this Angelique Beauvoir and he was determined to make that happen as soon as possible. As he drove toward the border of Haiti, he passed the *Parque Nacional Jaragua* on his left, a diverse mix of mangroves, shrub, and dry forest. Finally, he arrived in the little former mining town of Pedernales.

The border crossing wasn't what he was expecting. Officially, it wasn't a border crossing at all. It was a small gate, the only thing between himself and Haiti, but there was no way to drive through it. You could only pass through on foot.

He weighed his options. One idea was to park the 4Runner and walk across, then try to secure transportation into Port-au-Prince. Or he could drive north to Jimini. After speaking with a local woman selling plantains at the crossing, he understood that rental cars were not allowed into Haiti. She agreed to watch over his 4Runner for twenty bucks. She lived right next to where he had parked, in a shack made of old scrap wood and aluminum siding.

So, the decision was made, and he tipped the border guard ten bucks to open the gate. The gate clanked closed hard as soon as Rick stepped through and the guard locked the heavy padlock as he crossed the border into Haiti.

As he journeyed deeper into the impoverished country, he was bombarded with locals trying to sell him anything they had or offer transport on moto conchs—small 125cc motorcycles that he would have to ride on the back of.

He crossed a dry riverbed beside a small footbridge into town. The first building he encountered was the immigration bureau—nothing more than a shipping container with a door cut out, and the officer out front didn't give him a glance at all.

Women balancing huge baskets filled with sticks and branches on their heads walked down the gravel street, as men on motorcycles drove past him, dodging potholes and rocks.

Hundreds of tents and makeshift houses were lined up next to the main street. It reminded him of a border town in Mexico he'd visited, only much, much poorer.

The Haitian side of this Caribbean island was a stark contrast to the DR side. The center of town was about two and half kilometers away, and as he made his way toward it, he noticed one-story buildings identified by government signage over their doorways. Deforestation had taken a toll on the country; only a few lonely palm trees waved near the soccer field as he walked past it.

The town was devoid of any public services—no electricity, running water, museums, libraries, restaurants or villas. Nothing.

Near the beach, a local guy was cutting up fish on a broken piece of plywood. Rick gestured to him as if he were driving a car, while mouthing the words "*Port-au-Prince.*" The guy laughed and said something in French that Rick couldn't understand, then mimicked riding a motorcycle and pointed toward the end of town.

Then he said, "*Tap-tap.*"

Rick pulled out his English/French phrase book and found that *tap-tap* was a Creole word for *camionette*. *Camionettes* turned out to be gaily painted buses. So now he finally understood and realized he could either ride on the back of a motorcycle or take a *tap-tap*. The trip would take about five hours. After spotting potholes the size of Volkswagens in the road, he opted for the *tap-tap*.

When he arrived at the painted bus, the driver was leaning against the front fender. Luckily, he spoke English—sort of—more of a mixture of broken English and Creole.

"When does the bus—the *tap-tap*—leave?"

The man looked at his watch and pointed at the bottom.

"Ah, 10:30?" asked Rick. The man nodded in agreement.

The bus resembled something out of a bad movie. Ratty bench seats lined both sides, the aisles were littered with a few cages of live chickens and boxes of produce, and fish sat on the roof rack. He grabbed a bottle of water from a street vendor, climbed into the little bus and plopped down on a seat in the third row.

Locals continued to board the bus, carrying everything from bags of fish to coconuts. One man walked on pulling a small goat behind him.

Two things had surprised him about Haiti so far. The people were much nicer than he had been led to believe, and, despite the looks of the bus, it left on time. The ride was miserable. Dusty, bumpy, and the smell was overwhelming. He couldn't wait to get out and take a shower. The *tap-tap* finally stopped on the outskirts of Port-au-Prince around 4:00 p.m., at a small village called Pétion-Ville. A sign with an arrow pointing up a winding road read "La Villa Creole."

The driver waved him off the bus and pulled back onto the road, leaving behind a cloud of dust and black smoke. Rick climbed up the twisting dirt path and was pleasantly surprised as he approached the hotel. It was quaint, yet appeared clean, judging by the meticulous grounds surrounding the entrance, which had a welcoming air about it.

Behind the check-in desk stood a guy who greeted Rick in perfect English. The man smiled and said proudly, "I am Pierre Henrissaint. Welcome to La Villa Creole."

Rick stuck out his hand and said, "I'm Rick Waters."

After Rick had greeted Pierre and commented to him on how well he spoke English, Pierre explained that he was born in Haiti but had studied in the U.S. for several years before returning home. Later, Pierre would become invaluable to him.

Once in his room, Rick dropped his backpack on the bed and immediately turned on the water for the shower. He wasted no time getting undressed and climbing in. The water was hard and came from a well, but it was hot, and the pressure was good, excellent for removing the road grime and dust from his body.

After he changed clothes, he went back down to the lobby and asked Pierre to recommend the best restaurant nearby.

"Les Jardins du Mupanah, but they closed at four. They only serve breakfast and lunch."

Pierre thought for a moment, then suggested, "Magdoo's. It's an open-air Lebanese Mediterranean restaurant, and it's famous for its Wednesday happy hour. You are in luck for three reasons."

"Why's that?"

"One, it's Wednesday, two, it's a quarter to five, and three, I get off at five and I'm heading there, so I'll give you a ride."

"Perfect. Do you also know where I can get a car rental?"

"Well, I have a Toyota Tacoma I usually rent for thirty dollars a day. How long do you need it?"

"Probably just a few days. Hard to say."

"I'll tell you what, Monsieur Waters. If you buy the first round, I will just let you borrow it as long as you bring it back full of petrol. Deal?"

"Wow, thank you, Pierre! That sounds like a plan. I'll see you back here in fifteen minutes."

Rick returned to his room and shoved his passport into the front pocket of his jeans along with his cash, which was rolled up in a rubber band. He put the rest of his valuables in the safe and headed back down to the lobby.

Pierre was waiting near the front door of the hotel and waved Rick over. They jumped into Pierre's work car, a Toyota Corolla, and left the hotel. It was only about two and half kilometers to the restaurant. Pierre pointed to a small, well-kept house on the left side of the road as they were driving.

"That is my house, and there's the Tacoma," said Pierre.

"Sweet. Should we grab it now?"

"No. Parking is a little tight at Magdoo's and I will need to return home after happy hour anyway."

"Makes sense."

The place was more sophisticated than Rick had expected, according to his impression of Haiti. Beautiful long, white curtains, tied in the middle, created a break between the open-air restaurant and the outside garden.

It was buzzing with activity. Two seats at the bar had just opened up and Pierre quickly grabbed them. They both sat down as the jovial bartender brought two menus to them.

"*Que voulez-vous boire?*" asked the bartender.

Pierre looked toward Rick. "Two mojitos?"

"Sure, sounds good," Rick agreed.

Pierre ordered the mojitos and said something in French to the bartender.

"I also ordered us hummus and meat sambousik. They are like little fried patties with meat inside," Pierre explained.

"You're the boss, I'm just visiting," Rick declared with a smile.

They did the "ha-ha, clink-clink" thing for an hour and both felt fat and happy. Pierre pulled out his wallet, but Rick waved him off.

"I only asked you to buy the first round," Pierre objected.

"It's my pleasure."

Rick paid the tab, and once they'd driven back to Pierre's house, Rick's new friend dug through the glove box of the Tacoma, looking for a map.

"Are you sure you want to go into the city tonight? The roads aren't great, and it can be dangerous if you don't know where you are going."

"Yeah, I need to go tonight."

Pierre began to give Rick directions on the map, using the flashlight he kept in the glove box, then stopped suddenly.

"My wife is visiting her sister up in Cap-Haïtien. I'm off tomorrow and Friday and have nothing better to do. Would you like a tour guide? My treat."

Rick thought about it for a second and said, "Sure, that'd be great."

"Hold on a second. I need to grab something from the house," said Pierre.

He returned with a backpack over one shoulder.

"If you don't mind, Monsieur Waters, I'll drive. I know Port-au-Prince like the back of my hand."

"Sounds good to me," replied Rick.

Pierre nodded in agreement as Rick hopped in the passenger seat and they took off.

"Where to first?"

Rick felt as if he could trust Pierre and needed an ally, so he let him in a little on the reason for his visit to Haiti.

"Pierre, I'm a private detective, and I'm looking for clues to solve two murders, one in St. Croix and one in Texas, that I think are connected. Have you heard of Angelique Beauvoir?"

When Pierre slammed on the brakes, Rick's head almost hit the dash. Pierre stared at him with a gaping mouth, and for a moment, seemed to have lost his words.

"Angelique Beauvoir? She is the *mambo asogwe*, high priestess, and a direct descendant of Max Beauvoir, who is believed to have been at the center of the Haitian revolution. She is bad juju, Rick!"

Rick smiled. "So you have heard of her."

Pierre nodded his head in agreement, but then shook his head no.

"You don't want any part of her. She is beautiful and seduces men, who wind up missing or dead. She is also deeply involved in the drug trade and has a lot of protection. People fear her for good reason. Whatever you think you know or have seen in movies about voodoo, forget that. She is the real deal and a real criminal."

"I need to find her regardless. Do you know how I can find her?"

"Her crew hangs out at the Casino El Rancho. It's really close. If I can't talk you out of it, I will drop you off at the front, but if you're looking for her, I don't want to be seen with you. Trust me, ask around and she will find you."

"Fair enough."

"I will come in a few minutes after you go inside and look for you. I will keep my distance and observe, so do not approach me. She is too dangerous, and I have to live here, but you can just leave and go back to the States."

Rick understood and agreed as they headed out.

When they drove into the parking lot of the casino, Pierre opened his backpack. From inside, he withdrew a small .38-caliber handgun and handed it to Rick.

"Just in case."

Rick took the gun and tucked it on the inside of his right boot. "Thanks. I'm sure I won't need it, but you never know."

Pierre dropped him off at the front entrance. "Good luck," he whispered, shaking his head.

Once Pierre drove out of sight toward the parking area, Rick entered the crowded casino. The building was old but had been beautifully restored and maintained.

The craps table, as usual, was a hive of action, but Rick wasn't there to gamble, although he really wanted to jump in and get his hands on those dice. Instead, he approached a small, four-seat bar and sat down. A few minutes later, on the far-right side near the entrance, he spotted Pierre, who was sitting at a slot machine that had a direct line of sight to where Rick was sitting. Pierre nodded toward Rick and then pulled the handle.

At the end of the short counter, the bartender was blending frozen drinks for two local girls. Rick waved him over, plunked down a ten-dollar bill, and indicated the drink-of-the-day special on the table tent.

"Hi, I'm Rick," he began. "I'm a reporter from the U.S., doing a story about the history of voodoo. Do you know where I can find Angelique Beauvoir?"

The man took the money Rick had laid down but didn't answer him and abruptly returned to his register, from where Rick could see him texting on his phone as he made Rick's drink.

In need of a bathroom, Rick looked around and spotted a sign and headed to the back of the casino. As he stood at the end urinal, two large men in suits entered; one stepped into a stall, and the other one approached the sinks. A moment later, when Rick turned on the tap to wash his hands, everything went suddenly black. With a heavy thud, he hit the floor.

When he came to, he found himself in the trunk of a fast-moving car. His hands and feet had been tightly tied, his mouth duct-taped, and a cloth bag covered his head. He tried to move but it was no use. His brain felt foggy, and the pounding pain in the back of his head was not helped by the car's jolting and the covering over his eyes.

The car suddenly stopped, and he heard two doors open. Then someone jingled keys in the trunk latch. The men who opened the trunk were speaking French. And then, he felt the prick of a needle in his arm.

He woke up groggy a few hours later, tied to a chair in a semi-dark room. His mouth was still taped, but the bag was off of his head. As his eyes slowly adjusted to the candlelight, he became aware of the smell of clove incense that permeated the room.

Almost no furnishings surrounded him, except for a small table against the wall. Symbols of voodoo similar to those he'd seen at Laney's crime scene sat on it, including a long, curved knife. He could hear the sound of voices speaking Creole in a nearby room.

Burning candles lit the space enough that he realized the table served as an altar. Through the crack under the door, he could make out shadows moving across the floor in the adjacent room.

As the door slowly opened, he squinted against the light from the other room. Someone walked in and closed the door. Once his eyes adjusted to the sudden bright light, he beheld a beautiful Creole woman in a long, flowing white dress who stood in front of him. Large hoop earrings hung from her ears, and a red silk bandana covered the top of her head, from which flowed long, black dreadlocks. Black lipstick and long black nails matched her dark eyes. She was stunning.

She seemed to almost float toward him, and then suddenly reached down and ripped the tape from his mouth.

"Where am I?" asked Rick.

"Never you mind. I ask de questions. Why is you looking for me?"

"I'm a reporter and I'm doing a story on the history of voodoo. I was—"

Before Rick could finish, she slapped him with the back of her hand and one of her rings scratched his face.

"Don't lie to me. You lie, you die; you tell de truth I may let you live."

Rick sat there silently for a moment, finally deciding he was out of options. So he said, "Ok, ok. My name is Rick Waters. Well, you already know that, since I can tell you took my passport and money from my pocket. I'm a private eye, investigating two murders. Both crime scenes were surrounded by symbols of voodoo, so your name was brought to my attention. You are Angelique Beauvoir, aren't you?"

"Who was murdered?" she asked angrily.

"Cara and Darren Johnson. A sister and brother. Darren was living under the alias of Laney Smith in St. Croix."

Recognition lit her face. "I know dis Laney, but I didn't murder him. If I murder someone, I tell you. I am not in de murder business. I am in de trade business."

She reached down, caressed Rick's neck and wiped the blood from his face.

"Are you sure you is not a cop?"

"No, I'm a PI. I could care less about your drug trade. I just want info about the murders."

"How dey killed?"

"They were both shot in the back of the head three times, and one was burned."

"If I take another soul, I look dem in de eye as I bury de knife deep into der chest," she said, as she picked up the big curved knife on the table and ran it delicately from Rick's shoulder to the center of his midriff.

"Life and death is one. Dey is same and killing someone while looking dem in de eye can give me dere power as dey cross over. It is coward to kill from behind."

She pulled back the knife as Rick took a deep breath.

"I tell you more, den you must pass de test."

"What test?"

"You shall see. I inflict a great fear into de boy, Laney. He was a runner fo' a man in Texas. He suppose to bring my shipment in a small boat upon de water to faster boats but he never arrive. I be told he had a change of mind and refuse to make de delivery. So I place upon him a great spell. The animal sacrifice I lay before him bring him strength to tell de truth. He hide de drugs deep in de hold of de boat but wanted to keep for hisself. I blow the powder upon him and took my supply back. I let him sleep, but I DID NOT kill him!"

Rick listened intently as she told him the details.

"Who is the man who placed the drug order with you?"

"I not know his name, only dat he live in Texas. He pay me tru a wire transfer, and always place orders in code."

"Why have you agreed to tell me all this?"

"I no fear you or de man who order de drugs. I have many followers who protect me, plus you must pass de test to live and if you do, you will never want to return or cross me."

"What's the test?"

She slowly opened her closed fist toward him and blew a white powder onto his face. Rick's whole body began to shake, and a numbing sensation began at the top of his head and traveled all the way down to his toes. Angelique moved toward him with a large box, from which she extracted a giant tarantula. When she placed it on his thigh, she cackled like a witch.

Rick tried to shake it off but realized he couldn't move. He wasn't asleep, but felt himself in a dream-like state, completely frozen stiff. He could see and hear everything but couldn't move a muscle. His heartbeat slowed; his breathing was shallow.

The spider crawled up his chest and onto his neck. If she was trying to scare him, it was working. It crawled up his face onto his head and down his back. He was trembling inside, but his body couldn't react. Eventually, the spider climbed down his legs and onto the floor. He wanted to stomp it, but movement was impossible.

Two men came in and began to hit him on the back and chest with strips of leather studded with round lead balls. He watched them swing over and over but felt nothing. The larger man hit him in the face with his fist, repeatedly. He wanted to flinch, but his head stayed motionless as the man connected to his jaw again and again. They began to beat his legs, and though his brain wanted to fight back, it was futile.

They finally left for a while but came back. The shorter man put a bag over his head as the bigger guy cut the zip ties around Rick's wrists and ankles. He grabbed both of Rick's feet and dragged him off the chair and across the room. The back of his head slammed against the hard floor, although he didn't feel it. They threw him in the trunk of a car like a rag doll.

After a long, winding drive, the car stopped, and the trunk popped open. Angelique's goons took the bag off his head, pulled him out of the trunk, and carried him to the side of the road, where a steep hill covered with high weeds angled downward. He heard them count as they swung his body back and forth.

"*Un, deux, trois.*" they chanted together as they launched his body down the hill. His face hit gravel and rocks as he rolled down the slope like a tire, finally settling near the bottom on his side. He lay there, motionless. The car drove away and out of earshot. When he opened his eyes, he could see the sun was setting. It would be dark soon.

Am I just gonna die here on the side of the road? His mind was racing, but there was nothing he could do about it.

The sun rose and fell three times. As he awakened on the third morning, he felt something crawling on his leg. He suddenly realized he'd regained sensation and was able to move. The creature was a lizard, which he swatted off his leg as the pain from the beating erupted throughout his entire body all at once. His head throbbed and his mouth was so dry he could barely move his tongue, but gradually, he sat up, reeling from the pain. His body seemed to have stiffened, as if rigor mortis had begun to set in. Awkwardly, and feeling dizzy, he stood, because in the distance, he could hear a vehicle approaching.

As quickly as he was able, he climbed up the hillside toward the road. It felt as if every muscle in his body was screaming, but he made it to the shoulder. On his knees, he struggled to raise his arm as high as he could. A man driving a truck carrying a few chicken cages in the back pulled to a stop in front of him.

Rick tried to speak, but nothing came out. His vocal cords had dried out. The driver handed him a bottle of water. After a long swig, he managed only one word: "Hospital."

CHAPTER SEVENTEEN

Rick awakened as a nurse wrapped a blood pressure cuff around his arm. There was an IV in his hand and saline slowly dripped from the bag beside his bed. His head didn't hurt as badly as before, but he ached all over.

"How many hours have I been asleep?" he asked her.

"Hours? *Deux jours*—two days, *monsieur*."

He tried to sit up in the bed, but his stomach muscles wouldn't cooperate.

"Someone gave you a righteous beatin'. You was robbed?"

"Yeah, something like that."

"Well, *monsieur*, you was in bad shape when you got here. We thought we might lose ya. You strong, doh."

"Thank you for taking care of me."

She wiped his forehead with a damp cloth and took his temperature.

"Is there a phone I can use? How about a phone book?"

She pointed to the phone on the countertop and put it on the dining tray across his bed.

"I be back, I tink dey is a phone book in de nurse's station."

She stepped out of the room and returned shortly with a directory, which she put beside the phone.

"Ok, I give you privacy."

Rick swiped the pages of the phone book. Even his fingers were sore. He found the number of the Villa Creole and asked for Pierre. After a few minutes, Pierre got on the phone.

"*Oui allo, c'est Pierre.*"

"Pierre, it's Rick. Rick Waters."

"Oh my God, man, what happened to you? One minute you were at the bar in the casino, and the next minute you disappeared."

"It's a long story. Can you come pick me up and get me out of here? I can tell you on the way back."

"*Oui*, for sure, but where are you?"

"I'm at the hospital. Hang on."

Rick realized he had no idea what hospital he was in, so he pushed the call button for the nurse's station. A nurse arrived quickly.

"What hospital am I in?"

"*Vous êtes à l'hôpital King de Port-au-Prince,*" she told him, and then said in English, "King's Hospital."

"Thank you."

"Pierre, I'm in King's Hospital in Port-au-Prince."

"Ok. I get off in about an hour. Sit tight and I'll get there as soon as I can."

"I ain't gonna move a muscle," he said, figuring he probably couldn't even if he wanted to.

After they hung up, Rick spotted his street clothes, obviously washed and dried, neatly folded on a chair by the door. His boots and socks sat beneath them.

With every ounce of strength and determination he could muster as the pain resonated throughout his body, he climbed out of bed and staggered to the chair, picked up his clothes and sat down. Even his eyelashes were sore. He dressed himself at a snail's pace.

I guess I passed the test.

He put his gown back on over his clothes, climbed into bed and pulled the sheets way up to his neck. He didn't want the nurse to know he was leaving, as he was sure she would protest and try to force him to stay, given his condition. The hospital fee wasn't an issue, as he'd read that Haiti had universal health care.

Pierre arrived about an hour and a half later.

"You ready?" Pierre asked. "You look horrible."

"I know I do; I have a mirror. Ready as I'll ever be. Let's roll."

Pierre helped him with his boots, opened the door and peered down the hall.

"The coast is clear," he reported.

Fortunately, they were on the first floor, since there were no elevators and he wouldn't have been able to manage stairs. Pierre had brought Rick's hat from the hotel, which he pulled down way over his eyes as they made their way, unnoticed, to the front door. With a groan, he climbed into the passenger seat and Pierre cranked up the Toyota.

"What happened?"

Rick told Pierre everything that had unfolded that night at the casino on the long, painful, bumpy ride back to the hotel.

"My gun?" asked Pierre.

"They took that—sorry—along with my passport, and all the cash I had on me. Luckily, I still have more cash in the hotel safe with my phone and a few other things. I'll repay you for the gun."

"I put your room on the DNR list, *Do Not Rent*. We do that when a room needs maintenance. No one has been in your room but me."

"Good, thank you. I don't know how I'm gonna get across the border now without my passport."

"I think I can help."

After they pulled into the hotel parking lot, Pierre helped Rick to his room.

"Can I get you anything?"

"A cheeseburger, ice and Tylenol." said Rick with a grin.

Pierre left and returned in half an hour with Rick's requests.

"Just relax, take a couple of days to recover, and I'll get you across the border. Don't worry about your room. I have it covered."

Rick sat on the edge of the bed. He hadn't eaten in days and was starving, but he was sure they'd fed him through a tube in the hospital because the back of his throat was tender and swollen. It hurt to swallow, but the burger was the best he'd ever tasted. At least he thought it was at the time, and he finished as much of it as he could.

His head hit the pillow and he slept hard, still in his street clothes. The next few days he spent lounging by the pool and spending a lot of time in the hot tub. He sent Jules an iMessage, told her that he was anxious to see her again, but that the case had become very complicated, and he would be sure to phone her as soon as he could. He didn't want her to hear his voice until he had fully recovered and felt safe once more.

He wanted to get back to the DR, report to Benjamin and try to make sense of all he'd found out, so once his body had healed a little, he met Pierre in the lobby and asked what the plan was for getting him back across the border.

"*Pas de quoi*, no problem. I can borrow a small plane. I have been taking flying lessons for a couple of years, and a friend at the airport has one I get my hours on. We just have to pay for fuel. I will take you, but we have to wait until tonight."

Rick returned to his room to gather his things. A few hours later, Pierre rang his room.

"Are you ready?"

"Yep, let's do this."

They arrived at the airstrip as the sun was setting and climbed into a de Havilland DHC-6-200 Super Twin Otter.

"Nice plane."

"Yes, my friend is incredibly kind to allow me to borrow it. I just filed a flight plan and pre-paid for the fuel. You can pay me back later."

"Don't worry, I got you covered. What's your mailing address?"

"You can just send it to the hotel. I'm there most of the time, anyway."

They took off and headed toward the border. Before crossing over, Pierre banked right and flew south toward Anse-à-Pitres.

"Where are you gonna land? I don't remember seeing any airstrips in Perdernales."

"*Oui*, that's the thing. I can't land there. I'm not allowed to take the plane into the DR."

"Well, how the hell am I gonna get across? I may as well have driven."

"Simple. You jump."

"Jump?"

Pierre pointed behind him at the row of parachutes on the wall of the plane.

"You've got to be kidding."

"It's the only way."

"How will I know I'm in the DR?"

"See the lights? That's Perdernales. The dark side is Anse-à-Pitres. Just head toward the lights," Pierre instructed him.

Rick shook his head but knew he had no choice. As Pierre straddled the border, he engaged the autopilot and helped Rick put on a parachute backpack. After a quick lesson as the jump point approached, Pierre strapped the duffel and backpack together and tied it around Rick's waist.

"The wind is still tonight, so just steer yourself toward the lights. We are coming in low, so as soon as you jump, pull this cord."

Pierre opened the big side door as the air rushed in. It was deafening. He patted Rick on the back.

"Godspeed, my friend."

"Thank you, Pierre. I am very grateful."

Rick hesitated, then took a deep breath, jumped, immediately pulled the cord and was jerked backwards hard. A sudden sense of calm overcame him as he drifted slowly toward the ground. He pulled the steering lines as Pierre had instructed him and quickly got the hang of it, but could only see lights or dark. He aimed for the lights, praying he wouldn't hit a building or something else.

He was coming in too fast and too close to a house, so he pulled hard on both lines. Doing his best to steer, he then pulled the right line and veered just past the roofline. But he could see he was now heading for a dark fence beside the villa. Closer, he realized it wasn't a fence after all, but a row of bushes, separating two villas. He slammed into the bushes and was dragged right through them, rolled on the other side and found himself on solid ground. His knees buckled from the impact, but glancing around, he was satisfied that no one saw him, because that side of the villa was dark, and no cars were parked in the drive of the house next door.

He unbuckled his parachute, pulled it in, wrapped it all up, and shoved it into the bushes as he unstrapped his backpack and duffel from around his waist. With his pack secured on his back, he flung the duffel over his left shoulder. His body still ached, and that less than gentle touch down certainly hadn't helped. The amount of pain he was still in only increased with the awkward landing.

Nothing seemed the same in the darkness that enveloped the little town, but he made it to a local hangout and told the bartender where he needed to go. The fellow told him it was about a mile and a half to the border crossing and gave him directions. As sore as he was, he was happy to walk there and just be back in a safer place.

When he arrived, his 4Runner was sitting right where he'd left it. He knocked on the door of the shack and the lady he'd left it with handed him his keys. Luckily, it was dark and she couldn't see his black eye or the bruises on his face. He gave her another twenty and thanked her.

The Toyota purred as he cranked it up and headed toward Barahona. An hour and a half later he pulled into the same driveway he had left a week before. The lights were off, and no one appeared to be there. He stuck his key in the door and stepped inside. The small pieces of paper he had left on the floor were gone, so he knew someone had been inside. Hopefully, just the maid.

As he moved into the master bedroom, he looked carefully at the screw on the painting that hid the safe. It was in the same spot. No one had checked it since he'd left. He took a shower and set his alarm for 4:00 a.m.

A rooster crowed and woke him up minutes before his alarm went off. After he'd locked the front door and stuck the keys in the lockbox, he headed toward Santo Domingo, arrived around 7:30 a.m. and grabbed breakfast at a local cafe in a hotel near the airport. He needed to get a new passport, and fast. The hotel was mostly empty, so he checked in, got a room right away, and then used the hotel phone to call Benjamin.

His client listened as Rick unfolded everything that had happened since leaving St. Croix. Most important, he explained about his stolen passport and asked him if her could have his truck picked up at the Dallas Park and Fly delivered to Possum's place in Houston, where he needed to fly back into instead of Dallas. Benjamin told him it would take a few days, but he thought he could source a counterfeit one to get him out of the country and take care of his Ford. Once he returned, he could apply for a new one, saying his had been lost. Rick gave him the hotel address and thanked him.

"By the way, Rick," Benjamin went on, "I got the results back from the dental records. It's definitely Darren."

"I'm so sorry, Benjamin. I'm gonna find whoever did this, I swear."

Rick hung up the phone and collapsed backward onto the bed. The enormity of what he had gone through in the past few days overwhelmed him and exhaustion took over.

There was no doubt that he was lucky to be alive, but now he had to follow up on the implications of all he had learned in Haiti. He was convinced that the key to solving the case lay in the papers he had mailed to Possum.

His buddy answered on the third ring. "Possum it's me. Did you get the box?"

"Yep, I got it. It's in my office under my desk."

"Ok, great. I'm counting on being able to put everything together based on the evidence in that box. I'll be back in a few days and explain everything."

"Ok. Are you all right?"

"I'm fine now. I'll be better once I set foot back in Texas."

Several days later, the front desk notified him that a package had arrived for him. Luckily, he still had his Florida driver's license with him to use as ID.

Once he returned to his room with the box, he found a brand-new passport inside, together with a note from Benjamin.

> *Here's the replacement passport you requested. Sorry it took so long. Your Ford is parked at Possum's place and he has the keys from the glovebox. I hope you're getting a lot of sun.*

The last part was obviously written to throw off any customs officers who might examine the contents.

He opened the passport, an exact match to his original one taken by the voodoo goons. It was even stamped by DR with the correct dates.

On his laptop, he booked the flight, and then he packed his stuff. Possum offered to pick him up when he called to give him his itinerary. He sent Jules another iMessage, saying how sorry he was to have to return to the States without seeing her again, but promising to be in touch soon.

He was a bundle of nerves going though security. The agent scanned his passport and hesitated. He looked up at Rick and then back down at the passport.

"This doesn't look like you."

"What?"

"The picture on the passport looks good, but you look like you've been beaten with an ugly stick," the agent said with a jovial laugh.

Then he passed the document back to Rick, who breathed a huge sigh of relief.

"Yeah, that'll teach me to mess with a local's girlfriend on the beach."

The agent grinned and waved his fingers, indicating "No, no, no!"

The plane took off on time, and Rick inhaled a long, deep breath, knowing he would soon be back on U.S. soil. He passed through customs and immigration with no issues in San Juan or Dallas—they just scanned his passport and waved him through.

"Welcome home, cowboy," said the gate agent. That Texas accent was music to his ears.

Rick met Possum outside of baggage claim, they headed to his house and on arrival went straight to Possum's office. After pulling on a pair of nitrile gloves, he opened the box.

He set the contents carefully on the desk. There were more photos of the deputy and Cara, and inside a small envelope he discovered a gold chain and locket. Inside was a photo of LeBlanc, and inscribed on the back were the words, "I love you always, James."

Rick opened the folder. It held a savings account booklet from Banco Popular. The balance was nearly $180,000.

How in the hell did a deputy's salary allow him to have this kind of money?

Also, in the folder was a copy of a paid-off mortgage for the villa in the DR and several other receipts totaling over $400,000, including one for a brand-new Corvette, paid in full.

There was a ledger showing payments going out, with initials or codes beside them.

150k to AB. 25k to DJ.

They were both dated a few weeks before Cara's and Darren's deaths.

It was all starting to make sense. If he was right, then Deputy LeBlanc was involved in a drug ring with both Angelique and Darren and it must've somehow gone south.

Rick could not wait another minute. He reached for his cell phone and called Deputy LeBlanc, who answered on the fourth ring. Rick got right to it.

"James, it's Rick Waters. Tell me, how's that 'Vette treating you?"

"What? What 'Vette ?"

"You know, the one you paid cash for, just like the villa in the DR."

After a moment of silence James said, "We need to meet. Can I see you, so I can explain?"

"Yeah, right. I can't wait to hear this explanation."

"No seriously, I can meet you wherever."

"Ok, tomorrow sometime around 9:30 a.m., at the boat launch where we exchanged numbers."

"Ok, I'll see you then."

Rick hung up the phone and turned to his friend.

"Possum, I'm heading back to Beaumont."

CHAPTER EIGHTEEN

Rick drove toward the boat ramp and got off at the Winnie exit on I-10. He knew there were no motels on FM 365, and he was still far too sore to sleep in the back of the truck, so he got a cheap room in Winnie, checked in, and prepped himself for the encounter with the deputy the next day.

On a notepad from the motel, he wrote down everything he had learned about the case up until then, including the time and place of the meeting with the deputy.

He put Possum's address on the envelope, together with a stamp he bought from the front desk and climbed into the Ford. If things didn't go as planned at the boat launch, at least Possum could follow through and implicate the deputy. There was a USPS collection box a mile from the motel.

After he dropped off the letter, he was hungry, so he drove past his motel to Al-T's restaurant, a longtime favorite of the area that served some of the best Cajun food around. He ordered the T's Trifecta, a combination of a boudin link, seafood gumbo and shrimp étouffée.

It was just as he remembered, spicy and delicious. He sat at the bar and chatted with the cute bartender, who was definitely flirting with him, but he was too sore and too tired to care, so he gave her a nice tip and headed back to the motel.

After his long hot shower, he rubbed Tiger Balm all over his body and examined his back in the mirror. It was the worst. There were more bruises than not, but the hot shower and Tiger Balm helped. The bed was soft, and he was asleep in an instant.

The alarm went off at 6:00 a.m. and, given the way he was expecting the meeting to go, he armed himself appropriately. He put his .44 in his rear waistband holder and the .38 in his boot. It was a little foggy as he pulled up to the boat ramp a few hours later, about 9:15 a.m., backed his truck to the edge of the fence facing the highway, and waited. The deputy arrived alone at 9:45 a.m. in his Sheriff's Department car, which surprised Rick, thinking he'd be in his own personal vehicle. LeBlanc stopped about ten feet from Rick's truck and stepped out of the cruiser.

He opened the door and unbuckled his gun belt, raising it up for Rick to see, and placed it on the seat of the cruiser. Rick had him dead to rights and the deputy knew it.

Rick took the .38 out of his boot and stepped out of the truck, holding the gun up with his thumb and index finger by the end of the handle with the barrel pointing downward. He raised it up high in the air, just as the deputy had done, then placed it on the seat of his truck.

He'd already hit the record button on his iPhone voice memo app when LeBlanc pulled into the parking lot. The phone was out of sight in the front pocket of his jacket, which was open.

They were the only two people at the boat ramp and approached each other cautiously.

"Waters," said the deputy, as he nodded.

"LeBlanc."

The deputy was carrying a small, zipped-up duffel as he approached Rick.

"What's in the bag?"

"It's for you. I hope we can come to an agreement," said the deputy, as he tossed the bag toward Rick's feet.

"Look, I'm sorry I lied about Cara. I had my reasons, but I swear to you I didn't kill her."

"I think you're lying. You know how I can tell? Your lips are moving."

"No, you've gotta believe me. I loved Cara. I would never hurt her. I think that voodoo bitch killed her to get back at me."

Rick threw the deputy a curveball.

"So, you didn't kill her, but you killed her brother?"

"What? Darren is dead?" said LeBlanc. He looked genuinely shocked, and then went on. "Look, by now you know I'm not a perfect cop. I can't make excuses for that. I met Darren through Cara a while back, but I didn't even know he was hurt, let alone dead. I haven't heard from him for a while, since he got cold feet.

"A few months before Cara disappeared, we flew to St. Croix and I met him at his house. She told me he was getting his life back together. I could tell he was using but I didn't let Cara in on it. When she left us alone, I asked Darren if he wanted to make some fast cash and get free blow for his own use. He jumped at the chance and practically begged me to cut him in on the deal. I started him off small. He would load his sailboat with a few kilos and sail down toward St. Thomas. A fast boat always met him there and they did the exchange. It went from two kilos, to four, then ten. I started to really trust him and set him up for a big score. It was supposed to be the last one I'd have to do, and I could quit the sheriff's department. Cara and I could move to the DR, away from her dad, and start a new life. She loved her dad, but he was overbearing and controlling. That's why we kept our relationship a secret. We were engaged and planned to marry, but no one knew. I'm telling you everything because I really have no choice and I truly want you to find Cara's killer. I hope what's in that bag will help you keep what I've told you to yourself."

"So, you used Darren to deliver coke to St. Thomas and then where from there?"

"I have a friend who's a baggage handler for American Airlines in St. Thomas. He would take the coke and repack it inside of coffee bean bags and print out luggage tags with the name AJ Hudson on it. AJ is a punk I caught making meth a few years back. In exchange for me not arresting him, we came to the agreement that he would be my courier from the airport in Houston. My airline buddy in St. Thomas would put the coffee bags inside large duffel bags and AJ would pick them up in Houston. It was going smoothly, and everyone was making money. I got an order for one hundred kilos and we knew it was too much to put on the plane, so Darren came up with the idea of putting it inside the new teak side walls of the sailboat he was restoring. He got cold feet, though, and said he wanted out. I hired Angelique Beauvoir to scare Darren into going through with the deal, not kill him. I still owe her for the hundred kilos. I had a buyer, but Darren never made the trip. I really think she killed Darren and Cara. We just have to prove it."

"That's quite a story James," Rick finally said. "Not sure I buy it."

"It's the truth. There's fifty thousand dollars in that bag and it's all yours if you keep quiet about what I told you, or at least keep me out of it."

Rick unzipped the bag. Bundles of hundreds were nestled inside.

"Keep your money, but if I find out you're lying and you had something to do with Cara's or Darren's death, I'm coming after you," Rick told him, kicking the bag back toward LeBlanc.

"I understand. Regardless of how it looks, we're on the same team. I would never hurt Cara. I didn't give two shits about Darren, but I didn't hurt him either."

The deputy picked up the duffel, slowly stepped backward toward his patrol car, climbed in and left.

Though he was anxious to pick up Chief in Dallas, he had a feeling that more vital information on voodoo was going to help him put all the pieces together, and New Orleans was the voodoo capital of the U.S. A face-to-face conversation with a practitioner might give him more background quicker than the hours of research he'd have to put in. It was only about a five-hour drive to the The Big Easy and he knew the city pretty well. At a gas station on the outskirts of Beaumont, he topped up his tank and continued east, past his exit for his old high school.

He pulled into New Orleans at 2:45 p.m. and parked near the corner of Ursulines Avenue and North Peters Street by the French market, then he moseyed up to the end of the street, grabbed a cab to the Bywater district, and stopped at Elizabeth's Restaurant.

He ordered praline bacon and a shrimp po-boy. Their praline bacon was famous. Bacon dusted in brown sugar and crushed pecans was unlike anything he'd ever tasted. Rick also added a sprinkle of cayenne pepper.

The place was starting to get busy the closer to happy hour it got. Rick paid his tab and spotted an elderly black guy sweeping the floor. He approached him and nodded.

"Hi, mister. I'm Rick from the Beaumont Enterprise newspaper. I'm doing a story about the history of voodoo. I've checked all the local spots, Marie Laveau's place on Bourbon and Reverend Zombie's House of Voodoo down on St. Peter, but they weren't much help. I felt like I was getting the runaround. You look like you've lived here a long time. Can you hook me up with someone who is really in the know?"

The old man studied him for a moment and then kept sweeping.

"I can't help you."

Rick pulled out a small notepad and pen, then wrapped a hundred-dollar bill around them both. He made sure the old man could see it.

"I'd be willing to pay for any information you can give me."

The old man thought for a second and gestured with his head for Rick to follow him. They stepped outside and he motioned him to the side of the building.

"They is a girl I knows, who practices. If'n I tell you how to find her, you must swear not to tell her I told you."

Rick handed him the hundred-dollar bill and mimicked locking his mouth and throwing away the key.

"Your secret's safe with me, mister."

The old man took the pad and pen from Rick and wrote down an address.

"Ok, now you best be on your way. Don't bother me again."

Rick nodded at the man and waved down a cab, then told the cabby to take him to his truck and wait for him. In his own vehicle, he pulled back the seat, grabbed his .38, discreetly tucked it in his rear waistband, and climbed back into the cab.

"Eight twenty-eight North Rampart Street." Rick told the cabby.

The cab driver looked at Rick in the rear-view mirror and shook his head.

"Ok, whatever you say."

It was almost dark by the time they arrived. The colorful little one-story house sat next to a closed-down, boarded-up, two-story building covered in graffiti.

A dog bolted to the side fence of the house, growling and baring his teeth at the gate. But when Rick knocked on the red front door, a young lady opened it and said cheerfully, "Don't mind him. He does that to everybody."

"Ok, good to know."

She took Rick by the hand and led him inside the house. There was a massive ornate round wooden table in the living room with a black candle burning in the center. He glanced back at the entrance door and noted the skull of a cow above the frame, with black symbols drawn on it. Above that was a large, round sign that read: "Voodoo Spirit Temple." Round and square bags of gris-gris hung on the large wooden door.

"Priestess Miriam will be right with you," she said, as she walked out of the room.

The same familiar smells as in that dreaded room in Haiti filled Rick's nostrils.

After a few minutes, a black woman adorned in a colorful dress and a headdress made of silk walked into the room.

"I am Priestess Miriam. How can I help you, young man?"

She was different, much friendlier than Angelique from Haiti. She had a sense of warmth and goodness about her.

"My name is Rick and I'm doing a story on the history of voodoo for the Beaumont Enterprise newspaper."

"Ahh, you want to tell the world how we sacrifice goats and practice spells on people to cause harm? I can't help you!"

"No, no wait," said Rick. He remembered reading that voodoo could be used for good or evil and was even considered a religion, with ties to the Catholic Church. Taking a chance, he said, "I want you to show me the good side of voodoo."

Her eyes lit up.

"Why didn't you say so in the first place? Voodoo has a bad name and folks don't take the time to learn about the good it can do. What do you want to know?"

Rick was encouraged by her sudden change of spirit and decided to play it out.

"Would you mind if I record our conversation?" asked Rick.

"My time is valuable, but I also don't want you to misinterpret anything I say."

"I understand." said Rick, sliding three hundred-dollar bills toward her.

"Please tell me how your temple differs from the voodoo shops on Bourbon Street."

She laughed, pulled a large book off a shelf behind her and set it down next to Rick. Then she began flipping pages to show him photographs she had taken when she'd visited West Africa. She explained that voodoo had started in Africa in what is now modern-day Benin. In the 16th century, slaves from West Africa were bought and sold and transported to the Caribbean.

Voodoo became a symbol of strength and was used in Haiti to build an uprising that eventually led to expulsion of the French from the country. Some of the colonists fled to New Orleans and their slaves, who practiced voodoo, brought it with them. It became an established religion in 1791, but was banned in the Americas, as was every other African religion. It was the enigmatic Marie Laveau's clash with local government that solidified the religion.

"We are a religion of peace," she said with smile. "We offer peace, love and wealth through herbal and spiritual means."

Rick listened intently and tried to keep an open mind. The candle was getting dimmer, so she replaced it with a new one. When she struck the match, she noticed Rick's black eye and leaned in closer.

"You are hurt, my child."

"I'll be all right."

"Nonsense."

She grabbed a bag of something off the shelf, put it in Rick's hand, closed his fist around it, and then told him to cup his hands together. When he'd done so, she laid both of her own hands on top of Rick's.

"I have given you a protection and healing sachet," she told him, as she bent forward to lay her forehead against the back of her hands, which still encircled Rick's. Her words were unintelligible; her body shook. Suddenly, she jumped back from Rick and stared down at him, aghast.

"You have seen the dark one! She has not a good bone in her body and is full of evil."

Rick sat amazed.

"You mean Angelique Beauvoir?" he asked.

She gasped. "Do not speak her name in this holy temple. She is the incarnation of evil and represents everything negative about voodoo."

"I'm sorry. I had no idea."

"You must not trust her, for her lies will betray you. She is wicked and capable of doing much harm to anyone who crosses her path," said the Priestess. "And you must leave."

"Listen, I believe she shot and killed two people in the same family, execution style. I need to know, is she capable of that?" asked Rick.

"If you are asking me if she is capable of murder, then yes. But she did not kill the people you are asking me about," replied the Priestess.

"How do you know that?"

"You said they were shot, correct?" she questioned.

"Yes."

"The dark one is evil and the only way she would take a soul is with her knife. She believes she can draw on the power of the soul she takes. It is always with her dagger. The long, curved knife dates back to the 1600s and is believed to have been passed down from the original West African priest Papa Legba, to the Haitian Priest Mambo, who started the Haitian revolution, and finally to her.

She stood up, crossed her arms and her entire body began to vibrate. With a stern look at Rick, she pointed toward the door.

"But I still have questions," Rick said. "Could you just…"

"Leave now and never return," she ordered, fire in her eyes.

As he walked out the door, she followed him, waving a chicken's foot over his head.

It was dark now and there were only a few cars on the street as he walked down toward what he thought was Bourbon. It was a bad area and there were no cabs in sight. Two guys in a dropped Monte Carlo with twenty-five-inch rims stepped out of their car as he walked past.

"Hey white boy, whatcha doin' down here?" said one of them.

"Just trying to get to Bourbon Street."

"Well dat's a long walk and you is on the wrong street." said the other, as he whipped out a butterfly knife. "Gimme yo' money."

Rick laughed. They both looked at him in confusion.

"All I got is this protection sachet," said Rick, dangling it in front of his chest.

When they moved closer, Rick tossed it up high, toward them. Then, as they both looked up in the air, he pulled out his .38 and pointed it at them.

"Now that's funny. Only a dumbass would bring a knife to a gunfight. So, step back and drop the knife," Rick said easily.

The guy holding the knife dropped it and they both took two steps backwards as Rick leaned down to grab the knife and the sachet. When he cocked the .38, they took off running.

Rick walked a few blocks further until he spotted a cab and took it back to his truck. He'd learned three things on this fishing expedition. One, voodoo, like witchcraft, consisted of both good and evil. And two, the back streets of New Orleans were just as dangerous as he had always been told. Lastly, he was fairly confident that Angelique Beauvoir was *not* the murderer.

CHAPTER NINETEEN

Rick hopped in his truck and drove toward Dallas to pick up his bird. It was an eight-hour drive and he wasn't going to make it in one day, so he made it as far as Shreveport and checked into the Comfort Inn just off I-49.

It was only 10:00 p.m. and he was wired. After he threw his gear into the hotel room, he searched on his phone for somewhere to grab a late-night meal. An hour later, feeling much more satisfied after some excellent oysters and a delicious filet, he was back in his room, and dozed off while watching TV.

A backfiring car awakened him at 5:00 a.m., so he decided to just get up and head to Dallas. He missed Chief.

When Rick arrived at the birdie hotel, they had only been open for about thirty minutes. The young girl working reception was on the phone and Rick waited as patiently as he could.

"Picking up or dropping off?" she finally said.

"I'm here to pick up Chief."

"Oh, he's so sweet. Everyone who works here adores him."

"He does that to people," said Rick.

She came out from the back with Chief in his travel cage. As soon as he saw Rick, the bird started bouncing up and down and raising the crown on top of his little white head. He was beyond excited. Rick took him out of the cage and kissed him on his beak, while Chief snuggled his head against Rick's chest and made whimpering sounds. Rick paid the girl and carried Chief's empty cage back to his truck with the bird snuggled inside his jacket.

A little more relaxed now, Rick figured he had money in the bank and needed to do more research on the case.

"What do you wanna do, Chief? I know. Let's go to PetSmart and have some fun."

"Cracker, cracker, step up?" said Chief.

Rick pulled out his phone, found the nearest PetSmart and copied the address into his GPS.

Chief held on tight as they entered the store. His bird always drew a lot of attention, especially from kids, and little ones were running up to Rick to get a closer look at his pet. He snapped a few photos of the kids playing with Chief, as did their parents, before he checked out with a few new wooden toys and bird treats.

"Well, Chief, we have a full tank of gas, a little money in the bank, how about we go uptown?"

Rick pulled up the address of the Ritz-Carlton and started driving. He valet-parked the truck, which stuck out like a sore thumb at the opulent hotel, then stepped up to the front desk.

"I'd like a room, king bed if you got it. I'm fixin' to relax in style."

Chief poked his head out just as the desk agent looked up.

"Sir, we don't allow pets at this hotel unless they're service animals."

"Why, this here is my seeing-eye bird, Chief." Rick declared, as he slid a twenty-dollar bill toward the man. "I suppose with that you don't see this seeing-eye bird or any bird at all, for that matter now, right?"

The man glanced over his shoulder and quickly folded the bill into his pocket.

Just as the manager walked up, the clerk motioned for Rick to close his jacket.

"Yes sir, king room on the top floor."

Rick tucked Chief back in and gave the man his credit card.

"The best room you have, please," Rick told him.

"I have the Uptown Suite on the seventh floor, 1675 square feet, two bathrooms, round-the-clock snacks, beverages and a large, oversized soaking tub. It also has a feather and down bed," whispered the agent.

After Rick told him that the room and the rate sounded fine, the clerk handed over the key in a small, folded paper holder.

"Enjoy your stay, Mr. Waters."

Rick thanked him and headed for the elevator.

"See, Chief, I told you we were going uptown. Even our suite is called the Uptown!"

The room was massive—all marble floors and countertops, and a beautiful living room area with a separate bedroom.

Rick opened his jacket for Chief to hop out, and the bird skipped all over the comforter, running his beak along the soft duvet like a bloodhound on the hunt. A basket in the center of the dining room table contained fruit and wine. Rick opened it, poured a glass of wine for himself and arranged a small plate of grapes and apple slices for Chief. The bird went to town on his treat.

The next morning, Rick dialed Possum's number.

"Yo, what's shakin', *hombre*?" asked his friend.

"I need to research a few books from your personal library about the treasure. I also want to follow up on a lead I have in Haiti. I'm pretty sure I can rule out one of my suspects, I just want to be certain. Cool?"

"Rick, why do you even bother asking? You know this is your second home, bro!"

"Do you think you can gain access to the FBI unsolved murders database, maybe ask Carson?" asked Rick.

"Yeah, Carson shouldn't mind," replied Possum.

"Do you think it's a U.S. or international database?" asked Rick.

"I believe it's linked to international crimes as well. The FBI has worked with Interpol, so I'm sure they share info, and I believe it is also shared with Crime Stoppers, so most of it is public record anyway."

"Great, I want to tap into Haiti's unsolved murder database and check a theory. I'll explain it all when I get there," said Rick.

Then he placed another call.

"Hi Jules, it's Rick. How have you been? I've been thinking a lot about you."

"Hi Rick! I'm great. It's so good to hear your voice. How's the case going?"

"Well, it's had its ups and downs and more questions than answers, but I think I've ruled out some suspects, which can only help me in the long run. What have you been up to?"

"Same ol', same ol'. I did apply for a grant for a job in Brazil. Dealing cards and craps is great money, but my true passion is cetology."

"Cetology? You've never mentioned that before. What is that exactly?"

"It's the study of dolphins and whales."

"Oh, cool. Do you think you'll get it?"

"It's a long shot, I have no idea, really, but I'll never know unless I try, right?"

"That's right, Jules. Good luck with it. Listen, I need to make this short. I have to leave for Houston. I'll try to call you in a day or so, ok?"

"I'd love that, Rick. Please be careful."

"I will. I promise. Talk to you soon."

Quickly disconnecting, Rick packed up his bags and Chief and set his GPS for the four-hour drive to Possum's place.

"Did you ever get a value on that watch?" asked Rick, once he'd arrived and settled in.

"The gold weight value of it is probably not a lot, but the historical value could be pretty substantial."

"I think I'll just keep it for good luck. It may help me find Fletcher's treasure."

They clinked their glasses together when Possum said, "Amen to that!"

Over the next few days, Rick studied all the books in Possum's library that related to treasure in Texas. He made lots of notes and carefully analyzed all the information Possum had collected over the years. But he couldn't shake the strong feeling in his bones that the area where he'd found the pocket watch was still worth searching.

Once Possum logged him into the FBI murder database, he used a link to the Haitian archive and did a query using the keywords *murder, Angelique Beauvoir* and *knife*. He discovered that she had been questioned about several murders in Haiti and was indicted in one, but the case was dropped when the star witness for the prosecution disappeared. Every murder that Angelique was ever questioned about or a suspect in involved a knife as the murder weapon.

The trip to New Orleans had paid off. Rick was now convinced that Angelique was not the killer in his case, and he could completely eliminate her as suspect, since both Cara and Darren had been shot at close range, not stabbed.

After a few days of research and physical rest, which did wonders for his bruises and sore muscles, he said his goodbyes to Possum, then loaded up Chief in the truck, bound for Hog Creek.

After refueling and picking up some groceries, he checked back into the Deluxe Inn and laid out his map on the bed. Even though he had already searched the waterfall, it was still worth going over again.

The alarm went off at five-thirty the next morning, so he fed Chief and told him he'd have to stay in the motel this time. Chief just munched on a grape and listened.

Once he'd parked in the spot he'd chosen on his previous trip, he trekked through the woods until he made it to Hog

Creek. On the bank, he laid out his dig bag and accessories, then pulled on his foul weather gear. His Garrett detector was all taped up and watertight, with a baggy around the head, ready to go.

He carried his metal detector, shovel and a probing rod into the waterfall, which felt cold as the water sluiced over his head. It must have been raining a lot upstream, because the flow was more intense than the last time he'd been there.

After moving stones and rocks out of the way, he tried to get some signals. He worked for hours until he felt he needed a break, so found a spot on the rocky bank and sat down to eat the sandwich he'd picked up earlier that morning. On the opposite bank, he spotted a cowbird sitting on a pair of large, pointed boulders. The big rocks looked like mini mountains jutting up above the stream.

After lunch, he dug out rocks and gravel from under the waterfall for several more hours. The only ping he got was from an old beer can wedged under the wet gravel. Feeling frustrated and tired, and knowing it would soon be dark, he decided to end his hunt for the day.

On his way back to the motel, he stopped and grabbed a burger and a six-pack of Shiner Bock. Chief munched on the french fries as Rick sat at the desk in his room, chowing on the burger and studying the maps.

Why would they draw a line from the bank with a W to the center of the waterfall? It must be in the waterfall. I'm just not digging deep enough.

His Garrett only had a range of about eight inches. His Pulse 8X had more of a range but was really meant for underwater search.

"Since the gravel's all wet anyway, I'll try the Pulse tomorrow, Chief, and you can come with me for good luck."

It was 10:00 p.m. when he finished his six-pack, so he lay down and got ready to do it all over again.

Before the alarm even went off, he woke up and loaded Chief and his gear into the truck. Once he reached the waterfall, he tucked the bird inside his foul weather jacket and pulled his Pulse 8X and shovel from the bag. The jacket was zipped up, but he left a crack for Chief to get some air and they plunged into the waterfall.

Once inside, he perched the bird on a flat ledge directly in front of where he'd be digging, so he could keep an eye on him. Chief didn't mind the occasional splash from the waterfall and seemed to enjoy it actually. Beginning toward the corner of it, he ran the Pulse over all the areas he had dug already and on the last sweep got a nice ping.

He hadn't worked this area much the day before because the water was rushing down in the corner and it was hard to dig there. The signal was strong, so he started to dig down, aiming to go at least three feet. He knew this would be a tough dig and his shovel would barely get through the wet gravel. Half the time he would have to use his hands for larger pieces.

For a solid two hours he dug and checked the signal every so often. It was getting stronger. Back and forth he went between digging with his hands and using his shovel. The hole was full of water and he was having a hard time getting the gravel out, but as he drove his shovel down hard, he heard a clink. He felt some resistance—metal to metal.

His back was killing him because he had been digging for almost three straight hours. But finally, he reached into the hole through the water and felt something long and metallic.

Gold bar?

With his fingers wrapped around the object, he pried it from the rocks. It finally came free with one last, hard tug. He pulled it from its watery grave, but the spray from the waterfall made examining it impossible. He rushed out from under the waterfall into the sun and looked at the bar as his eyes adjusted.

"A damn railroad spike? I've been digging for three hours for this?" Rick said aloud.

In frustration, he flung the spike into the stream and plopped down on the bank. He was done. That ping was the only one he had gotten inside the waterfall, and he concluded he was in the wrong place.

His back ached and his head pounded. His fingers were raw from digging through the gravel and his hands looked like prunes. He was cold, wet, and tired.

Beside the creek on the grass and gravel, he pulled out the map, then laid his head down in the soft grass. Holding the document up with both hands above him, he stared up at it, blocking the sun.

A crow cawed behind him on the other side of the creek. He leaned his head back, looking upside down across the creek at the crow that had landed on the two large pointed rocks. That's when he saw it. As he looked at the rocks, he could clearly see they resembled an upside-down W.

That's not a W on the map! It's a drawing of the two rocks! It's upside down because the map was folded there!

His heart was racing. He put Chief back in his cage and grabbed his Garrett, then ran clumsily across the shallow creek, almost tripping. All around the first big rock, he swept the detector. Nothing. When he moved to the other boulder, his detector pegged the needle!

Could it be? I've been digging for days only ten feet from the right spot?

He hiked back to the truck and grabbed the come-along he always stored behind the seat, as well as some rope he kept in a bucket in the bed of the truck. After he returned, he tied one end of the long rope around the large rock, looped the rope around a big pine tree, and then tied the other end to the come-along. He started to ratchet the small winch. Over and over, he ratcheted with all his strength until the boulder began to move.

It was now about two inches off the ground on one side. With his axe, he cut a thick branch off of a tree, wedged it under the boulder and laid the other end over the other boulder. He ran back to the come-along and winched a few more times. It was coming over. With all his weight, he pulled down on the far end of the long branch. His feet were coming off the ground when, suddenly, with a loud sucking sound, the boulder flipped over.

All he could see under it was mud in the hole. He grabbed his detector and swept it over the mud. It went off like the fourth of July. Clumsily, he ran across the creek, grabbed his shovel, came back and started to dig. The wet mud was sticking to the shovel. Every time he dug deeper, more and more clay stuck to it. At about twelve inches down, he drove the tool hard.

A loud thud stopped it. He'd hit something solid. Using his hand trowel, he dug all around it to expose the sides. It was a box—a large wooden box. He cleaned the clay off the shovel and raised it high in the air. Then, with all his force, he slammed it into the top of the box. The wood splintered and the box cracked open. When he reached down to pull the wood away, he uncovered a burlap sack, already wet from the water that had seeped into the box. The sack ripped open to reveal a leather bag. He grabbed the corner and pulled it as hard as he could.

His hands were slipping on the wet leather, and one side came free before the other. It was so heavy that he fell backwards as he lifted it out of the box and found himself clutching an old leather saddlebag. Chief watched comfortably from atop the other boulder as Rick used all his strength to drag the saddlebag to dry ground. The buckles were rusted, so he pulled out his Leatherman and cut the straps. Slowly, almost as if in slow motion, he opened the bag.

The light reflected brightly on a small gold bar with a V stamped into it. The V represented the weight of the bar, five ounces.

He screamed at the top of his lungs, "I found it! I found Fletcher's treasure!"

On the bank, he danced around like a crazy person until he fell back into the water. He didn't care. He reached up to take Chief down from the rock and swung himself around in circles with the bird holding on for dear life.

"We did it, Chief, we did it! You are my lucky bird!"

Rick dumped the contents of both saddle bags on the ground. Another V- stamped gold bar fell out of the other saddle bag, along with a bunch of rocks and a note inside a corked whiskey bottle.

Using his teeth, he pulled on the cork and slid out the note.

> *You are a lucky man to find the treasure*
> *But only two bars did you seize*
> *The rest was moved into a box*
> *But you will need the Keys*

To find the box, travel south
Beyond the Seminole
For at the bottom where railway starts
It's deep inside a hole
Fletcher

It wasn't just a poem; it was a riddle. Rick remembered that Marcy had told him her great-great-grandfather Fletcher loved to get the kids to go on scavenger hunts. Fletcher had placed some of the treasure under the rocks to ensure that the finder knew it was real but had moved the remainder of the trove to a different location.

He drove straight to Marcy Nobles's house and knocked loudly.

"Who's there? I ain't buying!" called Marcy from behind the closed door.

"Mrs. Nobles, it's Rick, Rick Waters, the treasure hunter guy," Rick answered.

"Oh, ok," she said as she slowly opened the door.

"Mrs. Nobles, I found something, and I need your help," Rick began. "You better have a seat."

Marcy moved some newspapers off the couch and sat down as Rick pulled the recliner closer to her. He reached into his jacket pocket, pulled out one of the gold bars and handed it to her. She gasped, eyes shining with excitement.

"You found the treasure!" she exclaimed.

"Well, some of it, and also a riddle in the form of a poem. That's what I need your help with," replied Rick.

"How much is this worth?" Her voice had dropped to a whisper.

"Each piece is worth about forty-five hundred dollars at the current gold prices."

She looked thunderstruck.

"Wait, Mrs. Nobles, there's a lot more, so please listen."

"Call me Marcy, please," she said as she lit a cigarette. She held the gold bar in her hands and caressed it, as if she was trying to polish it.

Rick read her the poem as she squinted and listened intently. She stared at the ceiling, trying to figure out what her great-great-grandfather had meant by it.

"Sounds like one of his dadgum scavenger hunts. You need the keys, probably, to open a treasure chest."

"That's what came to my mind as well at first. But when I read on to the part about *Beyond the Seminole*, I wondered if he was referring to the Florida Keys instead of keys to a lock? It especially caught my attention where he mentions where the railway starts. Maybe he's talking about the great Flagler Railroad that connected the Florida Keys to the mainland. To your knowledge, did he ever travel to the Keys?"

Marcy leaned back on the couch in deep thought, then stood up and grabbed a photo album off one of the shelves behind her. She opened it and rapidly flipped pages, then stopped and spun the book around toward Rick. In the middle picture John Fletcher Jr., who was John's son and Marcy's great grandfather stood smiling, holding a shovel. In the background, Rick could make out mangroves, but the most stunning part of the picture was an old railcar bearing the names Andrews and Flagler. That proved it. Fletcher Jr. had at least been in the Florida Keys at some point during the building of the railroad to Key West. Fletcher Jr. must've moved the treasure for his dad after his dad's death.

"Thank you, Marcy. May I take a quick snapshot of the photo?"

"For sure. No problem," she said.

Rick let himself out, telling her he would keep her posted on any developments in the search. As he drove away, he became more and more convinced that a trip to the Keys was the necessary next step in the search for Fletcher's gold. But for now, at least, he needed to get back to finding Cara's murderer. His instincts told him he was close to breaking the case wide open.

CHAPTER TWENTY

The next morning Rick was sitting on the edge of the motel bed, watching mindless TV when his phone rang.

It was Deputy LeBlanc.

"Rick?"

"Yeah."

"I just got a call. Someone using a voice modulator box claims to know what happened to Darren and Cara and wants to meet. He told me to come alone but I'm not comfortable with that. Rick, I think this lead is legit. He wants to meet at the site where we found Cara's body. How could he know where that is? This might be our chance to catch the killer, or at least find out who the real killer is. He wants to meet tomorrow at noon. Can you get out there early, do some recon, and maybe be my backup?"

Rick was really hesitant to trust the guy. If LeBlanc was telling the truth, it'd be a chance to nail the killer, but then again, he could be setting Rick up because he knew too much, and this would be a good way to make sure he kept quiet. He would have the advantage either way, though, by getting there early and staying hidden.

"Ok I'll get there a few hours before and case the area. I'll stay hidden. You won't see me, but you'll see my red Ford at the boat ramp and know I'm there."

"That's a good plan, Rick. Let's do this. And thank you."

They hung up and Rick set his alarm for 7:00 a.m. It was only an hour-and-a-half-drive to the crime scene. That would put him there about 8:30 a.m., plenty of time to get set up.

"So much for a late night, Chief. Let's hit the hay."

It seemed like just minutes after he'd fallen asleep that the alarm woke him. He grabbed his bags and Chief and headed to the lobby, where he knew they offered 24-hour coffee, grabbed a to-go cup and took off.

As they drove toward the crime scene, Rick ran through every scenario he could think of in his head. He knew there was a possibility the deputy was just trying to bump him off, but his gut was telling him that this was the real deal. There was also a chance the mysterious person who'd called the deputy was just trying to tie up loose ends, so he'd have to be careful... and stealthy.

After picking up his jon boat at the storage facility, he pulled onto the ramp at 9:15 a.m. and launched the boat. Since it was a chilly forty-eight degrees and the wind was cutting right through him, he pulled his camo coveralls on over his jeans and shirt.

Chief was in his travel cage, so Rick put him in the camper of the truck and wrapped a blanket around the cage.

"Sorry, buddy. It's too dangerous out there, and I need you to be quiet. Just stay here. I'll be back." Chief looked into Rick's eyes almost as if in agreement.

After locking up the truck, Rick stuck his loaded .44 into his holster and flung his .30-06 deer rifle, also loaded, over his shoulder. It had a high capacity magazine that held ten rounds, plus one in the chamber, and was deadly accurate. Rick hoped there wouldn't be a need for any gunfire today.

He cranked up the boat and started motoring toward the area where he had found the body a few months before. The location was still saved on his phone, so he had no problem finding it. As he got within a half a mile of the location, he killed the engine and dropped down his trolling motor. He could see the area where he had originally pulled his boat up last time. A gator lay there, motionless, soaking up the morning's sunrays.

The jon boat silently pulled about three hundred yards past the creature, and up to another flat spot on the bank. There was a dense blanket of fog just above the water as the sun peeked through. It would end up being a clear day once the sun was fully up.

As quietly as possible, he pulled the boat to the bank and carefully laid saw palmettos over the hull and engine. It was well hidden, so he slowly and silently trekked toward the area where he'd found Cara's body, being extra careful not to break any twigs or small branches as he stepped.

At the edge of the clearing, he found a spot with a great vantage point. Bracing his back against a tree, he propped the deer rifle against another tree beside him. Deep in the tree Rick buried his knife, then laid his rifle atop the makeshift brace and began to scan the area through the scope.

With a shotgun mic and his Sennheiser field recorder, Rick got a good level and placed the recorder on record and pause.

A small number of hungry raccoons worked the opposite edge of the clearing, digging in the mud for a breakfast of snails and crawfish. A few noisy crows overhead in the trees were cawing, and a bullfrog occasionally bellowed his morning call. It was a typical morning on the bayou.

As he waited, he pulled out a banana he'd picked up from the hotel and quietly ate it.

At about 11:45 a.m. he could hear the sound of an airboat approaching from the distance. He knew it had to be the deputy. It was ridiculously loud as it approached the field.

Rick could hear every sound LeBlanc made as he stepped off the boat and walked toward the clearing. There was really no need for stealth though, because he was expected to be there.

Since LeBlanc wore bulky street clothes, Rick couldn't tell if he was packing a gun. When he made his way to the center of the clearing where the body was originally found, Rick hit record on the field recorder and waited.

"Hello? I'm here. I'm alone, as you asked," called the deputy in a loud voice. "I'm unarmed."

An uneasy silence filled the air for a minute, and then LeBlanc repeated his announcement. You could hear a pin drop after he stopped speaking. Rick wasn't sure if anyone was going to show or not.

Then, in the distance, he heard another boat pull up. There was rustling off to the east side of the clearing and he could hear steps approaching. A figure started to take shape as it pulled aside saw palmettos and entered the field. The man had long, black dreadlocks streaked with red, and wore a long, ankle-length black jacket and black, leather-looking pants tucked into military-style boots. As he came into view,

Rick saw that his face was covered with a skull mask, and a top hat with a long feather in the side sat on his head. The mystery man did not speak as he approached the deputy.

LeBlanc stayed perfectly still. Rick looked through the scope at the bizarrely dressed figure and couldn't spot any guns. He breathed a small, silent sigh of relief. The stranger's back was now to Rick as he motioned for LeBlanc to sit down, so he seated himself on the stump beside the fire where Cara's body had been discovered.

"You have info about the murder?" asked LeBlanc.

The man just nodded, pulled out a leather-bound notebook and handed it to him. James took the notebook and began to untie the binding, but the mystery man shook his head no. The deputy stopped. The man reached up and slowly pulled the mask from his face. Rick had the scope centered on his back, his finger on the trigger, and he could see LeBlanc's face clearly as well.

As the mask revealed his face, the deputy's jaw dropped. Suddenly, the unmasked man reached into the left side of his jacket with his right hand and Rick saw the shimmer of light reflect off the blade of a machete.

Rick fired the deer rifle at the exact same instant the blade severed the deputy's head from his body and it rolled to the ground. His headless body sat motionless for a second before it began to fall, as Rick's bullet exploded through the other side of the man's chest. His body fell forward, just missing LeBlanc's, face down in the salt grass.

Rick jumped up and ran toward them. He carefully poked the body of the dead man with the end of his barrel. His bullet was spot on, but there was blood all over the leather book. Rick put on his gloves and pulled it away from the corpses. He straddled the mystery man and with his left arm began to flip him over. As he did so, Rick pulled back the hair from his face and it became apparent he was wearing a wig. He flipped the body all the way over and stood in shock for several minutes after he recognized the face.

It was Darren.

Finally, he gathered his thoughts, forced himself to open the notebook, and began to read.

> *Father, I wrote this journal both for myself, to give me peace, and for you, so you'd know why I killed your precious daughter. I killed Cara so you could feel the pain that I have endured throughout my life, while you always favored her over me. You treated her like a princess and me like garbage.*
>
> *You never suspected that I hid the home movie camera you bought me when I was nine years old in my bedroom. On this copy of the flash drive is the same evidence I left for the police and the entire world. Now they all will know what you did to me and other innocent boys. You should've never taught me how to use that camera. You thought I'd use it for practicing my baseball swings, but I found other uses for it. Now, you will face the charges and pay for what you did to me.*
>
> *Shipping me off to some Caribbean island may have been your idea of making it up to me, but we both know you only wanted me out of the way, so I wouldn't expose you and keep anyone from finding out about your depravity.*
>
> *The abuse you inflicted upon me as a young child will soon be known by all. I hope you burn in hell.*

Rick continued to read in shock and disgust as the whole mystery and murder plot was revealed. If Rick had not been on the scene, he was convinced Darren would have killed LeBlanc, then left the diary and flash drive for the police to find. He probably had every intention of returning to St. Croix or somewhere else to hide, and then would revel in having exposed his father to the world for what he really was. But he hadn't planned on Rick being there. Darren must've handed the book to LeBlanc to distract him so he could land his fatal machete blow to the deputy's neck.

Darren had lured Cara away from Casa Olé that fateful night by telling her that he and LeBlanc were meeting, and that James had a surprise for her. Darren knew she had been looking for a new cutting horse and told her James wanted to show her some papers he had on a promising mare.

When she arrived at the hotel, Darren had killed her and wrapped her body in a burlap sack, then carried her into the bayou. Initially, to inflict further pain and suffering on his father, he'd buried her in the clearing in the bayou so she would never be found, and his father would never have closure on this terrible tragedy.

The voodoo elements were just a last-minute addition to throw off the cops in case her body was ever discovered. He must've thought of that after his encounter with Angelique.

But once Rick had discovered Cara's remains, Darren's plans had changed. He still wanted his father to suffer, but getting mixed up in drug trafficking, and being terrified by Angelique Beauvoir had taken its toll on Darren's fragile mind. He figured that by killing Cara and revealing the sexual abuse he had suffered as a child, his dad would somehow feel the kind of pain he had experienced and might get locked away forever or possibly kill himself. Either way, he would get his revenge.

Rick was beginning to think that Darren had become psychotic from the combination of abuse, cocaine, and his brain injuries.

It all came together. When Rick moved closer to Darren's body, his mouth was hanging open and Rick could see that several of his back teeth were missing. He had pulled out his own teeth to fake his death in St. Croix.

The entire notebook was actually a journal but read more like a confession. Darren hated his father so much for showering all his love on Cara and sexually abusing him as a young child that he had committed the ultimate sin and taken his sister's life just to punish his dad. The motive was clear. He had killed his own sister out of jealousy, revenge and pure hatred of his father for the abuse he had endured.

The notebook implicated the deputy, Angelique Beauvoir and her crew, as well as the airline employee in St. Thomas in the drug trafficking. After Darren had killed a homeless guy in St. Croix and used his corpse to stage his own death, he'd hidden out in the mountains of St. Croix and planned his revenge on his dad. He also knew word would get back to Angelique that he was dead and she would finally leave him be. After she'd put him in that voodoo trance, he had become increasingly fearful that she would come back to St. Croix and eliminate him. It was all there in black and white and spatters of red.

Rick motored back to the boat ramp and loaded up the skiff on the trailer. For a while he just sat silently in his truck, trying to let it all soak in, then he pulled out his laptop and plugged in the flash drive. He wished he could un-see what he was seeing, but it was too late. Not only did he find a video of Benjamin sexually abusing his son, but there were also photos of young boys in compromising positions taken from websites on Benjamin's computer, as well as private messages enticing boys to meet his alias, DaddySugar15. The compilation on the drive documented a history of Benjamin being a sexual predator that sickened Rick to the core.

After taking several minutes to contemplate his next move, Rick called Benjamin and asked him if he was sitting down.

"What I have to tell you will come as quite a shock. I've solved the case, but before I go into detail, I want my payment. I will hang up now and wait for the deposit. This is no scam; the case is solved, and I will tell you who the murderer is once I receive the deposit. There is no room for argument or negotiation. Just make the deposit and you have my word I will call you back."

"I understand. A deal's a deal." Benjamin said quietly, then hung up.

Rick stood there, staring at his phone, wondering what Benjamin was thinking.

He called 911, gave them his location and waited for the deputies to arrive. Several sheriff department cruisers pulled up within twenty minutes and Rick explained how Darren had swung the machete at the deputy and how he himself had tried to stop him but was too late. He handed over the leather notebook and flash drive and told them he had more documents in Houston that he would give them.

His phone whistled and he glanced down to see a message pop up from Bank of America. When he opened the app, he read that a wire deposit in the amount of $400,000 had been made into his account. Benjamin had paid him the reward and then some. He was now sitting on a pile of cash.

Once again, he called his client.

"I made the deposit, Rick."

"I know. Now, listen, this is going to be hard to hear, but now that I know everything, so will you, and so will the rest of the people who have followed this case. Let me get through the whole story and don't interrupt me."

"Ok, I'm listening."

"The body I found in St. Croix was not Darren. I don't know who it was, but it was definitely not Darren. Darren is dead, though. I just shot him." Rick paused. "Now, about your daughter. Cara and Deputy Leblanc had a secret relationship. She wanted to marry him but kept it quiet because of your overbearing control of her."

Benjamin interjected, "Now just a minute, I never…"

Rick cut him off. "I said 'no interruptions,' remember?" The next thing you need to know is that Darren and LeBlanc were in business together. The drug business. Your son got greedy and tried to keep a shipment for himself, but Angelique Beauvoir found him and took back her supply. As you know, this woman doesn't mess around. She sent him into a powerful, drug-induced sleep state for several days, and in my opinion, he was not the same when he came out of it. He was developing some kind of psychosis anyway, and this just tipped the scales. He planned and carried out the murder of Cara and then killed Deputy LeBlanc just before I pulled the trigger of my rifle from my lookout point in the clearing, where there was a planned meeting between LeBlanc and someone with information about the murder. He was in disguise, wearing a wig, probably to get the jump on LeBlanc, who would have recognized him immediately. The reason Darren killed Cara was to get back at you. And you know why. I'm sickened that you abused your own son. You have an illness. There was a flash drive attached to the inside of the notebook and when I viewed the contents, I was in shock. Once the authorities see the copy of this flash drive, your life will never be the same. I'd say I'm sorry but I'm not. There's no excuse or pity for what you've done. You deserve whatever happens to you. I'm going to hang up now. Don't ever contact me again. Our business is done."

Rick disconnected and stared out of his dirty windshield, pondering what Benjamin would do. Would he kill himself? Would he flee? He definitely had the means to disappear.

EPILOGUE

Rick spent days in a funk, mentally and physically drained from the case. Since Benjamin had been arrested at the airport and was now in custody, Rick knew it was time to give up his obsession with the case, and staring through the window of the Beaumont Grand Spindletop Hotel he had holed up in, he suddenly knew just how to do it. He looked over at his bird and said, "Chief, let's buy ourselves a boat!"

Pulling out the business card he'd guarded carefully in his wallet, he called Jerry, the boat broker in Destin, and asked him if the boat he'd been interested in was still available. Rick knew in his heart it was the boat for him since he'd examined the sister ship in person at the boat show. When Jerry answered affirmatively, he was overjoyed, and next asked if he knew of any slips available.

"There are always commercial slips in the harbor, but they'll run ya a thousand a month," said Jerry.

"Can I arrange to have the boat delivered and put into a slip there? I can prepay a year's slip fees and pay a captain to get her there," Rick told him.

"I'll move her myself. There's a slip just a few down from our office," the broker told him. "I'd be happy to take care of all that for you."

He gave Rick the wire information for the bank and the final amount due for the closing, plus slip fees. Rick plugged Bank of America into his GPS and made his way to the closest branch.

After he arranged for the wire transfer and all the slip fees and taxes were paid, he still had more money in his account than he'd ever had before.

Now there was a long-overdue phone call he had to make. He'd put Jules and their magical time together out of his mind for the past few days, but knew that if he hadn't already screwed it up, this was a relationship that was worth pursuing. He dialed her number, fingers crossed that she wouldn't hang up on him. Just hearing her voice would be a breath of fresh air.

"Jules? It's Rick."

"*Hola*, Rick, how have you been? It's been so long since we've had a real conversation! I was beginning to think I was only imagining what we had."

"Jules, I'm sorry it's been so long. I texted when I could, and should've called sooner, but this case has consumed all my time and all my energy. I know it's not an excuse, so forgive me."

"Well, I'll think about it," she said, but Rick could hear a hint of teasing in her tone.

"Good. Thank you! I have so much to tell you. But let me start with the good stuff. I bought a boat—not just any boat, but the boat I've always dreamed of. It's a yacht, actually. A fifty-five-foot sport fisher with a beautiful interior, several nice cabins and a full galley. She's a beauty."

"I'm so happy for you, Rick. When can I see it?"

"When can you come?"

"You want me to come to you? I'd love to! I have some vacation coming. Just say the word."

"I'm heading back to Destin. I'll call you once I'm settled and book you a flight. It'll be so great to see you."

"I can't wait, Rick. I really want to see you."

"Me too, Jules, more than I can say. I'll call you in a couple of days, ok?"

"Ok Rick. Be safe. I look forward to talking to you soon."

Rick set his phone down and put his truck in gear, Destin bound.

He turned to Chief, handed him a grape, and said, "It's time to head for blue waters, buddy."

The End

ABOUT THE AUTHOR

Eric Chance Stone was born and raised on the gulf coast of Southeast Texas. An avid surfer, sailor, scuba diver, fisherman and treasure hunter, Eric met many bigger than life characters on his adventures across the globe. Wanting to travel after college, he got a job with Northwest Airlines and moved to Florida. Shortly thereafter transferred to Hawaii, then Nashville. After years of being a staff songwriter in Nashville, he released his first album, Songs For Sail in 1999, a tropically inspired collection of songs. He continued to write songs and tour and eventually landed a gig with Sail America and Show Management to perform at all international boat shows where his list of characters continued to grow.

He moved to the Virgin Islands in 2007 and became the official entertainer for Pusser's Marina Cay in the BVI. After several years in the Caribbean, his fate for telling stories was sealed.

Upon release of his 15th CD, All The Rest, he was inspired to become a novelist after a chance meeting with Wayne Stinnett. Wayne along with Cap Daniels, Chip Bell and a few others, became his mentors and they are all good friends now. Eric currently resides in Destin, Florida with his fiancé Kim-Cara and their three exotic birds, Harley, Marley and Ozzy.

Inspired by the likes of Clive Cussler's Dirk Pitt, Wayne Stinnett's Jesse McDermitt, Cap Daniels Chase Fulton, Chip Bell's Jake Sullivan and many more, Eric's tales are sprinkled with Voodoo, Hoodoo and kinds of weird stuff. From the bayous of Texas to the Voodoo dens of Haiti, his twist of reality will take you for a ride. His main character Rick Waters is a down to earth good ol' boy, adventurist turned private eye, who uses his treasure hunting skills and street smarts to solve mysteries.

FOLLOW ERIC CHANCE STONE:

WEBSITE:
http://www.EricChanceStone.com

FACEBOOK:
https://www.facebook.com/RickWatersSeries

Made in United States
Orlando, FL
04 September 2022